Fair Warning

**Center Point
Large Print**

**This Large Print Book carries the
Seal of Approval of N.A.V.H.**

Fair Warning

HANNAH ALEXANDER

CENTER POINT PUBLISHING
THORNDIKE, MAINE

This Center Point Large Print edition
is published in the year 2006 by arrangement with
Harlequin Enterprises Ltd.

The text of this Large Print edition is unabridged. In other
aspects, this book may vary from the original edition. Printed in
Thailand. Set in 16-point Times New Roman type.

ISBN 1-58547-808-3

Library of Congress Cataloging-in-Publication Data

Alexander, Hannah.
    Fair warning / Hannah Alexander.--Center Point large print ed.
        p. cm.
    ISBN 1-58547-808-3 (lib. bdg. : alk. paper)
        1. Large type books. I. Title.

PS3551.L35558F35 2006
813'.54--dc22

2006008544

Joan Marlow Golan, executive editor of Steeple Hill, runs a tight ship and is a constant encourager. This attitude infects the rest of her staff, and we are the ones who benefit. We appreciate you all!

Also going above the call of duty yet again is Lorene Cook, mom extraordinaire, who supports, encourages, runs errands and markets like a pro. Thanks, Mom.

Thanks to retired Battalion Chief Fred Baugher, who knows fire and doesn't mind his niece picking his brain from time to time.

Thanks to Captain Powell of the Branson Police Department for great information about the station and protocol.

Thanks to Susan May Warren, fellow novelist and former missionary to Russia, who gave us some great insights.

Thanks to Barbara Warren for your word-slashing ability, and to Jackie Bolton for personal insights.

We've been blessed yet again by help from a lot of intelligent people. Any mistakes are completely our own.

In loving memory of June James, born July 16, 1922, passed on to heaven January 29, 2005. Aunt June was filled with the life and laughter that inspired the character of Ginger Carpenter.

Chapter One

Willow Traynor's eyes opened to the blackness of deep night as the noise and flash of an overbusy dream receded into the mist of her subconscious.

She held her breath as her eyes adjusted to the square edges of the dresser across the room, the dim reflection of light in the mirror, the ghostly drift of gauzy white curtains above the heat register. Something had awakened her.

She knew the dream had not been a nightmare, because in the past two years it seemed as if nightmares had become her constant companions. She would have recognized the aftereffects. She didn't feel them now—no racing heart, no night sweats, no rush of relief upon waking to discover that she was still alive.

Something else, then. A noise? Perhaps a passing car, or a boat on the lake? The neighbors in the apartment complex? Sometimes the two little Jameson girls got rambunctious late at night, and Mrs. Bartholomew in the unit next door called to complain.

Willow sat up and peered toward the small digital numbers on the nightstand clock. Two-thirty, April 1. Probably wasn't the children.

It might be something as insignificant as the unfamiliar silence. Even after two weeks she hadn't yet adjusted to the move—or rather, the escape—from bustling Kansas City to her brother's rural log cabin six miles south of Branson in the Missouri Ozarks. Major change.

She had never lived this far out in the country. Although the eight-unit apartment lodge her brother managed meant they weren't exactly isolated from civilization, it was nothing like city life. Living in the cabin, situated on the shore of Table Rock Lake, was more like being on permanent vacation. Willow still struggled to come to grips with the comparative solitude.

As she stared into darkness, the square of sliding glass door at the far end of her room seemed to emit a pulsing glow. She blinked to clear her vision, but the glow increased. Headlights from a boat on the lake, perhaps? Except she heard no sound of a boat motor.

She turned her back to the light and plumped her pillow. "None of my business anyway," she whispered into the darkness.

Her brother, Preston, certainly didn't want her help keeping track of the renters. As he'd told her several times in the past two weeks, she needed to take a break and heal.

After a little more than twenty-three months, she'd almost given up hope of that. True, she no longer relived the night she'd received the visit from the police chief to tell her that her husband had been killed in the line of duty. At least, she didn't relive it every single night. Maybe more like once a week now.

And she no longer had the nightly awakenings to cries of her forever unborn child. Only a couple of

10

times a week did she cringe when someone invaded her personal space.

People did that all the time now, because her personal space had extended, in the past twenty-three months, to include whatever room she was in. She usually allowed people she knew into her personal space, but there were still those times when she could do nothing but withdraw from the world.

Since two attempts had been made on her own life after Travis was killed, she'd found herself suspecting practically everyone. She had known when she married Travis that he had one of the most dangerous jobs imaginable—not only was he a cop, but he was an undercover narcotics agent.

Here in Missouri, the Bible belt, the heart of the nation, a war raged against illegal drugs, particularly methamphetamines. She had never dreamed the danger would extend to the cop's family. But with Travis's death, it most certainly had.

She closed her eyes and breathed deeply, exhaled, tempting sleep with as much entreaty as she could muster, willing her body to relax. The art of relaxing had become a lost skill for her.

Since arriving here in the middle of March, she'd assured herself daily that the only things she had to fear in this place were her memories. If she died, it would be a side effect of the grief that had imprisoned her since the day she lost Travis.

There's nothing out there. It's your imagination. Again.

Wasn't that what everybody kept telling her? Even Preston. They hadn't exactly told her they thought she was imagining the attempts on her life, but after the investigations turned up no evidence of foul play, she had felt her friends and her brother looking at her differently.

Try as she might, her eyes refused to remain closed. A faint flash of light greeted her again from the wall. She sighed and rolled from the bed, irritated by her exaggerated sense of responsibility. Maybe one of the renters was wandering around the yard with a flashlight, or maybe there was a party going on.

She slipped noiselessly to the glass door and unlatched it. All she needed was to prove to herself that no one hovered in the shadows watching her, waiting for her to go back to sleep so they could pounce.

And yet, what if someone was there this time?

She slid the door open and frowned. She caught a faint whiff of smoke, with an underlying scent of something else, pungent and strong.

What was it? Turpentine? Like the bottle of stuff Preston had been using in the shed a couple of days ago? No. Not turpentine . . . kerosene?

No.

Her frown deepened. Had Preston left the door open to the utility shed in the back? He'd spilled some gasoline on his clothes yesterday when he was working on the boat motor, preparing it for the coming warm days of spring.

She sniffed again. Smoke. Fuel.

She caught her breath. Smoke? "Preston!" she cried over her shoulder. "Fire!"

She shoved the door wide and dashed onto the cold deck. The wood chilled her bare feet. The odor of smoke blasted her. She scrambled down the steps and around the west side of the cabin, racing between it and the east wall of the apartment lodge.

Light flared as she reached the front corner of the cabin. To her horror, she saw several jagged lines of flame streaking across the yard—snakes of fire, winding through the darkness.

She blinked and stared, stumbling in the grass, fighting confusion. What was going on? The flames pitched in headlong flight directly toward the cabin.

"Preston!" she screamed. "Oh, Lord, help us!" *Please, let this be another dream.*

She raced toward the front door. She couldn't shake the impression that she'd stepped into one of those B movies where a long, glowing fuse raced toward a bomb. Fuses. That was what those ribbons of flame looked like.

Before she reached the front steps, she saw her brother's dark form stumbling out the door onto the porch.

"Get away!" he called. "Willow, get—"

A curtain of flames suddenly blasted across the wooden porch with all the force of an explosion. Preston leaped free of the fire and caught Willow in a tackle that rocked her backward. They crashed into the privacy hedge separating the cabin's yard from the wider lawn encircling the entire complex.

He shoved her forward, through the hedge. She cried out as roots and stones bruised her bare feet. Preston kept pushing her farther from the danger.

They collapsed into the grass.

"Willow, you okay?" Preston asked, his deep voice harsh with alarm, breathing as if he'd run for miles.

"Yes. What's happening?" She stumbled to her feet and drew back the hedge branches to stare at the fire, nearly deafened by the roar.

He grabbed her by the arm and pulled her around to face him. "Listen, Willow, help me get the others out. I'll call 9-1-1 as soon as I get to a phone, so don't worry about that, just get the people out of here! Take the top level, I'll take the bottom, but keep a close watch on the fire."

She swallowed hard, her attention returning to the holocaust as if she were a human moth.

He took her by the shoulders, his fingers digging into her flesh with urgency. "Willow, go now. Hurry!"

Slipping on the damp grass, she scrambled toward the first unit. The lodge was built into a hillside, so both floors were at ground level, and both had scenic views of the lake below.

She reached unit One A and pounded on the door as she rang the doorbell, remembering the two little girls and their single mom who lived there.

"Sandi!" she shouted. "Get the girls and get out. Sandi, please wake up!"

She glanced over her shoulder. Preston was gone.

Fire engulfed the cabin. Smoke billowed into the sky, casting an eerie glow. It was crazy! Those streaks of fire . . . like fuses . . . what was happening? As she watched, headlights came on about a quarter of a mile away, brushing the treetops with their probing beams.

No one answered at Sandi Jameson's apartment. Willow picked up a decorative flowerpot on the porch and flung it through the glass pane in the door. The crash of shattering glass should have awakened anyone inside.

"Sandi?" she shouted through the gaping hole. "Fire! Get out of there. Now!" She reached through the window, fumbled for the door latch and snapped it open, catching her right arm on a glass shard as she withdrew her hand. The sharp point sliced through the tender flesh of her inner forearm.

Gasping, she bent over with the shock of pain. There was no time to deal with it. She shoved her way inside. No light, no one came running into the room. Could they be gone?

She rushed through a kitchen cluttered with dirty dishes and trash of unbelievable proportions, past the living room. She found her way to the bedrooms at the far west end of the hall.

"Sandi!"

She heard a startled squeal through one of the doors and burst inside to find Sandi's two little girls, Brittany and Lucy, huddled together on the lower level of a set of bunk beds. They wore tattered, oversize T-shirts for nightgowns.

"Girls, it's okay," Willow said, rushing to them. "We've got to get out of this apartment now. Where's your mother?"

"Sissy, she's bloody!" five-year-old Brittany wailed, clinging to her older sister.

Willow looked down at her right arm and saw the blood dripping at a rate that alarmed her. "It's okay, honey. I'll take care of it later. Right now we've got to get you out of here. Please tell me where your mother is."

"Not here," said seven-year-old Lucy. "We can't leave the apartment. Mom said never leave the apartment when she's not here."

"Your mother's gone?"

The girls stared at her, one pair of green eyes and one pair of brown eyes wide with apprehension.

"Your mother will want you to leave this time," Willow said. "I need to get you out of here to safety. You can trust me. I'm not going to hurt you." She reached for Brittany, who cried out and backed away, staring at Willow's arm.

"But what's wrong? What's happening?" Lucy asked.

"Preston's cabin is on fire." Willow forced her voice to remain gentle and reassuring, though she felt anything but calm. "We need to get you out of here because the cabin is too close to the lodge."

"A fire?" Brittany wailed.

"It's okay, I'll get you to safety." Willow would deal with the negligent mother later. She switched on the

16

overhead light and reached into the connecting bathroom for a towel.

In deference to the squeamish child, she wrapped her wound with the not-so-clean towel, then scooped the youngster into her arms and grabbed the older sister's hand. "Girls, you'll have to trust me. This way."

Brittany trembled in Willow's arms, but held tightly around her neck and burrowed against her shoulder.

There were more people who needed to be warned. Would she reach them all in time?

Graham Vaughn snapped awake at the first trill of his cell phone on the bedside stand. He wasn't on call tonight, but still he reacted instinctively, like one of Pavlov's beleaguered animals, when he heard that particular sound. Somehow he'd expected to break that unwelcome habit when he left the practice.

He'd obviously been demented to even consider such a possibility. After all, it wasn't as if he'd stopped taking patients—he'd just stopped getting paid for it.

He glanced at the numbers on his clock. Two thirty-five. He grabbed the cell phone, but didn't recognize the number on the screen. A patient in trouble? He pressed the green button. "This is Dr. Vaughn."

"Graham, it's Preston. I need help. My cabin is on fire and it could spread at any minute."

The news didn't register for a moment. "Uh, Preston?"

"Did you hear me?" The man's voice rose in panic. "Fire!"

17

Graham lurched from the bed and reached for the clothes he'd dropped onto the floor three hours ago. "I'll be there. Have you called 9-1-1?"

"Yes. Help is on its way, but there are two other fires in the Branson area tonight. They're shorthanded. Hollister's responding, but I think we'll need some extra hands to help us evacuate, and the renters will need a place to stay tonight. Can you get here in time?"

"I'm on my way now. Where are you?" Graham pulled on his jeans with one-handed awkwardness, then reached for his shirt, shoving his feet into a pair of sneakers. Preston was right—Graham couldn't possibly get there in time to help with evacuation, but he was ultimately responsible.

"Down below at Two B. I'm using Carl Mackey's cell phone." There was a sound of pounding, then Preston's voice as he shouted for the occupant.

Graham had purchased the lodge at a greatly reduced price last year and had invested a good deal of sweat equity in it since then. He'd spared no expense on safety, and in spite of the high rent, Preston, his manager, had filled all the units in record time.

People liked to live in the country, except for times like this, when help was farther away.

"Has it spread past the cabin?" he asked.

"Not yet," Preston said.

"It shouldn't. We took every precaution when we refurbished that lodge."

"You're right, it shouldn't spread naturally," Preston said. "But this monster doesn't look natural to me. I've never seen green grass burn either, until tonight."

"What are you saying?"

"I'm saying this doesn't look accidental. Look, I've got to go," Preston said. "Rick Fenrow's not answering his door, and I didn't think he was scheduled to work tonight. Carl's gone up to see if Rick's car's in the carport."

"Okay, but be careful. Don't let anyone go back inside for belongings. And don't *you* go back in for anything."

"No chance of that. My place is an inferno. If my sister hadn't awakened, we wouldn't have made it out. Got to go."

The connection ended. Graham shoved the phone into his shirt pocket, then immediately retrieved it. He pressed a number he knew well and grabbed his jacket on the way out the front door.

He ran down the hillside from his house and pounded across the wooden dock that stretched out into the private cove that fed into Table Rock Lake. He was jumping onto his jet bike when the groggy voice of his friend splintered a half-conscious greeting through his cell phone.

"Dane? Graham. Sorry to do this, but can I use your speedboat? I need to get to my rental lodge fast." He explained the situation in terse, shouted sentences as he revved the motor of his jet bike and raced from the protected cove to the other side of the lake. The chill of the moist, early-spring air bit into his skin, and he realized he'd be frozen by the time he reached his destination.

"I'm coming with you." Dane Gideon's voice barely carried over the noise of the jet bike. "I'll meet you down at my dock." The connection broke, and Graham shoved the phone back into his pocket as he faced the freezing blast of cold air that rose from the lake and mingled with the spray of lake water in his face.

Moments later, pulling up to the dock at the boys' ranch that Dane owned and managed, Graham cut the motor and drifted into an empty slip.

The echo of another motor drifted across the surface of the water from the opposite shore. He glanced over his shoulder and glimpsed a set of headlights bobbing a quarter of a mile west of his own place, from the municipal dock at Hideaway.

The residents of their small village, set along the shore of Table Rock Lake, depended almost as much on boats as automobiles for transportation locally. At this time in the early-morning hours, however, Hideaway slept.

Graham looked up the hill to see the bouncing beam of a flashlight. Footsteps rushed down from the huge farmhouse that provided shelter for twelve boys. Okay, he saw two bouncing beams.

"I called Taylor Jackson and Nathan Trask." Dane's calm but breathless voice sounded as he reached the dock, followed by Blaze Farmer, a college student and part-time resident of the ranch.

"Is that who's coming across the lake?" Graham asked.

"That's right." Dane's silver-blond hair gleamed in

the flashlight and headlight glow as he and Blaze released the *Mystique* from its moorings and pushed it from the slip. "Get in. They're going to follow us in Taylor's Sea Ray."

Blaze rubbed his ebony hands together in obvious anticipation. "I think they just want to race. They've been threatening to go head-to-head ever since Taylor got his pride and joy, but I never thought they'd do it at night."

"We're not racing," Dane said.

"Looks like it to me," Blaze said.

Dane waited until they idled past the no-wake zone, then gunned the motor and flashed his lights at the approaching boat. "We're just leading the way."

Chapter Two

As Willow ran to the final apartment on the top level, she glanced over her shoulder to see a knot of renters gathered in the large gazebo in the middle of the lawn, watching the inferno. She prayed with fervent passion that it wouldn't spread beyond Preston's place.

Something exploded within the maelstrom. Sparks rose in the night sky, mingling with plumes of smoke and flames. The roar intensified and the heat reached across the expanse of air to warm her skin.

She peered through the darkness at the empty porches. It had taken more time than she'd expected to rouse all the residents and get them outside to safety;

some were elderly, hard of hearing, and had removed their hearing aids to sleep.

Was Preston having this much trouble? Where was he?

She knocked on the final door, rang the doorbell, peered through the window, then heard the excited yap of a small dog inside. She knocked again, then tested the door. It wasn't locked.

If she remembered correctly, she'd seen an elderly woman entering this apartment three days ago, carrying a bag of groceries. Preston had called her Mrs. Engle.

Pushing the door open, Willow switched on the light. "Hello? Mrs. Engle, are you here?"

The dog, a tiny Pomeranian, yapped at her from the hallway to the right, then raced into the other room. Its fluff-ball form flitted in a ghostly shadow from the glow of the fire through the front window.

Willow followed the little animal to an open door on the right. "Mrs. Engle?"

Another explosion burst through the night. The windows rattled at the far side of the bedroom. The blast of light illuminated a frail-looking figure on the carpeted floor on the other side of the bed.

"Could you help me?" came a shaky voice. "I think I've broken my hip."

Willow switched on the overhead light and rushed to the woman's side. "Mrs. Engle, there's a fire on the property. We need to get you out of here." There would be no time to call 9-1-1 and expect a timely response, not in this place, so far from help.

"Honey, you're not going to be able to lift me," Mrs. Engle said. "Where's Preston?"

Willow peered outside. She'd been wondering that, herself. She unlatched the window and shoved it open. "I need some help in Four A," she called to the growing crowd that now huddled in the gazebo.

The people were too far away. No one heard her over the roar of the fire.

"Hello!" she shouted. "Can anyone——"

Another explosion shook the floor as a flash brightened the sky to day. Someone screamed, and the light illuminated a group of men running up from the direction of the boat dock. The roar of the boats blended with the roar of the fire and with another sound—the reassuring whine of a siren in the distance. Help was apparently on its way.

Willow went to the phone at the bedside stand and dialed 9-1-1. The dispatcher could immediately call the arriving firemen to help her with Mrs. Engle.

Living this far out in the sticks, emergency personnel were seldom just a phone call away. That was something Willow had seriously considered before deciding to come here, and she now questioned her sanity for her decision. She had hoped to find peace and safety here.

After giving her information to the dispatcher, she returned to the injured woman and knelt at her side. "Mrs. Engle, I don't want to move you if I can avoid it." As a former ICU nurse, Willow knew the damage that could be done if she tried to lift an injured patient.

She pulled a thick comforter from the bed and settled it beside Mrs. Engle. If the situation became desperate, she could wrap the comforter around the lady and pull her as gently as possible to safety. For now, however, that could wait.

The shriek of the siren drew closer.

Sharp tongues of fire stabbed the night sky, reflecting its fury across the surface of the lake as Graham rushed up the hillside from the boat dock. Emergency lights flashed red in the treetops in concert with the flames. A siren accompanied the crackle and hiss of the burning building.

The first fire truck pulled into the lot, and its crew rushed to connect to the hydrant. Unfortunately, it seemed Preston was correct about the firefighting personnel and equipment being spread thin tonight.

Graham glanced at the sky out of old habit from his E.R. days. Superstition or not, it had always been his experience that more chaos reigned on nights with a full moon. Tonight, however, the moon formed a crescent against the blackness of the western horizon. He'd have to blame something else for the tragedies taking place in the Ozarks this early April Fool's morning.

He cut across the lawn at the far corner of the complex and caught movement from the corner of his eye. He turned to catch sight of a tall, slender woman with black hair stepping from the entryway of Four A, Esther Engle's place.

24

The last time he'd seen that silhouette, the woman had been holding a camera, flashing pictures of a crime scene at a local music theater. Jolene Tucker called herself a photojournalist, and she passed up no opportunity to see her byline in a local paper. She had her finger on every pulse of gossip in the Branson community, but how had she managed to beat the fire engines here?

Though Graham had seen her only from a distance, he'd heard horror stories about the trouble she caused her hapless victims in her weekly gossip column.

Graham switched directions and marched toward her. She had no right to be here. Her presence endangered not only her, but any others who might feel called upon to remove her from harm's way. What was she doing inside *his* building?

To his amazement, when the woman caught sight of him through the darkness she gave him a frantic wave and started toward him across the yard. "Sir, are you with the fire department? I could use some help with—"

"Where's your camera?" he snapped.

She slid to a stop on the grass and stared at him through the smoky murk. "What are you talking about? Why aren't there more emergency personnel here? There's no time to—"

"Ms. Tucker, you've got some gall coming into a situation like this," he said without breaking his stride. He reached for her arm. "You're on private property. *My* property, and I want you off within the next ten seconds or I'll give the police a call."

She took a step backward, evading his grasp. "But you don't understand. There's a—"

"I don't want to hear it. If you want to complain, just write it up in one of your columns." He led her from the yard. "This place is dangerous, and you need to leave. It's an insurance risk."

She jerked away from him. "Insurance? That's all you're worried about?" She scrambled back across the dark lawn toward Esther Engle's front door. "There are still people who need help. Mrs. Engle's fallen in her apartment and we need a stretcher—"

"I'll take care of Mrs. Engle," he said, rushing after her. "You hightail it on home for once. Your nose for news doesn't belong here." He thrust his thumb in the direction of the parking lot. "Out!"

She gave a long-suffering sigh and did as he told her this time. "You'll get Mrs. Engle?"

"That's where I'm headed right now." He saw Blaze and Dane, Taylor and Nathan running up the hill and commandeered Taylor's help—Taylor Jackson was a tough Ranger with the heart of a paramedic. Often it seemed necessary to utilize the full range of Taylor's skills on the field when responding to accidents.

The fire seemed to have limited itself to Preston's cabin, though it could easily spread to the utility building east of the lodge. Graham prayed it would go no farther. When he'd refurbished the lodge, he'd made sure the building was above code. Now he would see if the additional efforts paid off.

Baffled and incensed by the behavior of the manhandling owner, who seemed to be confusing her with someone he knew, Willow waited until he and another man entered Mrs. Engle's front door. She stepped gingerly from the gravel to the grass to protect her feet, and rushed toward the small crowd of people who had left the shelter of the gazebo to watch the firemen spraying the flames. Another siren wailed through the trees. An orange-and-white ambulance arrived on the scene, pulling to a stop at the edge of the lot.

Willow waved at the driver and directed the crew toward Mrs. Engle's apartment when they stepped from the vehicle. Finally more help had arrived.

"Has anyone here seen Preston?" she asked Carl Mackey, who lived in the apartment below Sandi Jameson's.

The older man pointed toward the shed. "I thought I saw him headed in that direction just before the fire truck arrived. Figured he wanted to move the gasoline tank before it blew with the rest of the building."

"He didn't come back out?"

Carl shrugged. "Nope, and we called for him."

She heard the shouts of the firemen above the snap and pop of the flames and the sizzle of water from the fire hoses. No way would her brother go into that mess. He was brave and strong, but he wasn't foolish, and he didn't have a death wish.

Carl stepped to Willow's side. He wore bright orange flannel pajamas, and his hair stuck up in all directions.

"Young lady, you've got a nasty wound." He gestured to the bloodstained towel around Willow's arm. "Why don't we get that seen to? I grabbed my car keys on the way out the door, and I can get you to the hospital before—"

"Thanks, Carl, but I've got to find Preston." Willow rushed back across the shadows of the front yard. "Preston!" she called. "Has anyone seen my—"

A strong, firm arm caught her from behind and swung her around. She looked up into the angry face of the same jerk who had yelled at her before.

"You don't listen well, do you, Jolene?"

She yanked away from him. "Look, bud, you may be the owner of this place, but *I'm not* Jolene, whoever that might be, and if you don't get out of my face I'm going to kick you!"

The man's expression froze, mouth open mid-rant. He blinked at her, looked down at her torn, mud-and-grass-stained pajamas.

"Where's Preston?" Willow demanded. "Have you seen my brother?"

The expression of dismay on his face was priceless. For a fraction of a second she almost felt sorry for him. Almost.

Yet another explosion rocked the earth. Willow gasped, then turned instinctively in the direction of the sound, toward the building behind the burning cabin.

"It's the utility shed!" a fireman shouted. "It's collapsing."

"Preston was headed in that direction!" Willow cried

as another fire truck rumbled into the ruckus. *Oh, dear God, no. Not Preston!*

Graham grabbed the panicking woman before she could run across the lawn to the shed, and wasn't surprised when she fought him. So this was the gentle sister of whom Preston had so often spoken.

"We've got to get him out of there!" the frantic woman cried.

"The firemen are doing that." He gestured toward the two men in fire gear, who were already forcing back the flames and entering the inferno.

Preston's sister—what was her name . . . something about a tree . . . Rowan? No, Willow. That was it. Willow struggled from Graham's grasp, and as she pulled away a red-and-white towel unwound from her right forearm. Blood gushed from a deep injury in the flesh above her wrist.

"Hold it right there," Graham said, feeling like an idiot as well as a bully. Why hadn't he noticed this sooner? "You need medical attention." He reached for her arm.

She pushed away from him. "I need to see about my brother first. Is everyone evacuated?"

"Mrs. Engle was the only one left. Blaze has her dog."

Willow's eyes widened. "Blaze?"

"It's the name of a friend. The dog's in good hands," he said gently. "I'm telling you, that wound is actively bleeding."

29

She placed her hand over the cut and turned again toward the fire. "And *I'm* telling *you* that I want to see about Preston."

Graham caught sight of Taylor Jackson, who had just finished helping the attendants load Mrs. Engle into the waiting ambulance. "Jackson!" He waved to catch the attention of the tall man with a stern and caring expression, who had followed Graham, Dane and Blaze from Hideaway in his own boat.

"What's up?"

"Over here. I've got a patient for you. Is there another ambulance on the way?"

"Yep, ETA of three minutes or less," Taylor said as he hefted his backpack of medical supplies over his shoulder and carried it toward them. When he reached them, he frowned at Willow's arm and gave a soft whistle. "Looks like the E.R.'s going to be hopping tonight."

Willow gasped, then gave a weak, horrified cry. Graham looked up to see the two firemen carrying a limp man between them through the smoking, flaming shed. Preston.

His sister fainted. Graham caught her, then lowered her to the ground so she could lie flat. "Get a pressure dressing," he said over his shoulder. "And start an IV. She might have lost too much blood."

Taylor already had out a handful of four-by-four gauze pads. He placed them onto the bleeding gash and wrapped it tightly with gauze dressing with the swiftness of an expert.

"That should hold it until we can get it sutured," Graham said, checking her pulse. It was fast, but that could be from a rush of excess adrenaline. As he checked her more closely, he noticed her skin wasn't cool or clammy to the touch, and she had a good capillary refill.

"She doesn't appear to be in shock. Did you bring a cardiac monitor on the boat?" he asked.

Taylor nodded. "I prepare for the worst."

"Let's check her out, just in case."

Willow moaned and shifted. "No. I'm okay," she murmured, her voice barely carrying above the roar of activity around them.

"Let us be the judges of that. You're not in any position to complain," Graham said.

She raised her good arm, blinking against the light of the arriving ambulance as she pushed away from Graham. "No monitor and no IV. I need to get to Preston. Where is he?"

Willow had endured enough of this pushy man's attitude. She caught sight of the firemen loading a gurney into the back of the ambulance and saw a man with a blackened face turn toward her and open his eyes.

It was Preston. He was alive and awake. She had to get to him.

"We should call an ambulance for you, as well," the pushy man said.

"There's no reason why I can't ride with Preston, is there?"

"Sorry, not right now. They're only equipped to handle one patient at a time. You fainted, and that could be a—"

"From the shock of seeing my brother like that. Please," she said, pushing away the monitor line the tall newcomer was attempting to attach to her. She would stand up and walk to the vehicle without their help if they were going to be so obstinate. She scrambled to her knees, hand to the ground to retain her balance.

"Okay," said Preston's boss, obviously a trifle irritated now. "We'll help you to the ambulance. Just hold on, will you? I'd take you myself, but I don't have a car right now."

She allowed the men to help her to her feet, and glanced down at the dressing on her arm. Obviously someone knew what he was doing.

She blinked at the white of the dressing as her vision seemed to waver. So maybe she wasn't as strong as she'd hoped. She guessed she'd let these men help her to the ambulance, where she would sit quietly in the corner until they reached the hospital.

Chapter Three

Graham stepped down the western corridor of the emergency department of Clark Memorial Hospital, south of town. Even at four in the morning, more than half the treatment rooms were filled and the staff was kept hopping with everything from chest pain to broken arms to the unusual occurrence of a knife wound.

There were also the more common cases of croupy children and upset tummies. The emergency department was a way station for all the area's unwell, no matter how minor or serious the condition.

He entered the third treatment room on the right and found Willow lying on the bed, her face pale. A monitor was connected by wires to her chest. It beeped in steady rhythm.

She looked up as he entered, and her eyes widened. They were blue-gray, large, fringed with long dark lashes. She had her brother's bone structure, though more delicate and refined. There was a watchfulness about her—an almost fearful tension.

"How are you doing?" he asked.

"I'm fine—just waiting to hear about Preston's condition. They're working on him in the trauma room, and they refuse to let me in there."

"I just spoke with him and with Dr. Teeter, the E.R. doc," Graham said. "Preston's stabilized. X-rays confirmed multiple rib fractures and a pneumothorax. They actually have him in CT now."

She raised her head and tried to sit up. Graham pressed a button to raise the bed for her. "He's in good hands, Willow, and he's asking about you. I've assured him you're fine. Try not to worry. Dr. Teeter is pretty busy right now, so it may be a while before he can see to your arm himself, so we've decided—"

"Hold it a minute." She lifted her unhurt arm. "Why is it you know so much more about my brother's care than I do? And how do you know my name?"

"Preston and I are friends. He's told me about you." Though Preston hadn't mentioned the firm point of his sister's charmingly dimpled chin, or the vulnerable look in her dark-lashed eyes. "He said you're an ICU nurse."

"I used to be." There was a hint of bitterness in her voice. "That still doesn't tell me why you've been allowed to speak with him and I haven't."

"I'm sorry. I'll see if that can be arranged as soon as he returns from CT. In the meantime," Graham said, "please allow me to apologize for behaving like a total fool earlier." Now that he had a chance to observe her more closely, he couldn't believe he'd mistaken her for the reporter.

Whereas Jolene had closely cropped straight hair, so black it reflected blue lights, this woman had dark curls with a sheen of polished mahogany, the same shade as her brother's hair. She looked younger than Jolene by about ten years, though Graham knew that Preston's little sister was only two years younger than Preston. Since Preston was one year younger than Graham, that would make Willow thirty-six.

Graham gestured toward her right forearm, still wrapped with gauze. "Why don't we see about getting your wound taken care of while we wait for Preston?"

"We?" She blinked up at him, and that firm chin rose a few millimeters. "Mister, who *are* you?"

Again he could have kicked himself. *Graham, you moron, first you bully her, then you scare her to death and now you're ordering her around like . . .* "I'm sorry, I should have introduced myself much sooner. I'm Dr. Graham Vaughn, and besides being the jerk who mistook you for an unsavory local reporter, I'm the only surgeon here right now who has admitting privileges in this hospital and is also available to show immediate attention to your arm."

She stared at him for a full five seconds. "You're kidding."

"No. This is a busy place, and you'd be wise to take treatment when you can get it."

Her eyes narrowed only slightly, but he could still see the wariness in those blue-gray depths.

"As I said, Dr. Teeter has his hands full," he said.

She rested her head back against the pillow and closed her eyes. "I still have almost four hours to get sutures, and I'd like to be available in case they tell me I can see my brother."

"The six-hour rule only applies to wounds not prone to infection," Graham said.

"I'll take my chances just a little longer, if you don't mind."

Time to treat her like a frightened patient, because that was exactly what she was right now, and he'd added to her fears. "If I had sliced my arm open on a broken—what, window?—and then exposed it to all the dust and grime and debris at a fire site, I don't think I would want to push the golden hours past their limit."

Her eyes opened again. "You're really a surgeon?"

He grimaced at the lingering doubt in her expression. "You can ask the staff, if you'd like. Would you let me take a look at your arm? I promise not to bite. I'll even try to get you one of the popsicles our nurses hand out to children who have been especially good during the suturing process."

Her scowl would have withered a sumo wrestler.

He couldn't suppress a smile. She fully shared Preston's self-sufficient personality trait. "Please let me help you, Willow. Your brother is a good and trusted friend, and those are often hard to come by. I'm not going to jeopardize my friendship with him by hurting his baby sister, I promise. And I also promise to have you sewn up and ready to see him by the time he's able to see you."

Her response was a reluctant, heartfelt sigh. "Fine, then. Do your worst."

He grimaced. Not exactly the response he'd have hoped for, considering the circumstances, but if he had just gone through what she'd endured tonight, he doubted he'd be at his charming best, either. Time to make this lady's life a little easier.

Willow winced and stifled a cry of pain. She watched Dr. Vaughn stop and reach for a bottle of sterile saline solution, which he poured over the adhered bandage.

"I'm sorry," he said. "I didn't mean to hurt you. I should be able to get the rest off without any more discomfort."

36

She waited, noting with surprise the depth of the wound. He was right—it did need sutures soon. A nurse had already set up a sterile tray and assisted with the anesthetic and suture material, then left him to his work as she rushed to more emergencies.

This place resembled downtown Kansas City in Friday-evening rush hour. Why was it that some of life's worst catastrophes happened in the wee hours of the morning, when help was hardest to find?

He adjusted the overhead light to get a better look at her arm. She couldn't help noticing, for the first time, that he'd changed into surgical scrubs.

The guy wasn't really a jerk. She could tell that. In fact, he was probably a nice guy. Preston was a good judge of character. Graham Vaughn was even a nice-looking man with short, sandy-brown hair that had some silvering along the temples and eyes the color of rich toffee, with lines of friendliness around the perimeters. Preston hadn't bothered to mention his boss was a surgeon—he had, however, mentioned that he was single.

And she'd snapped at Preston for even hinting, in any way, that she would be interested in whether or not a man was single, since she didn't consider herself to be single.

She was a widow, and there was a big difference between being a widow and just being single. That fact was brought home to her nearly every night, when she discovered that her heart was still broken into splinters, and every morning, when she awakened alone.

"The edges of the wound are a little jagged, but still pretty well approximated." Dr. Graham Vaughn reached for a package of sterile, cotton-tipped swabs, startling her from the preoccupation that caught her so often in its grasp. "I'm going to explore the wound now. This could hurt some."

She braced herself. "Go for it."

He lifted one edge of the wound and inserted the sterile swab.

Willow caught her breath and stiffened.

After a quick probe, he removed the swab. "The cut extends to the subcutaneous fat, but the fascia over the muscles appears intact. I don't think there's any tendon injury or deep nerve or blood vessel involvement. Of course, I still need to check for that possibility."

He started his neurovascular exam by gently pinching each of her fingers, taking special care to also pinch the web space between her thumb and first finger, as well as check her pulse. "I'm screening for any sensory damage to any of the three major nerves that could have been damaged. Can you feel everything okay? Nothing feels dull to my touch?"

"Everything feels fine," she said. In fact, it felt better than fine. The man now focused so intently on her injury was a different man from the one who had come striding across the lawn, yelling at her.

Okay, so he hadn't exactly been yelling.

"Preston says you come from Kansas City," the doctor said, his kind gaze flitting over her with apparent interest. "Which hospital did you work in?"

"Truman," she said, touching each finger to thumb as Graham now turned his attention toward searching for any motor damage to the nerves. "But as I said, I'm not working now."

"You came down here for a rest?" He indicated for Willow to spread her fingers apart.

She performed the maneuver without difficulty. "Something like that."

He looked up at her with a brief question in his eyes, then refocused on his work. He had her flex her wrist, then her thumb, then each finger individually as he carefully observed the wound, looking for any evidence of a cut tendon.

Willow liked his thoroughness.

"Your brother loves you very much, and I know he's been worried about you these past few months."

She grimaced. How much had Preston told this man? "They say the grief process can take between two and four years. My husband died twenty-three months ago, Dr. Vaughn. It still isn't an easy subject to discuss."

He nodded, obviously already aware of her situation. "I'm sorry—believe me, I understand. Though I'm not a widower, I was plunged very reluctantly into the single world again after years of marriage. It's been three years for me, and I still haven't recovered."

She looked up at him with interest. Why was he telling her this? Was he just trying to hold a conversation to keep her mind off the pain? Pretty heavy discussion to hold with a complete stranger.

"Dr. Vaughn, I'm sorry to hear that. I don't know

what my brother told you about me, but he tends to be a little overly protective."

"Please call me Graham," he said. "Now, I'm going to numb the wound before I begin to clean it." He started to remove his gloves, obviously to change to sterile gloves.

"No, I'm a big girl." There were times Willow would have much preferred physical pain over the emotional pain she'd battled for so long. "You don't need to numb it until you start sewing."

He looked at her. "Are you sure? It can be very uncomfortable."

"I'm sure."

"Okay, but as soon as you think it's becoming too painful, you let me know and we'll take the pain away."

In spite of his gentle technique, Willow had to grit her teeth as he cleansed the wound, and she nearly asked for the anesthetic.

"Preston's been an answer to a prayer for me," Graham said as he worked.

"Hope you didn't tell him that," Willow said. "He probably wouldn't appreciate the designation."

Graham nodded. "He definitely isn't interested in talking about spiritual things, is he?"

"No."

"And you?"

"If you're asking if I'm a Christian, yes, but don't expect me to burst into song about the everlasting joys of living the spirit-filled life."

He gave her a look of inquiry, and she shook her head. How could she explain, without getting too maudlin, that she and God weren't exactly on speaking terms at this time? According to the books on grief written by the experts, she should be past that stage of the process. She'd left those books back in Kansas City. They were useless to her now.

"How was Preston an answer to prayer for you?" she asked, hoping to deflect the attention from herself.

"He and I met a few years ago at a weekend seminar on real estate investment, at Chateau on the Lake here in Branson. I discovered Preston wanted to work with rentals while he learned the business and earned the money that would make it possible for him to invest in his own property. I, on the other hand, needed to invest money immediately and needed a manager for my properties."

"He worked as an accountant and financial adviser in Springfield for ten years after graduating from SMSU," Willow said. "Then he got bored."

"Well, he doesn't have a problem with that now," Graham assured her. "In fact, until tonight, I was pretty sure he was having the time of his life."

"What are your renters going to do about a place to stay?" she asked.

"I've already made some calls, and they have rooms at a condominium down on Lake Taneycomo until they can return to their lodge. Preston's cabin was the only building destroyed."

"Any idea what caused the fire?"

"Not yet. I haven't had time to worry about that. I've had my hands full with other things. Though the cabin was a few years old, I had it checked out before I purchased it, and it was in good shape structurally."

"My uncle was a fireman before he retired," she said. "He told me once that the investigation begins as soon as the first fireman arrives on the scene."

"What first alerted you and Preston to the fire?"

"I saw a light outside. When I stepped out the back door I smelled something pungent, like turpentine or some kind of fuel. Then I smelled the smoke." She paused, remembering. "When I reached the front, there were streaks of fire shooting toward the house across the lawn."

He didn't pause in his movements, but she felt, rather than saw, his sudden, startled interest. "Streaks?"

She nodded. "I remember thinking at the time about fuses. You know, like to a bomb."

"Has anyone from the fire department or police department contacted you?"

"Yes, as soon as I arrived here with Preston, there was someone here to talk to me. I told him what I'm telling you."

"I'll have a talk with them. For now, you just relax." After cleansing the site and setting up for sutures, Graham changed into sterile gloves and picked up the syringe filled with anesthetic solution to numb the wound.

He completed a two-layer closure in less than ten minutes.

After wiping the wound one last time with a saline-soaked swab, he invited Willow to examine the finished job. She nodded with admiration. The guy was good.

Graham removed his gloves and excused himself.

Willow laid her head back and closed her eyes in silent, automatic prayer for her brother's life.

A moment later she heard a quiet footfall and jerked upright, eyes snapping open. A man in the doorway looked slightly familiar. In his mid-thirties, he had curly dark hair, a long face and warm, friendly brown eyes.

"Everyone okay in here?" he asked, taking a step closer to the bed.

"There's just me, and I'm fine," she said, frowning at him. Then she placed him. "You're Rick Fenrow. Apartment Three B, right? Did you know about the fire?"

"Yes, I heard. You're Preston's sister, aren't you?" He had a low tenor voice, with a northern accent.

"That's right. I didn't know until tonight that you worked here."

"I haven't been here that long. Did you know another tenant, Carl Mackey, works part-time at the hospital, as well? He's in the pharmacy. The way things are looking tonight, we could have the whole complex here by the time the sun rises."

"The fire hadn't spread to the lodge when I left," she assured him.

"That's what the fireman told me. It's a relief, too.

Everything I own is in that place."

"Are you a nurse?"

"Orderly. I usually work on the floor, but they were extra busy tonight, so I got called down here." He looked at the chair that held her pajamas. "Caught you off guard, did it?"

"I'd say."

Rick held up a hand. "I'll be right back." He winked and left the room. Moments later he came back, carrying a set of green scrubs. "These should fit."

"Thank you," she said.

"And don't worry about Preston—he's one tough guy. He'll get through this just fine."

"Have you seen Mrs. Engle?"

"She's in some pain, but they've already called an orthopedist. She'll be okay." He patted her foot, then turned and left the room.

Less than thirty seconds later Graham returned to Willow's treatment room. "Preston's ready to see you before they take him to surgery."

Holding her hospital gown with her good arm, she eagerly followed him into the trauma room, where Preston had been prepped for surgery. Blood infused through one of the two IVs in his arms, and a well-taped chest tube protruded from the left side of his chest, ending in an underwater seal device standing on the floor.

Preston's upper chest and forearms had reddened; his skin was mildly blistered. EKG electrodes, an automatic blood pressure cuff and a fingertip pulse oximetry unit all connected him to a portable monitoring unit, which beeped with steady rhythm.

Willow noted that Preston's blood pressure was a little low, his heart rate a little fast, but his oxygen saturation was excellent, and the cardiac monitor showed a strong, steady heartbeat.

"You get yourself into more trouble," she said loudly enough for him to hear over the mechanical noise.

He opened heavy-lidded eyes. "Sis," he whispered through his oxygen mask. "You okay?"

"Doing great. What's up with you?"

Preston sighed, closing his eyes as if he were drifting off. But he opened them again. "Seems the CT scan showed I have a fractured liver, and my spleen's bleeding." His voice deepened, sounding as rough as gravel churning in a concrete mixer. "They're taking me straight to surgery." His eyes closed again. "Not sure how a person fractures a liver."

"Well, if anyone can do it, you can," she said.

"Guess they'll have to put a cast on it, huh?" His voice drifted to silence. A snore punctuated the mechanical sounds of the room.

The nurse came to wheel him to surgery. Willow turned to find Graham stepping up behind her.

"You're being released," he said. "But you don't have anything to wear out of here except your filthy pajamas or that hospital gown." He gestured to her attire.

"Rick Fenrow brought me a set of scrubs to change into."

"He's on duty tonight? Preston was worried when he couldn't find him at the lodge. There's a private waiting room where you can relax until we receive word. You look as if you could use some rest."

"Thanks," she said dryly.

"You're welcome."

Back in her treatment room, she fingered the soft material of the scrubs and felt a flick of bittersweet memories. Would she ever escape them?

What *was* she going to do? Everything she had brought with her to Branson had been destroyed in that inferno. Her driver's license, her credit cards, her checkbook, even her cash were gone. The only thing she owned that had been spared was her car, because it was parked in the carport across the drive. And she didn't even have her keys.

This was a different kind of nightmare.

Chapter Four

A predawn light touched the western horizon when Graham entered the private room where Willow had been waiting for news about her brother. The lights had been turned off, and only the glow from the hallway and window filtered into the room.

Word had come a few moments earlier that the fire had been contained and the other buildings were out of danger. Now came the tedious duty of cleanup and paperwork. Graham hated paperwork.

He saw Willow lying on the sofa, her breathing soft and even. He hated to wake her. Still, she would want to see Preston.

Graham smiled to himself. He understood the strong bonds of family. His sister was on her way here now. He had high hopes that she could charm Willow, after his gruffness had brought out her iciest response at their first encounter. Though she had thawed considerably once she realized he wasn't the ogre she'd first deemed him to be, he knew she hadn't yet warmed completely. Her guard was up. He couldn't blame her.

For some reason he didn't want her to be alone right now. In spite of her self-reliance, there was something about her that seemed so . . . breakable.

Her soft, even breathing stopped for a few moments, then a moan seemed to shake her. Her eyes sprang open. She uttered a cry of such pain that he stiffened, wondering if her arm could be hurting her that badly.

"Willow, it's okay," he said.

Her lips parted in obvious alarm. She focused a terrified gaze on him, and he thought she might scream.

"It's okay," he said gently. "It's just me, Graham."

She shot a quick look around the room, then seemed to realize where she was. "What are you doing here?" she croaked, her voice tense and hoarse.

"Working on my bedside manner." He noticed she'd changed into the scrubs. "It's the least I could do after harassing you so mercilessly earlier."

She rubbed her eyes. "Preston?"

"He's doing fine, recovering in surgical ICU. I've

been working on my landlord duties. You have a place to stay, as of right now."

She blinked, then slumped against the overstuffed arm of the sofa. "Can't believe I fell asleep," she murmured softly, as if to herself.

"Bad dream?" Graham ventured.

She blinked again, straightened her shoulders and returned her attention to him as she scrambled out of the depths of the overstuffed sofa. "Nothing new about that." She winced as she accidentally placed her weight on her injured arm.

"I don't think you need to stay alone right now," Graham said.

She stood up, and for the first time he noticed she was nearly as tall as his five feet ten inches, maybe an inch or two shorter. "I'm not sure what I'm supposed to do about that," she said.

"I have a suggestion."

She grew still, silent. Again, that wariness. Was this a natural part of her personality or a result of her husband's death?

"My sister is staying with me in a house down on the lake near Hideaway," he said. "It's a large house, so there's plenty of room for you. When Preston gets out of the hospital, there will also be room for him to stay while he recuperates."

She wrapped her arms around herself, as if she were cold—or as if the bad dream continued to terrorize her. "How far do you live from this hospital?" she asked.

"It's a bit of a drive, but—"

"No. I appreciate your concern, Dr. Vaughn—"

"It's Graham, remember?"

She reached up with slender fingers and rubbed at her eyes again. At this moment she appeared closer to sixteen than thirty-six. "I prefer to stay close in case Preston needs me. Until I can get a new set of keys for my car, I'll find a room nearby so I can walk."

"That won't be necessary," Graham said. "I've already arranged for someone to make a set of keys for you. Everything's being taken care of, but I wish you would—"

"I'm sorry, Graham," she said gently as she edged past him and reached for the door. "It's so kind of you to offer, but you have plenty to keep you busy. I can take care of myself."

Without waiting for him to argue, she slipped through the door and let it swing shut behind her.

Willow stood by Preston's bedside and watched the rise and fall of his chest. His mouth hung slack, and the fan of his long black lashes seemed unsinged. His eyebrows hadn't fared so well, and a blister framed the left side of his face.

Unwilling to awaken him, she watched in silence. *I know better than to ask why, Lord. I know I won't get an answer. But how about a "when"? As in "When will it stop?"*

A film of tears blurred her vision. She sniffed and dashed them away, and when she returned her attention to Preston, his eyes were open.

49

"I didn't mean to wake you," she said.

He reached his right hand out to her. She took it gently, feeling the calloused ridge along the top of his palm from too many hours holding a hammer while working on one of his rental properties.

He looked down at the hand he held in his. "You're shaking."

"Do you blame me?" She attempted her usual dry, casual tone with him. It didn't come out right.

His gaze went to her bandaged forearm. "How bad?"

"Not too."

"Graham fix you up?"

"How did you know?"

"He told me, dummy." His teasing grin didn't quite reach his eyes, but she could see it through the oxygen mask. The eyes held only worry, deep worry.

She shrugged. "He's good."

He nodded, satisfied, then indicated her apparel with a look. "Did you get a job here?"

She grimaced as she glanced down at the green scrubs. "One of your renters took pity on me and found these for me." She gestured toward Preston's upper lip, also visible through the mask. "Your mustache is in awful shape." It, too, had been singed.

Preston shifted as if he would try to sit up.

"Don't even think about it," Willow said, pressing a hand against his shoulder.

"He still around?"

"Who?"

He scowled at her. "Who fixed your arm?"

50

"I don't know where he went. Would you just relax and focus on getting well? I'm sure he told you they've got the fire under control, and he seems capable of taking care of the renters."

Preston gave an impatient shake of his head. "I need to talk to him about—"

"You don't need to do a thing right now, my friend." A familiar baritone voice came from behind Willow's left shoulder. "I've got a handle on it all, and if I can't deal with it I know someone who can."

Willow turned and looked at Graham Vaughn, struck afresh by his solid, friendly appearance. He had that "smile with your eyes" trick down perfectly. There was a warmth in his expression that would, of course, serve to encourage his patients to trust him.

In spite of what she'd said to him earlier this morning, he did have a good bedside manner, and he did engender trust. Willow knew she tended to be a little grumpy when stressed, and she was working on that.

"Willow, there's someone I want you to meet as soon as you finish visiting with Preston," Graham said.

"Someone like who?" she asked.

"Someone who can take you shopping for some necessary items until you receive the keys to your car," Graham said. "You'll also want some cash, and the claims adjuster will have that to us later this morning. I've got surgery today, but my sister can—"

"His sister can speak for herself." A new voice spoke from the doorway.

Willow turned to encounter a fresh, smiling, freckled face. The woman, possibly in her late forties, had short, graying red hair the color of antiqued copper. She wore blue jeans and a chambray shirt that suggested she might have been working outside when she received the call from her brother and hadn't taken the time to change.

"I'm Ginger Carpenter," the woman said, stepping forward with an outstretched hand.

Willow took the hand, appreciating the firm grip. "Willow Traynor. I take it you're the sister Graham mentioned?"

"Guilty as charged. Graham offered me the opportunity to help someone else spend money. That's like a dream come true for me. We need to get you fixed up with some clothes, a place to stay until we can find something more permanent, and we've got some money to spend, courtesy of my brother's bank account until the checks arrive later."

"But I don't—"

"Insurance money," Ginger said. "I've turned shopping on a shoestring into an art form. You'd be surprised at the bargains I've learned to dig up in the Branson shops in the past few weeks. I could open your world to a new way of shopping."

Willow gave her borrowed scrubs another perusal. "I wouldn't mind a couple of pairs of jeans."

Ginger patted her own well-endowed fanny. "Honey, I'd give you some of mine, but you'd float around in them. Let's go paint the town green, okay? Looks like

Preston's in great hands." To Willow's surprise, Ginger leaned over the bed and gave Preston a quick, sisterly kiss on the cheek. "Loan Willow to me for a few hours, okay?"

Preston nodded. "You've got her. I'll take a nap."

Graham couldn't help observing Preston's watchful silence as Ginger cajoled Willow from the room. It was a foregone conclusion, at least to Graham, that no one but Ginger could have pulled off this feat. Willow tended to skitter away from people like a half-wild kitten. The woman was intriguing.

At this point, so was her brother. What was up with these two? Yes, they had been through quite an ordeal tonight, but Graham had noticed Preston's body language when he'd spoken of Willow recently. He was worried about her. Preston didn't worry about much, so when something concerned him, Graham homed in on it like a beacon.

With a final glance over her shoulder at Preston, Willow disappeared down the hallway with Ginger.

"I need your help," Preston said quietly the moment the women were out of earshot.

Graham returned his attention to his friend. "You've got it, you know that. Don't worry about a thing. Ginger can help with the renters until—"

Preston gave an impatient wave. "Not that. We can deal with the renters later. I've kept an off-site set of computer records for months now, so that's no problem." His voice grew raspy, and he raised his hand to his throat. "I need help with Willow."

Graham reached for a couple of ice chips and gave them to Preston. "Sorry I can't do any better than that, but you can't have anything else so soon after surgery. Why don't you stop trying to talk? You inhaled a lot of smoke, and you need to rest your voice."

Preston took the chips, coughed, shook his head. "I need you to know some things about Willow."

"You mean you haven't already told me everything there is to tell?" He had heard Preston talk about his sister for several months. Obviously Preston cared a great deal about her.

"I haven't told you everything," Preston said quietly. "She's afraid, Graham."

"Of what?"

"That's what we need to talk about. It's complicated." Preston placed the small ice chips in his mouth.

Graham pulled a chair over to the bed and slumped into it. Last night had been a hard one, and it didn't look as if he'd be getting much rest before his first patient today. "Tell me."

Preston closed his eyes. "Just remember, in my drugged state I may tell you more than Willow would approve of. Don't let this get back to her."

Graham shook off his drowsiness. "What's going on?"

Willow stepped into the hospital parking lot behind Ginger and immediately spotted a sign that advertised lodging.

"Are there several hotels or motels near here?"

"Are you kidding?" Ginger gave a snort that was barely ladylike. "Honey, you've got hundreds of rooms within walking distance, depending on how fast you walk and what kind of shape you're in." The freckled redhead gave Willow an appraising look over the top of her glasses, then nodded with satisfaction. "From the looks of it, you could walk a few miles to get here if need be, but Graham was hoping you'd stay with us at the house, and I'd love—"

"He didn't tell you that I'm planning to stay near the hospital to be with Preston as much as possible?" Willow asked.

"He did mention that, but since Graham drives into town every day you could easily come in with him."

"I like to be able to come and go in my own car. Graham says you live in Hideaway."

"That's right."

"It's a long way to Hideaway from here." Willow wasn't in the mood to move in with complete strangers, even if those strangers seemed trustworthy.

She'd trusted before—trusted that as long as she and Travis were doing God's will, they would not have to worry about enduring any of the shocking tragedies that so often took people by surprise. She now felt foolish for holding that irrational belief.

"As the crow flies, Hideaway isn't terribly far from here," Ginger said.

"I'm not a crow."

"The drive isn't that bad. You could get to the hospital from Hideaway in forty minutes—thirty if you catch the traffic right. Believe me, you'd be more than welcome to stay with us."

The woman was a bit pushy. Willow slowed her steps and fixed Ginger with a look. "You need to understand that I won't be doing that. While I appreciate the offer, my answer is no. Please don't argue with me." With some people it was necessary to establish her boundaries in the beginning. If they didn't like it, they could move on and rescue someone else.

To her surprise, Ginger chuckled. "Well, I see you're a lady who knows her own mind. Good. But as my brother reminds me often enough, I'm a nag. I'll try to keep it to a minimum. Now let's enjoy the morning."

Willow caught sight of a motel marquee down the street that announced vacancies. "I think I'll see if I can get a room over there. At least for a while." She refused to think of the multiple reasons she should accept Ginger's offer.

As she'd told Graham and the fireman that had interviewed her earlier, those streaks of flame she'd seen rushing toward the house—like fuses racing to a bomb—had definitely raised her suspicions and already found their way into her nightmare.

Those weren't just naturally occurring phenomena. They had a direction, an object of attack. She had seen headlights in the forest beyond the apartment complex. Someone else had been out there. She didn't need any further investigation to tell her that much.

She didn't want to be alone right now, but that wasn't

a good enough reason to move in with strangers. The fireman had informed her that there had been two other fires last night, and theirs had most likely been a random attack. As soon as they found the perpetrator, all would be settled.

Too bad she couldn't convince herself of that. She wasn't up to being logical this early in the morning with so little sleep after barely escaping with her life.

But she was a grown woman, able to take care of herself. She didn't need keepers.

She would go shopping with Ginger, enjoy the female company and buy some things she desperately needed. Then she would rent a room and settle in.

Graham listened to Preston's worries with growing concern. "Willow's husband was murdered?"

Preston shifted in his bed and took another ice chip. "He was killed in the line of duty during a drug raid, but Willow isn't convinced his death had anything to do with the drug raid."

"What does she think happened?"

"She's convinced of some kind of conspiracy, either within the department or from an old enemy from another case. The trajectory of the bullet was wrong, and the bullet didn't match any of the firearms confiscated after the raid."

"I'm sure there was an investigation, right?" Graham asked.

"Of course. No other shooter was found. It was decided that one of the perpetrators must have gotten away. End of case. But Willow can't accept it. Ever since Travis's death, she hasn't been herself."

Graham could tell the poor guy was miserable, but his heightened concern for Willow kept him vigilant even now, with the aftereffects of the surgery. "You're saying she still has some major emotional issues connected to her husband's death?"

"To put it mildly." Preston's eyes closed, and he grimaced with pain. "And that's not the only problem."

"We need to see about getting you some more medication," Graham said.

Preston sighed and nodded. "Okay, but please, please watch Willow for any signs of trouble." He caught his breath, then moaned softly.

"I'll make sure she's safe, though I don't have to tell you how independent she can be." Graham motioned for the surgical ICU nurse.

Preston opened his eyes again, and this time Graham could plainly see the fear in them. "Everyone knows that when a person is having some kind of emotional problem, they try to make sure that the last thing it affects is their job. Well, Willow lost her job six months ago."

"She was fired?"

"No, she quit. She hasn't worked as a nurse since. After her husband's death she started talking about these . . . bad dreams. She insists her husband's murderer is after her, and believe me, after what just happened, she's even got me spooked, and I should know better."

The nurse joined them and made note of Preston's vitals, then looked at Graham expectantly. "You wanted to see me, Doctor?"

"Yes. Did Dr. Glessner leave orders for pain meds? Mr. Black is having some pain."

"Of course. I'll set it up immediately."

As soon as she left, Preston reached for more ice, then fell back against the pillow. "You probably need to know this. Willow was pregnant when Travis died."

"She was?" That would be doubly tragic, for a child to be on the way when the father is killed.

"About a month after he died," Preston continued, "Willow was leaving work one morning after a long night and walked out in front of a car. It hit her and knocked her down. She lost the baby. She was convinced someone ran her down intentionally."

"Did they?"

"I don't know. She was irrational by the time I got to her in the hospital, out of her mind with grief, so I wasn't sure what to think. Maybe, at the time, I was so overwhelmed myself with the situation that I wasn't willing to consider her suspicions."

Graham felt a surge of sympathy for the woman who had endured so much tragedy. Now it was obvious why she held everyone at arm's length. He'd be suspicious, too, if he'd gone through that.

"One good thing about all this," Preston continued as the nurse returned with his medicine. "Willow happened to be awake last night, or we'd probably both be dead."

"Has she said anything more about what woke her?"

"We didn't have a chance to talk about it. She's been too worried about me. But mark my words, she'll be wondering about last night's fire."

Graham knew that, among other things, Willow had already been interviewed by the fire captain, and no one was talking about it.

"If it was arson," Preston said, "Willow will be convinced it was set by her husband's killer."

Graham felt a chill slither down his spine at the thought that there could be a murderer in Branson.

Chapter Five

Willow carried an armload of packages into the motel room that she had just rented for the week. Ginger followed close behind, also loaded down with packages.

"You're sure you want to do this?" Ginger released her burden onto the cheap, floral-print spread that covered the only bed in the small room. "The guest bedroom at the house where I'm staying is three times this size, the ambiance is—"

"I'm sure it's a paradise." Willow suppressed a smile, surprised by the rapport she had developed with this woman with the big mouth and the bigger . . . uh . . . fanny.

For the past three hours, after treating Willow to a generous feast at a breakfast buffet, Ginger had played tour guide between stops at the outlet malls. The woman had given a rundown of the shortcuts and back-streets that would help Willow avoid Highway 76—the Branson creep show during the busy months, when traffic crept along more slowly than the tourists on the sidewalks.

Ginger pulled some articles of clothing from one of the bags and spread them on the bed. "Well, anyway, as I said, I don't know that it'll benefit you much to stay right here so close to the hospital when you already know the shortcuts through town. Graham gave the other renters condo suites. Insurance covers it."

"Is there a condo nearby?"

"Here in Branson, there's always a condo nearby. There's a furnished duplex over on Blackner that's always looking for renters. The manager's a friend of your brother's. It'd be barely a five-minute drive to the hospital from there." Ginger quirked an unplucked, copper-bronze eyebrow. "However, the best place to stay is—"

"I know, I know." Willow chuckled. "Hideaway. You sound like a commercial for the place." She had almost weakened a time or two under Ginger's determined but sweet-natured onslaught, especially since she enjoyed this woman's laid-back attitude and up-front sense of humor.

But she couldn't allow others to control her life right now, no matter how well-meaning they were. They didn't know her situation, and *she* needed that control.

Ginger held up the one purchase she'd made for her-

61

self at the Dress Barn. "Mind if I use your bathroom to try this on?" She glanced toward the tiny room. "If I can fit into that broom closet. I want to see if our all-we-could-eat breakfast has affected my dress size in the past couple of hours."

While Ginger changed, Willow unpacked socks, shoes, jeans, T-shirts, toiletries and a flashlight, while listening to Ginger's comments, accompanied by an occasional grunt from the bathroom.

"This dress is the gift Graham's getting me for my birthday," Ginger said through the crack in the door, which she'd left ajar. "He just doesn't know it yet. I plan to spring it on him before he can buy me something totally inappropriate."

Willow unwrapped a package of socks. "When's your birthday?"

"Next Tuesday. I'll be fifty-three."

"No way."

"Big way. My age is one of the reasons I was forced to come back to America."

Back to America? "Fifty-three isn't old."

"It is to some people."

"Where were you living?"

Another grunt, then a low mutter about too many buttons. "Belarus. I'm a physician's assistant, and for ten years I worked at a mission clinic on the outskirts of Minsk."

"You're a *missionary?*" Now that she thought about it, Willow realized that Ginger hadn't talked much about herself today, nor had she asked any personal questions about Willow. What she had done was fill Willow in on the Branson hot spots and tell her all about the charms of Hideaway and its residents. And she'd called the hospital every hour for a progress report on Preston, who was still sleeping.

Ginger had been the perfect hostess, putting Willow totally at ease—quite an accomplishment. Until today, Willow would have thought that would be impossible.

"Was," Ginger said. "*Was* a missionary. Big difference."

"Why did you have to come back?"

"Heart problems. Mine got broken one too many times by some of the children who came through our clinic. Of course, the chest pains might've had something to do with it, as well."

"Chest pains?" Willow asked.

"Yes, and some big mouth told Graham about it, and he insisted I come back to the States for a workup. So here I am. I had the workup, found a little problem, nothing worth mentioning, and while I was away, some new med school grad replaced me." She came out the door, her face flushed from exertion. "But I'm not bitter."

She wore a leopard-print dress that made her look like a very fluffy female stuffed animal with Grand Canyon cleavage. "Well, what do you think?"

Willow tried to keep all expression from her face. "About what?"

Ginger held her arms out and did an ungainly model's pirouette. "How do I look?"

Oh, boy.

"Come on, give it to me straight."

"The color looks good," Willow said. "Excellent color choice."

"You really think so?" Ginger pattered barefoot to the small dresser and did another pirouette, straining to turn her head far enough to see the back of the dress. "You know, this is the first time in years I've had a chance to go shopping for something nice like this. I don't even know what's in fashion anymore."

"Nose rings and tattoos," Willow said dryly.

"That I cannot do. I'm not a fan of pain. So you really think this dress looks good on me?" She turned to face Willow, hands on hips.

No way was Willow going to lie to this woman. "Um. What I said was that the color is good on you."

Ginger blinked. "The color?" She turned back to the mirror and frowned. "Granted, I'd have to do something drastic to rein in the neckline, but don't you think the print gives me a certain flair?"

"Maybe a vertical tiger-print top with a slim black skirt."

"Oh-oh." Ginger patted her derriere, chuckling. "Looks like my love for pig fat, borscht and potato pancakes has caught up with me. You haven't lived until you've tasted *kholodets*."

"How long have you been back in the States?"

"Going on a month," Ginger said, turning again to check her reflection. "You don't think a nice wide black belt would do the trick?"

Willow made a face.

Ginger grimaced. "Didn't think so."

"What did you do before you went to Belarus ten years ago?" Willow asked.

"Oh, the usual. Had to get married at seventeen, was a scandal in our small hometown and a disgrace to the family. I was divorced at eighteen, got married again at twenty-five, was widowed at twenty-nine." Ginger's gaze sought Willow's in the reflection of the mirror. "Life does go on, even though I didn't want it to back then."

Willow held the gaze. She swallowed. "Any children?"

"Two boys. Twins. They were the reason for the first marriage, and the reason why I did keep going after the divorce and after their stepfather died. They've got families of their own now, teenagers and all, paying for their raising." She winked at Willow. "You?"

Willow closed her eyes and nodded. "I lost a little girl when I was four months along, a month after my husband's death. Pedestrian versus car." She didn't know this fun-loving missionary well enough to confess that she suspected the "accident" was no accident. Saying that in the past had earned her some uncomfortable looks, and even more disconcerting comments.

Ginger turned from the mirror and walked over to plop down onto the chair beside the bed. "Oh, honey, you've been through it, haven't you?"

Willow didn't want to sink into grief today. She

wanted to forget the nightmare for once and forget the reason she was here, doing this right now—because there had been a fire.

She'd become so lonely and overwhelmed by her dreams and her fears that she'd finally given in to her brother's insistence that she move in with him and forget about what was happening in K.C. He was worried about her emotional stability.

Her own brother probably thought she was neurotic, maybe even psychotic.

And now he needed her, and she wasn't even sure if he would be willing to accept her help, or if he'd try to micromanage her life, even from his hospital bed.

She realized Ginger was watching her closely.

"You doing okay, hon?"

Willow sighed, surveying the jumble of plastic bags and clothing strewn across the bed. "I'm just a little overwhelmed right now."

"You didn't get a lot of sleep last night. I think I'll change back into my comfy duds, repackage this wild outfit and take it back to the Dress Barn. That way I'll be out of your hair and you can take a nap."

Willow looked at the clock. It was after lunchtime, but at last check, Preston had still been sleeping. Maybe a nap would be exactly what she needed. "I think I could use some rest, but I need to get the key and pick up my car."

"You don't have to do any of that right now," Ginger said, patting Willow's arm as she rose from the bed. "I'm still full as a tick from that late breakfast, but how about an early supper in a few hours? I'm desperate for some girl talk. I love Graham, but he hasn't had a lot of time since I've returned to listen to my chatter."

Willow looked at the clock beside the bed, then nodded. "You've got a date. Give me a couple of hours?"

"I'll give you three. Try to get some sleep."

Graham completed the sutures on a five-year-old child who had run through a window, reassured the little boy's mother one last time that the wound should heal with very little scarring and handed her a sheet of printed instructions for wound care. He also made an appointment card for her, with the date for suture removal.

The phone had rung almost constantly since he'd begun the repair, and his assistant had gone to lunch early today to run errands for the clinic. He needed more help.

He'd thought about asking Ginger to fill in a couple of days a week. As he expanded the clinic—a necessity if he was going to keep up with the needs of so many patients—he would be able to utilize her skills. Right now, however, he needed another volunteer office assistant, someone to answer phones, make appointments, follow up on patient care.

An additional nurse would be great, as well, and a PA such as Ginger would be a blessing from heaven, especially if Graham had to start moonlighting in the E.R. for income.

That was a definite possibility after last night. He could lose renters over this. In fact, one of his renters, Carl Mackey, a transplant from up north, often pitched in here when he wasn't on duty at the hospital.

As the mother and child left the office, he finished his report on the little boy's accident, then checked his messages. He had fifteen.

He should never have come to the clinic today. But then, the woman who had just left the office would have incurred a major bill in the emergency department, particularly since she had no insurance. She could barely afford to keep a roof over her head as it was.

Winters in Branson could be difficult for people in the service and entertainment industries. The downtime put a lot of people on the unemployment lines between January and March. April and May were often catch-up months for those with financial struggles. Several of the units at the lodge had only recently been occupied by newcomers to Branson.

Graham rubbed his eyes wearily, then picked up the telephone and dialed the number of the last person to leave a message—the Hollister fire captain.

Graham had been in close contact with the fire department all morning.

As the phone rang, he thought again about Preston's remark that Willow would probably take the fire personally. She seemed like a perfectly sane, capable woman who was obviously wary of strangers. If she truly had experienced attacks from the person who had killed her husband, it would be a little strange if it hadn't affected her to some degree.

Preston's problem right now was his helplessness. Graham would be the one to make the decisions for him in the next few days . . . maybe even weeks. Those decisions might also affect Willow.

One of the messages on the machine was from Ginger, informing him that Willow had insisted on securing her own lodging, which was a motel near the hospital.

It disappointed him, but he wasn't surprised.

The phone was answered on the seventh ring. It was the fire captain.

"Hello, Captain Frederick. Graham Vaughn here. Do you have any good news for me this time?"

There was a long sigh, then the captain's deep voice, with nasal twang, came over the line. "Sorry. We knew pretty much from the first arrival that it was arson, Dr. Vaughn."

"Graham. Just call me Graham."

There was a pause. "Don't think so, Doc. You operated on my wife four years ago when she had that burst appendix. She was scared spitless, and you took such good care of her it was like she was your own. You're the Doctor."

"Thank you, Captain."

"So that's why I can't figure out why anybody'd want to hurt your property."

Graham closed his eyes. "Neither can I. How was the fire started?"

"Pretty simple. The perp used the old cigarette-and-matchbook trick. Attach a cigarette to an open book of matches, so the matches will ignite when the cigarette burns down, giving the arsonist time to get away. Looks like the perp took plenty of precaution—used four of these babies, after pouring a stream of lighter fluid from each matchbook to the house, which he had liberally doused with gasoline. It's no wonder Ms. Traynor smelled the fuel."

"Any leads?"

"Not much to go on right now. My men and women are good, and we've got a lot of help on this case, but we haven't found a culprit yet, only the sighting of a black sedan in the neighborhood sometime before the fire began."

"Who saw that?" Graham asked.

"A neighbor down the road from you, coming home from working a late party."

"There are a lot of people with black sedans," Graham said. "That doesn't tell us much." Carl Mackey had a black sedan, as did the Jasumbacks.

"You're right, it doesn't. We'll check out your renters, of course. We've already started the interview process. We did receive a call later this morning about Jolene Tucker. She was run off the road and injured when driving back into town after a trip out to your place for a quick photo shoot just before first light this morning."

Graham frowned. He'd known she would show up sooner or later. "Who would have run her off the road?"

"I can think of a few people who'd like to do it," the man muttered.

"Where is she now?"

"No idea, but she earned herself a trip to the E.R. via ambulance. She had a banged-up leg, was treated and released. She insisted it was deliberate."

"Did she get a description of the automobile that ran her off the road?"

"Sure did," the captain said. "We even have the vehicle impounded. It was a brown Ford Expedition stolen from a convenience store two blocks from Clark Memorial Hospital earlier this morning because some trusting idiot left his keys in the ignition while he went in to get a cup of coffee. Bet he doesn't do that again."

"So no leads there."

"Nope. The police found the vehicle abandoned later, also near the hospital. Might not be any connection to our fire, but we're checking all possibilities. You can bet the incident will be in tomorrow's paper. Jolene's need for attention might even be a good thing right now, if it attracts a witness or two."

Graham thought again about Preston's concerns for Willow and her fears that someone might be after her . . . and last night's case of mistaken identity. "What kind of car was Jolene driving?"

"It's a red Kia Sportage, which is the reason she didn't sustain any more damage than she did. Good little cars. My wife drives one."

As the captain lapsed into rhapsody about the delights of his wife's car, Graham closed his eyes and

71

recalled a detail from the fire last night. He'd come out of the apartment with Mrs. Engle and seen the row of vehicles in the carport across the drive from the lodge, specifically checking to make sure none had been damaged. He'd seen an unfamiliar small dark red SUV among them.

Coincidence? Had to be. But what if it wasn't?

"Doc, are you there?" Captain Frederick asked.

"Yes, sorry. Jolene did believe the wreck was deliberate?"

"She *said* it was deliberate, but we all know that woman likes to overdramatize everything."

"Something just occurred to me, Captain. I may be overreacting here, but it's possible that Willow Traynor might drive a red Subaru Outback. She looks enough like Jolene in low light that someone could have mistaken Jolene for her. I made that mistake myself."

"Where is Ms. Traynor right now?"

"I hope she's safely shopping with my sister, but I think I'll make sure. Meanwhile, a friend of mine was having a replacement key made for Willow's car. He had to get the particulars from Preston because I didn't have them. I wasn't involved in that conversation."

"Better keep your friend away from the car. We don't want to pass up any leads, even if they seem farfetched. We'll need to check out that car first."

"Check it out?"

"What if someone did intentionally run Jolene Tucker off the road because they mistook her car for Ms. Traynor's? If they were serious enough to do that

72

kind of damage, and if they discovered later that they had the wrong car, they might take it another step and set a booby trap of some kind. Stranger things have been known to happen."

"I'll call my friend now. Then I think I'll take a drive out to the complex."

"Can you get us the key?" the captain asked. "The officers can jimmy the lock with no problem, but it would be better if we didn't have to."

"If we have Willow's permission, I'll gladly give the police the key. I'll just have my friend meet us there."

"They'll get her permission before they make any attempts to enter the car, of course. I don't suppose Ms. Traynor would know about anyone who might have a reason to hurt her, would she?"

Graham thought again about his conversation with Preston. Would she? "It's possible, Captain."

"Well, this could be a long shot, but right now we don't have any other leads on any of the fires that were set last night."

Graham remembered the other fires that had spread the department so thin last night. "Are you telling me they were all arson?"

"That's right. All three of them, same M.O., same everything."

"Was last night the first time this has happened?"

"First I've ever seen. How's Mr. Black doing?"

"He's in a lot of pain right now."

"Think he might have made an enemy? Maybe a former renter?"

"We haven't had any complaints."

"Well, you just let me know as soon as you find Ms. Traynor, will you?"

Graham promised to do so, then hung up, praying that he was jumping to faulty conclusions, praying that they all were.

He pressed Ginger's speed dial number, hoping against past experience that this time, for the first time, she would actually be carrying the cell phone he'd given her.

Nope. Not Ginger. She'd probably left it in her car somewhere, relegated to the glove compartment, or perhaps beneath the seat.

He left a message on her voice mail, knowing she probably wouldn't check it. In fact, her phone could even be out of juice.

And he needed to talk to her right now.

Chapter Six

*D*ark *eyes hovered in the thickness of night, staring up at Willow from the coffin, their depths drawing her down. Something . . . they wanted her to know something . . .*

Those eyes repulsed her, and she backed away. Too much. It was all too much. Other people . . . innocent people . . . helpless people depended on her for protection. But how could she protect them? If only she knew.

The rhythm of a heartbeat sang through the room in mechanical tones, a familiar sound she worked with every day. She could do this.

She was in her element . . . until the man in the coffin opened his mouth and moaned. Then she lost her strength.

Willow's eyes snapped open. She knew immediately she had been dreaming. Not just dreaming, but fighting her way out of another nightmare.

This time the man in the coffin had been so real, and for a moment she wondered if she weren't receiving some supernatural warning that she might be dead soon. Or maybe someone she loved would be dead.

"Stop it," she muttered impatiently. If she kept this up she'd be seeing omens in every cloud in the sky. She had always been cursed with an active imagination.

Still, couldn't her subconscious be trying to tell her something?

But it wouldn't come. Would she ever be able to sleep normally again? Without the aid of sleeping pills? Without the haunting memories that plagued her?

"Oh, Travis," she whispered. "Why didn't you just take me with you?"

Immediately she knew the futility of that line of thought. She couldn't wish for death.

She wanted to fight. She wanted to defeat the mysterious evil that had accosted her at times she least expected it since Travis had left her, since her baby had died, since she'd lost her reason for living.

And yet she couldn't fight an invisible enemy.

She turned over in bed and looked at the clock. In five minutes the alarm would go off anyway. She snapped off the switch and lay thinking.

Who was the dead man in the coffin? This was a dream she'd had before and, as always, it confused and frustrated her. Why did that particular dream come to her so often? And why now?

Frustrated with Ginger's failure to answer her cell phone, Graham disconnected and called Blaze. At least he could depend on the communication-savvy college kid to be accessible.

Blaze answered after the first ring. "I was just getting ready to call you, Graham."

"Where are you?"

"Parked alongside the road at the entrance to your complex. The police have got the driveway roped off. Something's going down, because there weren't this many people here earlier, when I came to get the identification number from the car so I could have a key made. Mind telling me what's up?"

"I will when I get there. Who else is there?"

"The place is crawling with police and firemen and news crews and onlookers."

Graham groaned inwardly. News crews. A rental property owner did not need this kind of media attention. "You have the key, then?"

"Yep. I had to go through fifteen gazillion hoops to

get it, but after a call to the police to verify my story, and a call to my guardian to make sure I was legit, and a call—"

"Blaze."

"Yeah?"

"Don't give the key to anyone until we know Willow has given permission for her car to be entered."

There was a pause, then he said, "Can I stay and watch the excitement?"

"Sure. I'll be there in a few minutes. Just stay out of the way."

There was an impatient sigh. "I'm not a kid, you know."

"Sorry. I'll see you soon." He disconnected. This would be a wild-goose chase. He hoped.

Once more he pressed his sister's speed dial number. He'd tried her at home and she wasn't there. He could only hope she was still shopping with Willow. If only, miracle of miracles, she had thought to recharge the phone this time. He nagged her about it enough—she should know by now.

One could always dream.

He turned onto the tree-lined driveway of the complex behind the fire chief and noted that Blaze hadn't been exaggerating. Three police cruisers lined the drive, as well as two fire trucks. Jolene Tucker stood at the periphery with a camera and a hand-held recorder, finding plenty of people to talk to about the excitement.

At least most of the renters were now safely settled

in their temporary dwellings and weren't on hand to be interviewed.

Blaze Farmer also stood watching with obvious interest, pacing up and down the road.

Ginger finally answered Graham's call. "Yes?" She sounded harassed.

Graham sighed with relief. "Did I catch you in traffic?"

"How'd you guess? It's okay. I'm on 76. It'll be slow for a while. Don't even ask me how I got caught in this turtle race."

"I won't. There's no time. Is Willow with you?"

"No, she's taking a nap in her room. Did you get my message about that? She insisted on getting a room near the hospital."

"Yes, I got the message."

"I'm on my way there now."

"I thought you, of all people, could convince her to stay with us."

"Sorry," Ginger said, "but she's a pretty spunky young woman, if one is allowed to use that word these days. I really like—"

"You're on your way to see her?"

"Yes, though I'm early. She was going to visit Preston before we went to supper."

"Listen, we've got a complication. Keep this under your hat for now, but a car resembling Willow's, with a driver who resembles Willow, was run off the road this morning. The police are checking out Willow's car."

"Oh, great, that's just what she needs," Ginger muttered.

"The authorities are sure the fire was arson."

"Do they have any suspects?"

"None yet, but that incident on the road this morning sounds a little too close to be coincidence. It's possible someone could have been trying to hurt Willow."

Graham parked and got out of his car, watching the police search the ground near the carport. In the light of day he saw one of the lines of scorched grass that led from the driveway to the destroyed cabin.

"Graham?" Ginger said. "Do you think Willow is in danger?"

"I don't know how to answer that right now. She could be. I think she's convinced of it, too. Preston told me a few things about her situation. Did she mention anything about her life in Kansas City when you were with her?" The crunch of gravel was loud beneath Graham's shoes as he walked toward the crowd of officers around the carport.

"Very little, except for the loss of her baby soon after her husband's death. I got the feeling she wasn't in the mood to share with a stranger. Not that I blame her."

He tsked. "Sis, you're losing your touch. Where's she staying? Do you have a number for the hotel?"

"It isn't a hotel. I told you, it's a motel, tiny and old, one of the few buildings that survived the reconstruction. I tried to get her to at least stay in a condo, but she was in the mood to make her own decisions. After everything that's happened to her, I can't say I blame her."

"You don't know the half of it yet."

"Oh, really? Mind filling me in?"

"Preston says she's convinced that someone not only murdered her husband, but also tried to kill her."

There was a soft gasp over the line. "Oh, Graham. She never said a word about anything like that."

"But Preston is also afraid she might be imagining things due to the onslaught of grief at the time."

"Why don't you let me tell her about the problem with her car when I reach her?"

"You're stuck in traffic—it could be a while. The police will need her permission to search her car for any possible tampering."

Ginger told him the name of the motel.

"You wouldn't happen to have the number, would you?"

"Nope. It'll be in a phone book," she said. "I still wish you'd let me get to her and break the news to her, myself."

"She'll be fine. Will you please keep your cell phone on you?" Graham asked, none too gently. "And keep it charged."

"You got it. Let me know what the police find."

"I'll be sure to call you."

Willow dabbed away the last droplets from her shower and towel dried her hair, glad she'd recently cut it short enough that her natural curl would take over. She didn't like to spend much time on styling, and all she had to do with this was wash and dry. Now she would have time to walk to the hospital and check on Preston before dinner.

She selected a newly purchased pair of black jeans and a flowing, red gauze blouse and realized, with surprise, that she was actually looking forward to early dinner. Ginger had been the first person in months who'd made her laugh.

How long since I've made a new friend?

She'd drifted away from most of her friends after Travis was killed, burying herself in work to avoid facing the loss. She'd attempted to stuff her grief with fatigue from too many hours on the job, particularly after the miscarriage.

Working most Sundays, she'd lost contact with church family, even though they called and attempted to keep her involved. Her relationship with her in-laws had atrophied from neglect, as well. After all, she'd had no children to keep the family connected. She couldn't blame Travis's parents and siblings for giving up on her.

These past two years she hadn't seemed to even have a life, which had made it so easy to pick up and move in with Preston.

Poor Preston.

Until this morning's shopping trip with Ginger, Willow hadn't realized how much she missed having friends. Could it be that, after two years, the trauma of the fire had finally shocked her out of her shell?

She slipped her feet into new black leather sling backs and was removing the tags from a new purse when the telephone rang on the bedside stand.

She picked up, expecting to hear Ginger's voice. Instead, it was the deep voice of a man who identified himself as Detective Abrams asking to speak with her.

During his quick description of the accident last night with a car much like hers, Willow felt herself growing weak. She sank onto the bed, listening to the man explain the situation.

"You want my permission for you to search my car?"

"Yes, ma'am."

How did she know he was the police?

On the other hand, if he wasn't the police, he would have no reason to call for her permission. "Of course, you have it. You actually believe someone might have sabotaged me?"

"I'm sorry, ma'am, we don't know that this is the case, but we also don't want to take chances, in light of last night's fire."

"How will you obtain access?"

"We have a young man here by the name of Blaze Farmer who had a key made so he could return your car to you today. Dr. Vaughn had requested his help."

"Okay, then. I'd appreciate an update when you can call me. I'll be in the hospital with my brother, if you call within the next thirty minutes."

After disconnecting, she sank onto the bed and clasped her hands together to keep them from trembling. What was happening?

Graham recognized Detective Trina Rush working beneath the rear hatch of the dark red Subaru Outback as he approached the crowd. She was about fifty, with graying hair and a kind face. At the moment, however, her usually serene expression held dismay. She stepped back and looked at the crowd over her shoulder.

"I don't believe what I'm seeing," muttered one of the firemen.

Graham worked his way through the small crowd of firemen, policemen and onlookers. The mat that covered the spare tire for Willow's car had been pulled out, along with the tire—the detectives had been thorough in their search for any kind of booby trap.

In the tire well was a gallon-sized plastic Ziploc bag. It held a pack of Virginia Slim cigarettes and several books of matches. And a can of lighter fluid.

"Willow Traynor has some explaining to do," Detective Rush said softly.

Willow stepped from the elevator onto the third floor and walked down the corridor to ICU. The hospital scents and sounds seemed to assault her, and she felt haunted by the familiar look and feel of the place, wistful for the activity. She'd missed that routine so badly these past months, grieving not only the loss of her family, but the loss of the job she'd loved.

But the patients in those beds deserved better than a sleep-deprived nurse who started at her own shadow and burst into tears without provocation. As she'd reasoned with herself throughout the few excruciating weeks before she'd turned in her resignation, how would she endure it if she made a mistake on medication or an error in a patient's care? An ICU nurse was held to an even higher standard than a well-trained floor nurse.

After quitting her job, Willow had practically become a recluse, living on her savings and the interest from her investments of Travis's life insurance policy.

Meanwhile, she had thrown herself into the remodeling of the home she and Travis had shared, keeping him alive in her heart as she attempted to make some of their dreams come true. She'd learned how to wield a hammer against a nail instead of her thumb and fingers. She'd painted and wallpapered and even knocked out a wall. She'd planted a garden and tended flowers instead of human beings, telling herself she enjoyed it.

Right now she missed nursing with a deep ache.

She found the correct room and entered, finding her brother awake at last.

He gave her a heavy-lidded look. "It's about time you got here," he said thickly. "I've been awake at least fifteen minutes."

A PCA pump stood beside his bed, and she could tell he'd made use of the pump with the painkiller. She saw the swell of a chest tube beneath his hospital gown and an automatic blood pressure cuff on his left arm. Wires connected him to the heart monitor overhead, and his vital signs were excellent.

He tugged at the plastic tubing that ran oxygen through his nose.

She pushed his arm away. "Don't pull it out, you need it."

He scowled at her. "I think I felt better before they brought me to the hospital."

"You'll be in pain for a while. That's why they gave you the pump. All you have to do is press the button."

"I did. When are they taking this tube out of my chest?"

"Not for a couple of days. You had a dropped lung, and they need to keep your chest tube to suction so your lung doesn't collapse again."

His scowl deepened. Preston had never been the best of patients.

"I thought you were dead last night," she said. "It terrified me. What made you enter that shed when you knew it could go at any time?"

"The gas tank. I thought I could move it before it exploded."

She clamped her lips shut to prevent herself from castigating him for his stupidity. He had a hero complex—had been that way for as long as she could remember.

"You're staying with Ginger, aren't you?" he asked.

She suppressed a sigh. "No. I didn't want to be that far away from you."

He groaned, closing his eyes. "Willow, I don't need you to take care of me." Irritation edged his voice. "That's what the doctors and nurses and machines and medicines are for. I'm in a hospital, remember?"

"And I'm a nurse, remember? Who better to take care of you than your own . . ."

His eyes opened. "You quit that job, and we both know why," he snapped. "You didn't want to risk the welfare of your patients, so why are you suddenly willing to risk the welfare of your own brother?"

Willow caught her breath at the sting of his words. "You're a grump when you're on medication."

"I'm a grump when I do everything I can think of to keep my sister safe and she puts herself in danger anyway."

"*You're* jumping *me* for putting myself in danger, and you rush into a burning building?"

"And you're staying alone, unprotected in a motel room?"

"I refuse to have this conversation. When you're off the morphine and back in your right mind, we'll talk. You're being irrational."

His attention shifted to the entrance of the room. "Willow."

She turned. In the doorway stood a graying brunette woman in a dark blue pantsuit, with a troubled expression on her face. Behind her stood Ginger, Graham Vaughn and a uniformed policeman, looking through the observation window.

"Mrs. Traynor?" the woman said softly. "I'm Detective Trina Rush of the Branson Police Department. We need to ask you a few more questions about last night's fire. Please come with us."

Willow gestured toward the two extra chairs in the room. "Couldn't we just talk here? My brother might want to help out with details. I'd be glad to—"

"I'm sorry, ma'am," the woman said, "but we need you to come to the station with us for questioning."

"The *station?* But why?"

"With your permission we searched your car this afternoon," Detective Rush said. "We found items that could be incriminating."

"What items?"

"Incendiary devices."

"Willow?" Preston said, trying to sit up. "What are they talking about?"

"I don't know. Don't get up—you'll hurt yourself."

"Mrs. Traynor," the detective said, "we'd like more information about where those items came from and what they were doing in your car."

"But I don't even know what items you're talking about."

"We'll discuss it at the station. You have a right to remain silent—"

Willow gasped. "You're arresting me?"

"Not at this point."

"Then why are you reading me my rights? I thought police only did that when they were arresting someone."

"Not necessarily, Mrs. Traynor." As the woman continued to read Willow her Miranda rights, the room seemed to spin around her. This couldn't be happening!

Chapter Seven

Graham paced the parking lot outside the city hall, unable to sit inside. He had had dealings with Detective Trina Rush before, when the clinic was burglarized a few months ago. She was logical, methodical and smart. If anyone could catch the arsonist, she could. She was also a tough antagonist. A person didn't want to cross her.

A few minutes ago Graham had overheard someone in the station mention that Willow's car door showed signs of being jimmied. He wasn't surprised, but he was concerned. Why would someone want to place incriminating evidence in Willow's car?

Obviously Preston was worried about her, but his behavior indicated something more than that of an overprotective brother. There was something he hadn't confided. Yet.

Ginger came out the city hall's glass door. "How long should this questioning last? It's already been an hour. You don't think they're running bamboo beneath her fingernails or anything, do you?"

"Have you heard any screaming?" he asked.

"Not a sound."

"Then she's obviously holding up well, and they have a lot of questions." He thought about it. "Either that, or they have a soundproof room for stuff like that."

Ginger glared at him. "That's not funny."

88

He turned and paced away from her down the sidewalk toward Veteran's Memorial Park, which faced the busy street of Business 65. "Relax. Trina Rush is just trying to get to the truth. It's what we all want. They aren't going to bully her or—"

"Or play good cop, bad cop?" Ginger asked.

"Well, maybe, but—"

"You know something? You're not making this any easier. Would you stop pacing for a minute and talk to me?"

He sighed and turned back to face his bossy, frowning older sister. He loved her dearly, but if Ginger were allowed, she would mother the whole world in those sturdy arms of hers.

"Ginger, don't jump into the deep end with this one, okay?"

"I'm not jumping into anything. I was called up here in the first place by a certain meddling doctor who couldn't deny his need to help some desperate people in a desperate situation. And now you're warning me to back off?"

"I didn't say for you to back off. I just don't want you to get too bossy. I don't think Willow's the type to appreciate it."

"I'm not bossing anyone. In case you didn't already know it, Willow's been through a horrible time, and she was just beginning to come out of her shell this afternoon. Now she's likely to retreat back into that shell and cut herself off from the help she needs."

"That's the kind of talk that makes me nervous. All

89

that going in and out of shells. Like she's a turtle. Or a psych case. First Preston, now you."

"I didn't say she was a psych case," Ginger exclaimed. "I'm talking about grief. Remember that emotion? When your whole world seems to crumble to nothing? Don't you dare try to tell me you didn't experience some of those wild emotions when Dena left you."

"Dena has nothing to do with what we're dealing with here."

"Your experience with the breakup of your marriage has everything to do with it. If nothing else, you can surely remember how you felt then."

"I'm not likely to forget."

"Then you can empathize with Willow." Ginger frowned. "Wait a minute. What's that you just said about Preston? Are you saying he thinks Willow's a psych case?"

Graham hesitated. He probably shouldn't have said that, but Preston wasn't his patient, he was a friend, so this wasn't a case of doctor-patient confidentiality.

On the other hand, Willow was, technically, his patient.

"You might as well tell me," Ginger said. "I'm not backing off. Preston surely can't believe Willow has any out-of-the-ordinary psychological problems."

"I think he's afraid something might have snapped with her after she lost so much in such a short period of time."

"Why would he think that? Awful as it is, people all

over the world lose that much or worse on a daily basis, and they don't snap. You saw her at her worst this morning. Did she seem like someone who had snapped?"

Graham gazed out at the busy street. "I'm a surgeon, not a psychiatrist. I know how to reassure a patient who is afraid to go under the knife and how to comfort a patient when I have to relay bad news, but I'm not exactly an expert when it comes to reading a person's mental state."

"You know more than you think you do," Ginger said. "Give Willow a chance. She's on the verge of starting a new life for herself. I can see it in her eyes."

"Oh, yeah? What else do you see?"

Ginger glared at him for the sarcasm in his tone. "Obviously, a lot more than you can. For instance, she's starving for human companionship, but she's afraid to trust. She loves her brother very much and is desperate for his well-being. She needs a lot of moral support right now."

He sank onto one of the concrete benches that encircled the flagpole. Ginger joined him.

"I don't guess they'd let us see her right now," she said. "To give her a little moral support."

"I don't guess."

"Well, we can at least take her out to dinner after this, remind her she isn't alone," Ginger said.

"I have a meeting with the Stone County fire captain tonight."

"Fine, then I'll take her myself. You just go on your

merry way and leave us girls in peace."

Graham sighed heavily. He wouldn't have Ginger any other way, of course, but sometimes she could test his patience. "I'll go with you. I don't have to meet with the captain until later, anyway. The police should finish with Willow in a few minutes." He hoped.

"Fine. I'll go check."

"No, you stay right here until she comes out. The last thing she needs is for some avenging angel to go storming into the interrogation room and demand a few minutes for a pep talk. The police don't take kindly to that type of interference."

Ginger took an exaggerated breath and exhaled slowly, letting him know he was trying her patience, as well. But she didn't move from her seat on the concrete bench.

"We need you to try again to explain about the items we found in your car this afternoon," Detective Rush told Willow.

"I'm sorry, I can't explain them. I have no idea how they got there."

"So you don't smoke?" Detective Rush asked.

"No, I never have."

"Then can you tell me what you were doing with a pack of cigarettes and books of matches and lighter fluid in the cargo hold of your car?"

"They weren't mine. I've never seen them." She glanced at the items in question, which the detective had set at the end of the table.

"You do own a dark red Subaru Outback?"

"Yes." Willow suppressed her irritation with difficulty. She knew this woman was just doing her job, and she knew this line of repetitive questioning was a tried and true method of getting a suspect so confused they would blow their story. Only, she didn't have a story—she just had the truth. Why couldn't this woman accept that? She seemed determined to prove Willow was the arsonist.

"When was the last time you drove your car?" the detective asked.

"Yesterday morning," Willow said, "to church." Lately she had attended services only by force of habit. Perhaps she'd subconsciously been attempting to appease Him with her obedience.

"Look, Detective, I think you can see I'm not hiding anything."

The woman smiled suddenly, changing gears. "I know this is difficult," she said, "but there may be some memory lurking within you that you don't even realize you have. Something you might not realize could be related to this case at all. My job is to attack that memory from every possible angle just in case we can unearth some vital clue that could help us find the arsonist."

"Okay, but as I've told you, I've only been in Branson a couple of weeks. I don't know anyone, and I don't get out much. I don't smoke."

The detective leaned forward. "Willow, does your brother have any enemies?"

"He hasn't mentioned anyone to me." Willow felt a prickling of dread erupt in gooseflesh on her arms. She must still be dreaming. Preston wasn't the one with enemies. *Please, God, wake me up!*

The camera observed her from overhead, in the corner of the small interrogation room—or at least she thought it was a camera. She glanced at the window which no doubt was a two-way mirror. Was someone standing guard, watching her, waiting to see if she would break?

She stared at the slender pack of cigarettes and the five books of matches. They smelled of lighter fluid. In fact, the odor was so strong it permeated the room.

"Can you tell me how long you'd been staying with your brother at his cabin prior to the fire?" the detective asked.

"Two weeks as of yesterday." Hadn't she just said that moments ago?

"And how many of the renters have you spoken with or had contact with during that time?"

Willow closed her eyes, trying again to recall exactly which of the renters she had encountered on the grounds. "As I've said, I'd met Sandi Jameson and her little girls, Brittany and Lucy, because Sandi dropped by to pay her rent one day last week when Preston was gone."

"Does Preston keep his car in a garage?"

"No, he keeps his car in the carport, just like everyone else."

"Then I'm curious why Sandi wouldn't have realized he was gone."

"Apparently she hasn't been in her apartment very long, maybe a month, so maybe she hadn't learned to recognize his car."

"Or maybe she was curious about you."

Willow shrugged. "Maybe."

"Has she gone out of her way to talk with you or connect with you at any other time?"

"Not after that, but maybe it's because I explained to her that I was his sister."

The detective nodded and jotted some notes on her pad. "Anyone else you've met at the complex since you arrived?"

"I saw Mrs. Engle a couple of times, but never actually spoke with her. I knew who she was because Preston talked about her."

"She's the one who fell in her apartment and broke her hip?"

"That's right. I also spoke to Mrs. Bartholomew on the telephone when she called to complain about the noise in the next apartment. I knew who Carl Mackey was because he, too, came to pay his rent while I was there. I understand Carl works part-time in the hospital pharmacy. He hasn't been in the apartment long, either. Preston told me there was a dearth of renters over the winter months, and they've just begun filling the lodge again since March."

"Who else have you met?"

"There's Rick Fenrow, who also works at the hospital and was on duty when the fire started. I didn't exactly meet him until I saw him in the E.R. this morning, but I'd seen him coming and going."

And so the questioning went.

"It seems to me that the only possibility is that someone planted those items in my car," Willow said at last. "Which, of course, I've already said at least ten times. Were the other fires in Branson last night started the same way? Is there any such thing as a serial arsonist?"

The detective folded her hands and leaned back in the straight-back chair, her gray eyes looking tired, the lines of her face looking a little deeper. "Of course there is, but it's been a long time since we've had that kind of problem here in Branson."

"So the other fires were started the same way?"

"Yes, that's why I'm on this case instead of some poor sap in another jurisdiction. Ordinarily, the sheriff's department would handle this." She suddenly smiled at Willow again. "Has it occurred to you that I should be asking the questions?"

"Yes, sorry. But it stands to reason the same person, or group of people, who set the fires in town also set fire to Preston's place. Whoever did that obviously decided to play a little joke on me while setting the fires."

"Reason doesn't often work as a motive for crime," the detective said dryly. "In fact, reason seldom enters into it at all—just plain old human meanness and greed. Whoever jimmied your car door and left these items left no evidence behind that we've found."

Willow slumped with relief. Was it almost over? "So you believe me?"

Detective Rush leaned forward with her elbows on the table. "Willow, how well do you and your brother get along?"

"Pretty well. He's a grouch right now, and he's over-protective, but he's the one who insisted I come down to stay with him for a while."

"Why did he do that?"

Willow certainly didn't want to delve into that whole subject again. They'd covered it twice already. "Because I was having nightmares and I wasn't dealing well with the death of my husband and my miscarriage."

The detective's eyes filled with genuine sympathy. "It's been almost two years since your husband's death. Why did he wait so long?"

Willow shrugged. "I never asked, but I think he felt I should have recovered from the loss. Some people like to put a time frame on these kinds of things, and when you don't fit your life into their time frame, it upsets their world."

There was a long, waiting silence. Another tactic that Travis had once told Willow about. Most people are uncomfortable with extended silence, so they fill it with words. Often those words spoken during unguarded moments can reveal more than can be uncovered during hours of intense questioning.

Willow wasn't uncomfortable with silence.

"I don't suppose you know anyone who would want

to frame you for this?" the detective asked at last.

"As I said, until today I didn't know anyone in town except my brother." Yet hadn't someone shown a marked desire to hurt her? Would that same person be so desperate to get to her again that he would go to all the trouble to track her down and follow her here to Branson?

She glanced once more at Detective Rush. Detectives were paid to give the impression of solidity and trustworthiness, but Willow didn't know this woman. *Can I trust her?*

And yet, if the police couldn't be trusted to get to the bottom of the matter without accusing the wrong person, then they didn't deserve their jobs.

"May I ask you a question, Detective?"

"Go ahead."

"How far back are you willing to investigate my life, in case this arsonist was singling me out?"

Detective Rush's eyes narrowed. "Why? Is there something you feel warrants investigation?"

"I'd like to know more about my husband's death, and how thorough the investigation was for a killer. And if there was a killer, someone with whom Travis might have crossed paths in his job as an undercover narcotics agent, then I'd like to know if he might still hold enough of a grudge against Travis to try to take it out on me, Travis's widow, this long after his death."

The detective sat in silence, holding Willow's gaze intently. "You believe there might be a connection between your husband's death and the fire?"

Willow spread her hands. "I hope not. There have been incidents in the past, twice since Travis died that make me suspect someone was trying to kill me. I was hit by a car, an intentional hit, and lost my baby. I could never prove it was intentional. There were no witnesses. I can't help wondering if someone from my husband's past might have hated him so badly that they still want to kill me."

The overhead lights hummed in the long silence as the detective waited to hear more. Willow believed she'd said enough.

"Okay, Willow," Detective Rush said at last. "To be honest with you, reopening an investigation isn't likely. As overworked as we have been lately, we wouldn't be able to spend a lot of time researching an old case, but I can make a couple of calls."

"Thank you." Those would be calls to the police station in Kansas City that had handled the case. Willow had received no answers from them, and she doubted this detective would, either.

"Now, we have another detective in our force who works with voice analysis," Detective Rush said. "If you're willing to take a voice stress test—kind of like a lie detector test—we may be able to get you out of here sooner."

Willow sagged with relief again. "Why didn't you bring that up earlier?"

"It's only used as an adjunct to questioning, so the results aren't a deciding factor."

"Let's go for it."

Thirty minutes later the voice stress test was over.

"You're free to go," Detective Rush said at last.

"I'm not going to be charged?" Willow asked.

"No, but I trust you will remain in Branson for the time being."

"As long as my brother's in the hospital, I'll be nearby."

"And you'll help me, if I decide to pursue research into your late husband's case in Kansas City?"

"Of course."

"I can't make any guarantees. We hope to find our arsonist before that becomes necessary."

The detective escorted Willow from the police station into the atrium foyer of the city hall building.

"May I ask you another question?" Willow asked as she climbed the steps behind the woman to the park entrance. "Why was I even under suspicion? If I had known those arson supplies were in my car, don't you think I'd have refused permission for the search in the first place?"

Detective Rush gave Willow a quirky half grin over her shoulder. "Hypothetically speaking? When the police are searching for a possible booby trap somewhere in your car, and you refuse permission, don't you think that's going to raise red flags?"

"Then if someone produces a warrant for the search, I'd look doubly guilty."

"You got it." The detective pointed toward the glass double doors, to the two shadowy figures who paced outside, within the circle of light from the building. "I think your friends are waiting for you," she said. "If not, I can take you back to the hospital or to your motel room."

Willow shook her head. "I think I'd rather walk. It's only a few blocks to the hospital from here." She needed some time alone to deal with all this.

And yet, in a way, she had never felt more alone in her life.

Chapter Eight

The moment the glass door opened and Willow stepped outside into the deepening April dusk, Graham could tell she had been through a difficult ordeal.

Ginger rushed to Willow's side. "Honey, I've been out here praying for you. How did it go? Was it awful?" She reached for Willow.

Before her arms could encircle that slender form, Willow withdrew, shoulders stiffening, chin raised. "I'm fine. Thank you for waiting. You didn't have to, though. I think I'll just walk to the hospital to prove to Preston that they didn't throw me in the slammer."

To Graham's relief, Ginger had the wisdom to give the woman some space. He couldn't always predict what she would do. "Why don't we call him?" He pulled his cell phone out of his pocket. "Then we can grab a bite to eat before you starve."

"Good idea," Ginger agreed. "Unless they served you a meal in that place, I doubt you've had anything since our late breakfast."

Willow forced a smile that seemed to twitch across her lips as if powered by an inconsistent electric current. "It isn't as if they resorted to starvation and torture. I had a candy bar."

"How about a nice healthy bowl of soup or chili to go with that?" Ginger asked, this time obviously taking great care not to throw an arm around Willow's shoulders. Graham knew his sister. She was in a mothering mood. She did that with him often enough.

"Really, I feel like some exercise." Willow picked up speed as if she would leave them behind.

Business Highway 65, which the city hall overlooked, was noisy with a rush of evening traffic, and Willow quick-stepped south along the sidewalk.

Graham might not be a touchy-feely person like Ginger, but he knew humiliation when he saw it written in body language.

He caught up and fell into step beside Willow. "I'm sorry, but I can't let you do that."

Her pace picked up. "I've already been held against my will for half the evening. It isn't a fun feeling. Don't try to tell me what I can and cannot do."

"I'm sorry, I'm not trying to be bossy," Graham said. "Ginger's the bossy one in the family."

"Excuse me?" Ginger protested from behind him.

He knew the three of them must look a little silly racewalking along the narrow sidewalk. "Obviously the detective believed you or she wouldn't have allowed you to leave."

"She had to believe me, because I passed her voice test."

"Of course you did." Ginger already sounded out of breath. "You're innocent. Why didn't she do that when you first arrived?"

Willow shrugged. "She needed information. It's what the police do—they gather information. I was perfectly willing to talk to them—I just wasn't expecting to become a suspect." She glanced at Graham and Ginger. "Really, you two don't need to walk with me. I'm a totally competent person, capable of finding my way home."

Graham heard the defensiveness in her tone. "No one's questioning your competency."

"You mean Preston hasn't already convinced everyone I'm hopelessly unable to care for myself?"

Graham thought about his discussion with Preston earlier this morning. "He hasn't convinced me of anything except that he's worried about you."

"Since you two are such good friends, I'm sure he's told you why."

Again Graham heard the defensiveness in her voice. He also caught a trace of bewilderment. Wow. Ginger was rubbing off on him.

Tentatively he touched Willow's arm. "Please, come to dinner with us. I promise we won't interrogate you. Everyone needs a friend now and then. You've got two right here."

"Absolutely," Ginger agreed. "And we're dying to know what happened in there."

Graham shot her a warning glance. "Didn't you hear what I said? We are not going to interrogate her."

Ginger rolled her eyes at him. "Anyway we've all got to eat tonight. Why not do it together?"

At last, at the busy bridge over Lake Taneycomo, Willow's steps slowed. She glanced up hesitantly at Graham, and he could see in the headlights of an oncoming car that her face shone with tears he hadn't realized were falling. So much for his skills of perception.

"You know they impounded my car?"

"Normal procedure," Graham said. "They have to make sure they have any scrap of evidence they might need. Whoever placed those items in your wheel well could have left something behind that could eventually be a clue."

"Meanwhile we can rent you a car," Ginger said. "Or you could use my car, and I could use Graham's old farm truck."

"What I could really use right now is a cup of hot chocolate," Willow said.

"I know just the place for that," Ginger said. "And it's only a short distance from here." She glanced over her shoulder at Graham. "They've got hot roast beef sandwiches made with freshly baked yeast bread and brown gravy that'll make you think you've died and gone to heaven."

Only then did he realize how hungry he was. He looked down at Willow. "Is that okay with you?"

She glanced down the road in the direction of the

hospital, then back at him. She shrugged. "You'll call Preston?"

He held out his cell phone. "Right this minute."

She nodded. "Lead the way."

Willow sat across from Graham and Ginger in the downtown diner, cupping the warm mug of hot chocolate in her chilled fingers. She hadn't realized until now that she'd been trembling for several minutes. Maybe even since leaving the police station.

She couldn't put a finger on what, exactly, was causing her to tremble so. Anger? She was certainly outraged by the insinuation by the police that she could be guilty of arson. She had never before been hauled to the police station for questioning. She felt like a criminal.

She picked up a spoon and dipped it into the swirl of chocolate syrup that decorated the dollop of whipped cream on top of her drink. It was laced with peppermint, and it warmed her.

She glanced up at Ginger, who sat across from her, indulging in her own cup. Then she looked at Graham.

He was right—she needed a friend. She needed to talk.

She raised another spoonful of the whipped cream to her lips. Twenty-five months ago, she would have savored the chocolate-mint flavor. How long had it been since she'd enjoyed her food?

Lord, when will this nightmare end? Why are You

allowing this to happen? What have I done to make You so angry with me?

Rationally she knew this was an unfair accusation. But in her heart she felt punished. Though she knew God didn't work that way, she also knew He had allowed all these tragedies to enter her life.

But why?

If Travis were still alive, he would have reminded her not to ask "Why me?" but instead to ask "Why not me?"

Once more she glanced into Graham's friendly amber-brown eyes, and then she looked at Ginger, whose attention had focused on a group of teenagers entering the restaurant in a lively throng.

"This brings back a lot of memories," Willow told them at last, bracing herself, weighing her words, wondering how much she could safely divulge.

Both looked at her simultaneously, with interest.

"My father always gave Preston and me hot chocolate when we'd had a bad day at school, or when . . . when things weren't going well at home."

She paused and sipped her chocolate, wishing the warmth would stop her trembling.

"Things sure aren't going well for you right now," Ginger said softly.

Willow shook her head. "You'll have to forgive my brother. As you've already noticed, he's overprotective. But he's also worried about me for other reasons."

Graham and Ginger both waited.

How could she even dream of confiding in these

people, who until this morning had been strangers to her?

"My brother has too many childhood memories of my mother." She stared at a dribble of cream that had slid down the side of her cup and pooled onto the table. They were generous with their portions at this restaurant. "My mother suffers from a mental illness that isn't always controlled by medication. She has schizophrenia."

Ginger caught her breath audibly. "Oh, honey. That must be hard on your family. Was it very bad when you were growing up?"

Willow shrugged. "Sometimes. That was when Dad whipped out the hot chocolate. He always believed the world's problems could be solved with a good, rousing round of prayer followed up with hot chocolate."

"Your father's a believer?" Ginger asked.

"My parents are both believers. That didn't magically take away Mom's illness. And because it didn't, my brother rejected God a long time ago."

"And now this," Graham said, his voice and eyes betraying empathy. "So Preston's watching you closely for any signs of trouble that would mimic your mother's."

Willow nodded. "When we were kids we guarded the secret as if we were desperate criminals. It was as if we were convinced that if anyone found out about her, we would be rejected by friends and carted off to the asylum. A lot of people seem to believe that's where all people like Mom belong."

"If I'm not mistaken," Graham said, "studies show that the illness will usually reveal itself by forty if it's going to manifest at all. You're what, thirty-six?"

Willow gave him a wry smile, empty of humor. "Preston told you?"

"Only your age, when he seemed to be doing some . . ." Graham paused, and if Willow hadn't known better, she would have sworn his face took on the slight flush of embarrassment.

"Some matchmaking?" she guessed.

"Exactly."

She watched him with interest. For a doctor, he embarrassed easily. "Preston has been concerned about himself, as well, but he's been even more concerned about me, especially after Travis was killed. He's been afraid the emotional trauma might trigger a psychotic response."

Graham leaned forward, elbows on the table, and Willow was suddenly aware of the solidness of his body, the broad shoulders. It would be nice to have someone . . .

"I knew Preston was concerned about your emotional state," he said, "but he didn't say anything about your mother."

Willow sank back into the cushioned booth seat, listening to the crackly sound of the vinyl as it shifted beneath her, to the chatter and laughter of other diners, which occasionally reached deafening proportions. She smelled the scent of frying onions and burgers.

"Honey, you don't have to talk about all this if you

don't want," Ginger said. "You don't have to talk about anything. I was just kidding you a while ago. You've got enough to deal with, anyway. We don't want to pry, but we'll be a sounding board if you need one."

Willow refused, this time, to allow tears to surface. None even stung her eyes. She gazed into the warm brown eyes of this friendly, kindhearted woman, and allowed herself a soft sigh. There were lines of comfort in that full-featured face. Ginger had obviously lived through a lot of struggle in her own life, and she'd allowed the struggle to deepen her well of compassion.

"Thank you," Willow said softly. She needed to talk, but before she could speak, a waiter arrived with two platters of hot roast beef sandwiches for Ginger and Graham, and a bowl of steaming country chili for Willow, with a side order of deep fried okra.

Though Willow had no appetite, it was time to eat.

"You'll definitely need a car," Graham said, picking up on the conversation they had discarded earlier.

"I'll wait," Willow said. "I can walk anywhere I need to go."

He cut a bite of his open-faced sandwich and discovered it to be every bit as good as Ginger had promised.

He took another sip of the hot chocolate. "Okay, sis, you want to fill us in on how you managed to discover this place in a month, when I've known this town intimately all these years, and didn't have a clue about the food?"

Ginger winked at Willow. "I've got good taste, and I

know a bargain when I see it." She reached out and tapped Willow on the arm. "I should warn you, Graham doesn't take no for an answer. I'll turn my keys over to you and let him drive me home tonight."

"I can't let you do that," Willow said.

"We don't want to leave the car parked on the street overnight, though, do we?" Ginger leaned back. "I'm not driving it home. End of discussion."

Graham ate his meal in silence as he listened, with some amusement, to Ginger and Willow spar verbally, with gentle gibes that revealed a friendship already in the making. Willow exhibited a dry sense of humor, and those slender hands waved gracefully in the air as she attempted to make a point with Ginger.

She had a lilting voice that every so often, even under these heavy circumstances, caught itself in a brief chuckle.

Ginger had that effect on people. And Graham was startled to realize Willow had begun to have an effect on him. He found her fascinating.

Eventually the argument ended with Ginger as victor—Willow would accept the car only until she could receive a replacement credit card and rent an automobile—and the subject became serious once more. Willow ate only half her generous bowl of chili, then set the spoon down and stared into the contents.

"I can't continue to depend on others for help," she said.

"Is that pride talking?" Ginger asked archly.

Willow blinked up at her, dark brows drawn together

until furrows formed in her unlined forehead.

"We've all got to depend on someone else at some time in our lives," Ginger said. "I've done my share of leaning."

"But then you've spent ten years of your life helping others on the other side of the world," Willow said.

"If I hadn't swallowed some pride and accepted help when I needed it, though, maybe I'd never have gotten to the point where I could help others. Did you ever think of that?"

The furrows disappeared, and Graham realized how very pretty Willow was, with gamine features, a short, turned-up nose, a generous mouth, eyes that changed from blue to gray, depending on the light.

"I seem to remember that you're an ICU nurse," he said quietly. "I'm sure once you get back on your feet you'll want to make a go of that again."

She glanced up at him briefly, then returned her attention to her bowl. "You make it sound so easy."

Ginger opened her mouth to speak, and Graham gave her a pointed look. She raised her eyebrows at him, then closed her mouth.

"After what Preston tells me you've been through," Graham said, "I wouldn't be so stupid to imply that, Willow."

She looked up at him again. "He thinks I'm imagining things. He hasn't seriously considered the possibility that someone really did try to kill me."

"Yes, he has. I think he's in denial, but the fire has made him start thinking about it more seriously. Your husband was killed during a drug raid, right?"

Willow nudged the bowl away from her and picked up her water glass. "He was shot in the back—not from the direction of the raid, but from across the street, behind a thicket of brush and trees. They never found the shooter, and though several arrests were made that night, no one admitted knowledge of the crime."

"Oh." Ginger breathed softly.

"Two days after the funeral I received a call on the telephone. The caller never identified himself, but he said, 'How do you like widowhood? I'm giving you fair warning, you're going to pay.' And then he hung up."

"Did you call the police?"

"Of course, but the call came from a pay phone at the airport. It could have come from anyone, and I couldn't prove what was said."

"You don't think it was from some sicko who had read the paper about Travis and decided to torture the widow a little?" Graham asked.

Willow narrowed her eyes at him. "You sound like Preston."

"Only covering all options."

"How about this option, then?" she said. "A month later, when I was four months pregnant, I was crossing the street on my way to my car after work when I heard an engine. I looked up just in time to see a car veering across the line, coming straight toward me. I jumped to get out of the way, and the bumper grazed me, knocking me to the ground. I miscarried. Two days later I received a call on my new cell phone. I recognized the same caller's voice."

"What did he say?" Ginger asked.

"He said, 'I gave you fair warning.'" Willow's voice caught with a mixture of despair and anger.

"Preston said you were concerned about two attempts that had been made on your life," Graham said.

She nodded. "The other happened at the lake, where I used to go swimming a lot with some coworkers. One day last fall I was out doing laps from the dock to the buoy when I felt a tug on my feet. Someone tried to drag me under."

"What did you do?" Ginger exclaimed.

"I screamed and kicked and managed to land some well-placed jabs, apparently. I was released and I got away."

"Did you ever see anyone surface?" Ginger asked.

"Never. When I told my friends about it, they reported the incident to the State Water Patrol. No one was ever found. By that time I had begun to sound like the boy who cried wolf."

Graham stole a glance at Ginger. Sure enough, her eyes were filmed with unshed tears.

"Preston mentioned your dreams," Graham said to Willow. "You're still having nightmares about the deaths?"

She gave him a look of pure exasperation. "What has Preston been doing, downloading my whole life story?"

"Just trying to keep his macho image from becoming too tarnished. He knew he wouldn't be able to be there for you while he's in the hospital, so he—"

"He thought he should line up another watchdog," she said.

"You were telling us about the nightmares," Graham prompted.

"Actually, I wasn't," she said dryly. "*You* were telling *me*. Did Preston also tell you that I lost so much sleep it began to affect my work?"

"He mentioned you had to quit your job."

"I was suffering from terrible insomnia and was always sleepy during my shift. One night I fell asleep and a patient of mine stopped breathing. Had it not been for one of the other nurses, my patient would have died."

"You worked nights?" Graham asked.

Willow nodded. "So you see, going back to work isn't an option for me until I stop having these nightmares."

"What about daytime shifts?" Graham asked. "Or perhaps shorter ones."

"I'd like to try again," she said. "Not now, but maybe after all this is settled."

"When did the nightmares begin?" Ginger asked.

Willow stared once more into the uneaten contents of her bowl, as if trying to find an answer in the shape of the ground meat, tomatoes and black beans. "I've had bad dreams for years. It's a curse in our family, though the dreams come from my father's side. This particular dream began soon after Travis was killed."

"Same dream?" Graham asked.

She nodded and looked up at him. "Same one."

"You know," Ginger said, "sometimes God uses dreams to tell us things we wouldn't ordinarily pick up on during our waking hours. Do you recognize anyone in the nightmare? I mean, anyone on this side of the sleep curtain?"

Willow shook her head, obviously troubled by the long-fought battle with her subconscious. "No recognition. Only the dead, white face of a man in a coffin. And then he sits up and points at me, as if he's accusing me of doing something. As if I put him there."

Willow clasped her hands hard in her lap, unable to believe she had actually just blurted out so much to these two virtual strangers. Six months ago she had sworn she would never tell another soul about her experiences. She was tired of the awkward looks and the uncomfortable silences.

No one was ever willing to believe that someone they actually knew could be a victim of attempted murder.

She'd just been so desperate to explain her situation to someone who might understand this time. Now what would they think?

"I'm sorry," she said. "I think I should leave before I open my mouth one more time and remove all doubt in your minds about my sanity." She scooted to the end of the booth and stood.

"Don't you even talk like that," Ginger said as she and her brother followed.

While Graham paid, Ginger stood beside Willow and took her hand in a warm, firm grip. "Honey, this stuff you're going through has intrigue written all over it. There are times in our lives when we doubt ourselves, doubt our own perceptions. It happens to a lot of people. It sure happened to me."

"But you didn't have a schizophrenic mother."

"Nope, just a wayward heart. Of course, I don't know exactly what's going on in your life right now, and you don't, either. But whatever it turns out to be, you've got to realize you're not alone."

"I thought you said you weren't a missionary anymore."

Ginger pursed her full lips. "This isn't missionary work. It's a little thing you call friendship and it works both ways."

"Yes," Willow said softly as she felt herself smiling. "It does."

She glanced out at the busy downtown street, which looked much as it might have looked fifty years ago, held back in time by the efforts of the shopkeepers who wanted to draw the crowds back to a simpler era.

But the past century had not been simple. Willow's past had been anything but simple, and she fervently wanted to escape its clutches. She just wasn't sure if she could.

Chapter Nine

Though Willow remained reluctant to borrow Ginger's car, Graham insisted, and the two of them saw her off at the parking lot in front of the city hall.

"She gave me the impression tonight that there are times she doubts her own sanity," Ginger said as she settled in beside him in his Dodge 4X4. "I'd sure like to convince her she's just as sane as you or I."

"Don't tell her that."

Ginger paused as she buckled her seat belt, and he could feel her glaring at him through the darkness. "What's that supposed to mean?"

"It won't help your credibility if you promise her something that might not turn out to be true," he said.

"Please don't tell me you think she could actually be psychotic. Does she act like a psychotic person to you?"

Graham started the engine and put it into gear. He was tired. It had been a very long day. He still had a meeting to attend at the clinic, and tomorrow promised to be even longer as he played catch-up with the patients he'd had to cancel today. He wasn't in the mood to argue.

"Well?" she asked.

"Did I *say* I thought she was psychotic? All I'm saying is that you aren't qualified to make any promises about her mental health, so don't."

"Is that what I was doing?"

"Yes. When I reassure a patient, I take pains not to promise them something I can't deliver. Just let her know you'll be there for her. In the long run that will be more comforting to her than insisting everything will be all rosy and perfect. That'll only convince her you don't want her any other way. Then she'll worry that you'll no longer be there for her if she does show signs of emotional turmoil. What she needs is reassurance, acceptance."

He turned onto Highway 76 and drove nearly two minutes in blessed silence. Amazing.

"Pretty insightful for a macho surgeon," Ginger said at last.

He grinned. "Thank you."

"How long do you think they'll keep her car impounded?"

"Maybe a few days, unless they turn up any other evidence. Legally they can keep it as long as they want, but they've probably decided she's innocent. They'll comb the car for any possible evidence that could lead to the real culprit, then return it to her as soon as they can."

"What about you?" Ginger asked. "Are you convinced she's innocent?"

He stopped at the traffic signal just before the Highway 65 overpass. "I trust the police. They've decided she's innocent. That's good enough for me."

"I'm not talking about trusting *them,* I'm talking about trusting *Willow.* Do you believe the things she told us tonight?"

For several moments Graham continued to drive in silence. Every fiber within him had told him to believe her. "Do you?" he asked at last.

"Of course I do," Ginger said. "I think it's criminal that she's had so much trouble convincing anyone about what happened."

"It wasn't proven."

"But if it's true—which it is, I know—then Willow could very well be in danger right now."

"The police are aware of that," Graham assured his sister. "I spoke with Captain Powell while you were powdering your nose, and they'll keep a cruiser close to the motel where she's staying."

"That isn't good enough," Ginger said.

"I know. I'd much rather take her to Hideaway with us, where she'd be farther from harm's way."

"Want to know what I think?" Ginger asked, shifting in her seat to look at him through the dim glow of the console.

"Sure." He knew he would find out whether he wanted to or not.

"I think your instinct tells you to believe her."

"I don't believe in instinct. I believe in evidence and cold, hard facts."

"You sound like a die-hard cynic."

"It's taken me several years to become this cynical, and I'm not about to lose my objectivity in the middle of this mess."

"What makes you think you'd suddenly lose your objectivity? You're a logical, intelligent man with all

119

kinds of objectivity, so why suddenly be afraid that you'll lose it now?"

Graham didn't reply. She was circling around a particular point, getting ready to step in for the kill, and he knew better than to try to derail her now.

Ginger waited until he had turned south on Fall Creek Road, then said softly, "Willow is a very appealing woman."

"That isn't exactly a news flash."

"Even after so many years apart, I can tell when you're settling into your protective gear."

"I like my protective gear. It's only failed me once."

"With Dena," Ginger said. "It's time to forgive and get on with life. Dena isn't a bad person—she just places her priorities in the wrong place."

"Yeah, money."

"That's her problem, not yours."

"Sure it is." Graham could hear the bitterness in his own voice. "Have you seen the divorce settlement?"

Ginger reached out and touched his arm. "You know what? It's been three years. You need to let it go."

"Talking to that woman is like jumping off the top of Table Rock Dam. She's deadly."

"When's the last time you called her and tried to settle your differences?"

"Why do I have to settle anything? The court did that for us."

"And you've lived with bitterness ever since," Ginger said. "It's coloring the way you look at other women. It's coloring the way you look at life. You've never been like this before, Graham. This isn't you."

"I've learned a little caution. I think that's a good thing."

He could feel his sister's glare. Yes, he knew better. One did not carry a grudge. One settled differences in order to be in a right relationship with others, and especially with God.

Maybe that was why he didn't feel as if his prayers had been getting through lately. Dena had been particularly antagonistic the last time he'd called her about some papers he needed her to sign to release funds in a joint account they had overlooked in the divorce settlement.

How could it be that the woman he'd trusted and loved, and with whom he'd shared his heart, had become such a monster—if not in reality, then in his own mind?

"You're right," he told Ginger at last. "I could do with a little less bitterness."

"Understatement of the week," Ginger said.

They pulled into the clinic parking lot, where the fire chief and an investigator were already waiting. One more meeting, then home to bed.

Willow didn't immediately return to her motel room when she left the parking lot, but circled the area to get her bearings. She caught herself instinctively glancing in the rearview mirror every few moments to see if someone was following her, either police or someone more sinister.

She saw neither.

Finally she parked in the hospital parking lot, within plain view of a security guard, then went upstairs to ICU to see her brother.

"Where've you been?" he asked. "Until Graham called me, I thought they'd booked you and stuffed you into the hoosegow."

"Well, thanks so much for your loving trust in me. After an interminable interview, they did the voice stress test and I passed and got to go home."

"Home where?" He shifted stiffly on the bed.

"I got a room not far from here."

He groaned. "You've decided you're going to stay there, after all? Could you please use your brain for once?"

"I could do worse," she said. "I could pull some strings and have you sent to St. John's burn center in Springfield. Keep you out of Branson for a while. In fact, maybe I'll talk to Graham about it tomorrow."

A tight smile aimed in her direction told her he knew she was teasing—albeit darkly—and that he wasn't in the mood for it.

She leaned over and gave him another kiss, then turned to leave.

"Where are you going now?"

"I'm going to do a little investigating."

"Oh, no, you don't. Willow Traynor, you get back in here this—"

She walked out into the hallway and closed the door behind her. She wouldn't argue with Preston tonight.

She needed to take some precautions for some innocent little ones who were unable to fend for them-
selves—though they were apparently being expected
to.

While talking to Graham about the lodging arrange-
ments for the other renters at the complex, she had discovered that he had put Sandi Jameson and her daughters up in a brand-new condominium unit on the shore
of Lake Taneycomo.

With a Branson map in hand, she found the place
easily. She recognized Sandi's car, took note of the
numbered spot and found the corresponding unit.

Three minutes after parking, she was being welcomed inside by two lively little girls who appeared
overjoyed to see her.

"It's the fire lady who saved us!" the youngest child,
Brittany, cried out as she danced through the expansive
living room, obviously suffering few effects of the
fright they'd experienced in the early-morning hours.

Brittany's seven-year-old sister, Lucy, was more cir-
cumspect with her welcome, but she tugged on
Willow's unhurt arm and urged her to the sofa. "Does
your arm still hurt?"

"It's fixed. It'll be better soon."

"Did you have to get stitches?" Lucy asked.

"Yes."

Lucy shuddered theatrically.

Brittany snuggled close, her long tawny-brown hair
tangling over Willow's left knee as she burrowed her
head beneath Willow's arm in an effort to cadge a hug.

Willow grinned and rewarded the child's efforts by drawing her more completely into arms that often ached to hug little children just this way.

"Did you get a shot?" Lucy asked. "Did it hurt?"

"Yes, I got a shot, but it didn't hurt that much."

"Did you cry?" Brittany asked. "When I get a shot I always cry so they'll know it hurts, because if I don't cry, maybe they'll stick me with a bigger needle next time."

"That isn't the way it works, sweetie." Willow glanced around the generous proportions of the living-dining area, then glanced toward the other doors. Was Sandi already off working again?

But her car was parked outside.

They definitely needed to talk.

"Did you have to stay in that hospital?" Brittany asked, crawling onto Willow's lap and snuggling against Willow's chest. How did anyone resist this little charmer?

"Mama said she heard the police took you to jail," Brittany said. "Did you go to jail?"

"Silly," said Lucy. "She didn't go to jail, or she wouldn't be here, would she?"

"Maybe." Brittany gently tugged Willow's arm back over her slender shoulders. "Maybe she broke out of jail."

Willow chuckled, hugging Brittany against her. "I didn't break out of jail, because I never even saw a jail cell, though it might have been interesting, don't you think?"

"No!" Brittany exclaimed. "That's where they put the bad guys forever. Mama says people die there, and that we must never go there."

"People don't die at our police station," Willow assured the children. "It's just a holding cell where they put people they don't know what to do with. But I was only at the police station because they wanted to ask me some questions to see if I had answers to help them find the bad guy who started the fire."

She had their attention immediately. Brittany looked up at her with adoring green eyes.

"How cool!" Lucy, with long dark hair braided in slender pigtails, had large brown eyes that sparkled when she was excited.

Willow hugged Brittany to her once more. "Girls, I need to talk to your mom."

The children looked at each other, and suddenly their exuberance dulled.

"Is she at work right now? I could go talk to her there."

Again came that look of complexity between the children that tore at Willow's heart. These little girls shouldn't have to cover for their mother.

"She was just going out for a while tonight," Lucy said. "For a walk. That's what she said. She'll be back any time." As if to prove a point, the child glanced toward the door.

So Sandi had impressed upon them how they should never let on that they'd been left alone. Maybe she really was just out walking. But if so, couldn't she take her children with her? Hadn't she learned last night how quickly they could be placed in danger, especially with no one here to watch them?

"While we're waiting, why don't you tell me about the neat playground I saw outside and the swimming pool?"

"And the lake!" Brittany exclaimed. "If I could swim, I'd swim in the lake all the time!"

"And a big television in the clubhouse," Lucy said.

"Lots of places to play," Brittany said. "And a swing set and . . ."

The chatter continued for at least fifteen minutes before the front door opened and Sandi entered. The girls fell silent immediately. Willow felt Brittany stiffen in her arms.

Sandi was a pretty woman with her younger daughter's tawny-brown hair and green eyes. She had dramatically slanted eyes and brows, high cheekbones and a voluptuous figure without being overweight. At this moment she was flushed, her eyes bright and snapping. Somehow Willow had the impression the woman was distracted, upset about something besides the fact that she had unexpected company.

"Hi, Mama," Lucy said. "Look who came to visit!"

Sandi glared at her daughter. "I thought I told you never to answer the door when I'm not here."

"But this is the fire lady. She saved us from the fire."

Sandi seemed to deflate. She glanced into Willow's eyes briefly, then looked away. "Girls, go get ready for bed."

After a few seconds of little-girl whining, Lucy and Brittany did as they were told. Once more shy with Willow, they said night-night softly before they trotted down the hallway, turning on all the lights as they went.

Willow stayed seated, embarrassingly aware that Sandi waited for her to say good-night and leave. Sandi didn't sit down, but stood by the door, arms crossed over her chest, looking anywhere but at Willow.

Since Willow's first meeting with Sandi, they had crossed paths a few times. Sandi had been polite, but withdrawn. According to Preston, she kept to herself. In fact, he had mentioned Willow and Sandi might make good friends, since neither of them seemed to like to mingle with other people.

As Willow watched her now, the woman cleared her throat and strolled toward the bar that divided the kitchen from the living area. "Would you like a soda or something? I haven't had a chance to stock a lot of food, but—"

"What I'd like is to have a talk with you," Willow said. "Because you and I have a problem."

For a moment Sandi froze with her back to Willow. When she turned around, her expression was once again distracted. She didn't meet Willow's gaze. "I don't know what you're talking about."

"In all the excitement, no one has picked up on the fact that you weren't at home with your children when the fire broke out."

At last Sandi looked straight at Willow, then sank into a chair by the front door, arms still crossed. "But you got them out anyway, didn't you? They're safe. The fire didn't even spread."

"What if it had? And what if I hadn't been there? What if no one had checked on them?"

Sandi's shoulders seemed to hunch forward. "Nothing would have happened to them," she murmured, defensive.

Willow gave a frustrated sigh, in the back of her mind acknowledging that what Sandi said was correct. Preston's cabin had been the only target for the fire. None of the other units had been touched. In fact, if things went well in the next few days, it was possible all the renters, except for Willow and Preston, would be able to return home.

"Did you know I was a nurse?" Willow asked at last.

Sandi frowned at her. "How should I have known that?"

"No reason. But when I worked as a nurse, I would have been legally compelled to report the situation with the girls."

"What do you mean?" Sandi's voice tightened with resentment—and possibly fear.

Willow leaned forward, elbows on knees, hating the confrontation, but unwilling to back down. "Sandi, your little girls are too young to be left at home alone overnight while you work. They need adult supervision and protection."

"They live in a lodge with other people just next

128

door, and they know my telephone number if anything happens."

"That isn't good enough," Willow said.

Sandi leaned forward, watching Willow with sudden, fearful keenness. "But you aren't a nurse anymore, right? So you don't have to—"

"I have to make sure the girls are safe. Knowing what I know, I can't allow them to be left alone at home for prolonged periods of time. It's too dangerous for them, as was proven this morning."

Sandi buried her face in her hands. "What am I supposed to do? I've got to work two jobs to make a living. I don't have a choice. I can't afford a babysitter."

"Their father can't help you financially?"

Sandi stiffened at those words. "My little girls don't have a father. The man who helped me make them was a vicious loser whose only interest in them would have been to use them to get back at me. We never even got married."

"He should still be paying child support."

Sandi gave Willow a withering look. "Excuse me, but welcome to the real world. Women like me don't get child support. They get grief from people like you who tell them to watch their kids better."

"I'm sorry, I don't want to cause you any more hardship." Willow honestly was sorry. Still, she couldn't, in good conscience, let the children be alone.

"What do you think I ought to do, then?" Sandi snapped. "Quit my jobs and let my children starve?"

"I think there are people who would be willing to watch them for a few hours while you're working at night."

"Oh, yeah? Give me some names. And cost. It isn't like I can afford a nanny."

"What are your hours? I could sit with them until you can find someone you can afford." The words were out of Willow's mouth before she could stop them. She certainly hadn't intended to say that.

Sandi's lips parted, eyes widening with obvious surprise and some other, less apparent emotion . . . perhaps dismay? Remorse that she had spoken so brusquely?

"So what do you say?" Willow asked. "I don't charge anything except the company of the girls."

Sandi blinked, looked away, then back at Willow. "I work Wednesday, Thursday and Friday nights this week. Graham said we should be back in our own homes by Friday, if everything goes well."

Willow suppressed a sigh. What had she gotten herself into? "I'll come here and sit with them. I could just plan to spend the night."

"No need. I'm usually home by two in the morning."

Willow said good-night and stepped out into the chilly spring air. In spite of her chagrin, she looked forward to time in the company of the two little girls.

Besides, what else could she do? Sandi needed a job, and the girls could not be left alone again, as they most likely had been countless times before. What a mess.

Chapter Ten

By Friday morning, April 5, Graham was finally able to breathe more deeply, with fewer telephone calls from insurance claims adjusters, contractors, police, fire investigators and renters wondering when they could have their homes back. His calls so far today had mostly been from patients, begging to get in to see him at the clinic.

At least he'd caught up with those surgeries he'd had to delay due to the fire and the fallout afterward. He didn't perform nearly as many procedures now as he had when he belonged to a physician group, but he had his share.

The only difference between the surgeries he'd done three years ago and those he did now was the lack of income for his work. Now his patients paid only the hospital charges. Graham waived his fee.

Someday he hoped to have his own outpatient surgery, complete with paid staff, rather than simply follow-up care for his patients. That would be a long time in coming, though, and right now he had more important things to do than dream of a rosy future.

He entered the familiar hospital lobby and took the elevator to the fifth floor. Preston and Mrs. Engle were on the same floor, making it easier for him to stay in contact with both of them.

Both were coming along fine.

He owed a great deal of thanks to Willow and to

Ginger, who had both spent several hours a day helping him catch up with his month-end paperwork for the rental properties and had helped him in the clinic.

Ginger had even taken several of his patients. As a physician's assistant, she had the skills and authority to treat many of his patients under his license, leaving him free to catch up with the more complicated cases.

This morning, as soon as Graham entered Preston's room he noticed that his friend was anxious. Preston had tossed his blanket back and was sitting on the side of the bed.

"You look ready to go jogging this morning," Graham said, sinking into the chair beside Preston's bed.

"I'm about to demolish the place. I'll be climbing the walls if I have to stay here another week."

"Then we'd better see about getting those walls reinforced, because you're not ready to be released yet."

"What ever happened to managed care limits?" Preston complained. "You know, where they patch you up and kick you out the door to get well at home."

"You're doing well to be sitting up after what happened to you Monday," Graham said. "Stay here and heal. You don't get a break like this too often."

"Have you spoken to Willow?" Preston asked.

"Of course, every day. She's been a lifesaver for me."

Preston's expression lightened. "Has she?"

"Yes, she has. You could stand to place a little more confidence in her."

"Have the police released her car yet?"

"Just this morning."

Preston slid from the bed and walked gingerly across the room. He looked disheveled, with unshaven face, hair sticking in every direction, eyebrows not yet grown back in and a scrub of a mustache.

Willow had purchased several sets of pajamas for him so he wouldn't have to make do with the hospital gowns. She also brought him at least one meal a day so he wouldn't have to live on a constant diet of hospital fare.

He sat gingerly in the chair by the window. "She's really holding up okay? I thought maybe she was just putting on a good act for me."

"You can stop worrying about her," Graham said. "I don't know what I'd do without her. She's organized, compassionate and she seems able to read my mind. I have trouble imagining why she thought she should quit nursing. She's a natural."

Preston fidgeted on the chair, obviously trying to get comfortable. "She always has been. She knew she wanted a career in medicine since she was ten. I, on the other hand, was a goof-off."

"Tell me about her."

"Have I mentioned she's headstrong? That has a tendency to drive a guy crazy trying to keep up with her."

"Independence seems to be a strong trait of hers," Graham said. "What else?"

133

"She was ten when she started bringing home stray birds and squirrels," Preston said. "Later, when she was in high school and college, she dragged home lonely kids without families for dinner and holidays."

Graham grinned at the thought of Willow bringing home an injured squirrel to nurse through spring break, or dragging other students from her dorm to her family's Christmas celebration.

"So your mother's mental illness wasn't so debilitating that Willow hesitated to bring visitors home with her?"

"She always knew to call first and check with Dad or me."

"What if there was a problem?" Graham asked.

"Then she took her friends to our aunt's house three blocks away."

Graham chuckled. "I'm sure your aunt appreciated that."

"She loved to see Willow, and she understood the situation. Everyone usually knew when my mother had a breakout episode, when her medication wasn't working, or when she neglected to take it. It was very obvious and very public."

"Preston," Graham said, leaning forward in his chair, "do you think it's possible that your experiences with your mother had such an impact on you when you were growing up that you're hypersensitive to Willow's every move now?"

Preston frowned. "Of course. That's exactly what I'm doing. I know it is. But did you ever stop worrying about Ginger when she was off in a foreign country alone for ten years?"

"Once or twice. Probably no more than that."

There was a knock at the open door of Preston's room, and both men looked up to find Carl Mackey standing in the doorway, a derby hat in his hand, gray hair slicked back neatly, wearing his usual tan jumpsuit.

"Came to see how the landlord's doing," the older man said, nodding to Preston, then to Graham. "I'm awfully glad to be moving back into the place today, but where are you going to stay when you get out of here, Preston?"

"I've been working on my own place in the woods just north of the complex," Preston said. "It shouldn't take long before I can move in there."

"That right? Shoreline property?"

"Nope," Preston said. "Give me the woods any day. It's quieter and less populated."

"Guess that's right. Well, I'm off to make another visit. I'm getting my car worked on today, so the Jasumbacks dropped me off to visit while they're in town." He waved his hat at them and left.

Graham wasn't as acquainted with Carl as he was with some of the other renters. "He's fairly new, isn't he?"

Preston got up stiffly from his chair and walked back to the bed. "He moved in about six weeks ago. You know we have several new renters. He's a retired pharmacist from Minneapolis. Said he wanted to move where it was warmer in the winter, and when his wife was alive they always came to Branson for two weeks every summer to see the shows."

Graham studied Preston for a moment. "Do you know all the renters that well?"

"Sure, it's my job."

"I don't suppose you'd suspect any of them of arson."

Preston hesitated a second too long. "Their references all checked out."

"So why do I get the feeling you're not quite convinced?"

"No good reason. I've just had a gut feeling the past couple of weeks that something isn't quite right with Sandi Jameson."

"How?"

Preston considered his answer for a moment, then shook his head. "Forget I said that. She just acts a little whacked sometimes."

"Whacked how? Are you talking about drugs?"

"I've had my suspicions, but I've never seen any material evidence, just her behavior. But I wouldn't suspect her of arson. Especially not with her little girls alone in the apartment."

Mrs. Engle looked deceptively small and weak in the hospital bed, but her eyes lit with delight as Willow entered the room and sat in the chair next to the bed.

"Rehab," the lady said. "They're taking me to the sniff unit on Monday if I keep doing as well as I have been, and then they'll start rehab. I plan to make the most of it. Mind telling me what a sniff unit is?"

Willow grinned at her. Visiting the lady this past week had been a joy, and Willow felt as if she had made a friend. "Skilled nursing facility. Congratulations. It sounds as if you've made a lot of progress this week."

"I plan to make a lot more." At eighty-two, Esther Engle had the drive and determination of a woman half her age.

"Ever thought of nursing in a rehab center?" Esther asked.

"No, but I plan to visit you there, so I'll learn something about it."

The lady nodded, obviously pleased. "You're a good nurse. You've spent enough time in here with me this week, so I can tell."

"I enjoy spending time with you."

"So if you enjoy it, why not get paid for it?"

"That's a long story. Maybe I'll get back into it someday."

Esther shrugged. "Don't suppose they found the arsonist yet?"

"Not yet."

"They might not, then. Fella's probably in another state by now. Ever figure out why he did what he did?"

Willow shook her head. "He obviously targeted Preston's cabin. I was told that the other fires that night were started in the same way. Not high-tech or anything."

"Maybe just a couple of delinquents out for a good

time?" Esther asked.

Willow thought about the items placed in the cargo hold of her car. She shook her head. "I think it was more than that, but I have no idea what it could be."

"Did Graham also tell you most of the renters are moving back into their apartments today? That there's a man who knows how to get what he wants."

Willow nodded. "There was no reason to keep them away any longer. The cabin sustained the majority of the damage. All the lodge suffered were some broken windows from the explosion, some places on the roof where burning material landed and did a minimum of damage." She was actually surprised they'd kept the renters out of their homes as long as they had.

"Guess Graham's pretty relieved," Esther said. "Can't be comfortable, waiting to see if his livelihood will continue to pay off."

"I doubt he needs the income from those rentals for his livelihood. From what I've seen, he has a thriving practice."

Esther gave Willow a quick look over the top of her glasses. "I thought you told me you'd been helping out in his office."

"Yes, but—"

"And all that time you didn't realize his patients don't pay?"

Willow sat back in her chair. "How could they not pay? What do you mean?"

"He doesn't get paid." Esther raised a hand of honor. "Hasn't for a while. You didn't know that?"

"I only worked in the treatment rooms with the patients, and I didn't see any charge sheets. I've always worked in ICU, so I'm not well acquainted with the business side of clinic work. I suppose I just figured insurance—"

"Insurance, my foot. The people Graham takes don't get insurance. That's why they're seeing him—other than the fact he's a good doctor. One of the best general surgeons in southwest Missouri."

"He works free?" How could she not have known that? Preston had never mentioned it, though. Neither had Graham or Ginger.

"Free as sunshine," Esther said. "Why do you think he's got all the rental properties?"

Willow shrugged. "Investment for retirement?"

Esther smiled and shook her head as she laid her head back against her pillow. Day by day her complexion had grown healthier, and Willow had come to realize how strong this lady really was.

"Does he receive some kind of federal or state money to help him?" Willow asked.

"Not a penny that I know of. Granted, he earned good money when he worked with the surgical group at the clinic across the street, and I guess he always knew how to save and invest. Still, when he left the group and decided to start the free clinic, he sure got the opposition." She shook her head and tsked. "Man took a beating in divorce court."

Willow glanced at Esther. "How do you know all this stuff?"

"Honey, this is Branson, not L.A. or New York City. It might look like we've got a huge population, what with all the tourists we get each year, but really, we're just a small town."

"I hadn't noticed," Willow said dryly.

"Well, you should've. Folks here vary from high-priced entertainers to retirees to cooks and food-service people. And then we've got lots of medical personnel taking care of the retirees, and there are some big-time investors sticking their noses into everything."

"The population definitely runs the spectrum," Willow said.

"Even so, we're probably closer to each other than folks in some other towns, because we have to support each other when we deal with all the outsiders coming in and interrupting our lives."

"So that means I'm probably the last person in Branson to know Graham's clinic is a free one?"

"Probably. Especially since that poor, misguided, insecure wife of his filed for divorce, hoping to force him to reconsider."

"Ouch!"

Esther nodded. "Pretty nasty. He refused, and she fought him."

Willow raised a silencing hand. "Is this something I need to know?"

"Only if you want to know what everyone else already knows around these parts. Eighteen months after Dena filed for divorce, she ended up with the house, car and half the savings. He used his half of the savings to purchase rental property, plus he ended up with a great house near Hideaway when a resort developer was forced to sell due to bankruptcy."

Already, this early in the morning, Willow was tired. With Esther Engle, she felt as if she were always just a few days behind the rest of the world. Being a native definitely had its advantages.

Esther nodded, as if to emphasize her words. "That clinic's his baby, start to finish."

"Okay, so the guy qualifies for sainthood."

"Except for the chip on his shoulder that's been there since the divorce," Esther said softly. "I've not been divorced, but if anything would make me bitter, I think that would."

Willow thought of her own recent experiences, and realized why Graham had so kindly supported her. He'd had his life placed under a microscope, had been subjected to anger and rejection from the one person who should have loved and accepted him the most.

The ordeal might have made him a more compassionate person, but he was obviously that kind of person to begin with. It seemed to run in the family.

How she appreciated that compassion right now.

Friday afternoon Graham sat behind his desk in his clinic office, sorry he'd ever gotten up this morning. His best nurse was quitting.

"I'm sorry, Dr. Vaughn." The tall, rawboned woman with short salt-and-pepper hair sat across from him, elbows on the desk. "I never thought this would happen, but Wilburn has this job offer he just can't turn down. We need the money. I can't drive all the way from Knolls for a shift."

"I wish I could pay you, Till." Graham sat back in his chair and tried hard to look happy for her.

Wilburn and Till Fellows, both nurses who worked full-time at St. John's in Springfield, had always been supportive of Graham's dream to start this clinic. Though Wilburn hadn't volunteered as often in the past few months, he had been a godsend for Graham when he needed help the most.

"How about getting your sister to help out for a while?" Till suggested. "The patients will love Ginger."

"She's a PA, so I'd still need a nurse. Besides, she's helping out at the clinic in Hideaway right now."

"I'll talk to some friends of mine at St. John's," Till said, "but most of those who would be interested in volunteer work are doing it in Springfield."

"Thanks, Till." It would be impossible to find someone as willing to help out as Till had been. Without pay.

And yet God was in the business of doing the impossible. Prayer would be in order.

One person came to mind quickly. But first, prayer.

Chapter Eleven

Friday evening found Willow back at the lodge where fire had raged the first of the week. All the other renters except Preston and Willow had been able to return. Graham was still trying to decide whether to rebuild the cabin. If he didn't, he might be able to take the money from the loss and, with help from the bank, build a fourplex on the site.

For the third time this week, Willow saw Sandi out the front door, then settled onto the sofa with the two little girls. This time, however, it was later in the evening, and instead of being lively and talkative, Lucy and Brittany were subdued and sleepy.

One girl cuddled up on either side of Willow, and she sat quietly for several moments, treasuring the feel of the warm little bodies snuggled close. It was times like these that she felt such a powerful ache to hold her own child in her arms, she nearly wept with longing.

She closed her eyes and leaned her head back against the soft sofa, picturing Travis in her mind—the square jaw, heavy with evening shadow; eyes of darkest brown that were always a little too serious; shoulders that looked as if they could always carry any burdens she needed to lay on them.

She'd been thirty-one when she and Travis had married—the first time for both of them. Travis had waited because of a painful childhood spent shuffling back and forth between feuding, divorced parents.

Willow's reasons for avoiding marriage for so long were all about her mother. Sometimes it seemed as if too much of her life had been lived because of her mother.

It had taken her and Travis two years of friendship, dancing around both their work schedules to find time to date, then convincing each other that marriage wouldn't have to be patterned after the failures they'd experienced.

And marriage had been wonderful. Beyond wonderful. Travis had even convinced her that they shouldn't delay starting a family simply because she wanted to be sure she wouldn't develop her mother's mental illness.

As he'd pointed out, she was a perfectly rational, happy woman. If she was worried about passing on the family traits, they could adopt, but that didn't guarantee healthy children, either.

With Travis, she felt safe. She had wanted children for many years, and so she had become pregnant.

And then life fell apart.

Tears filled her eyes and blurred her vision. She sniffed and wiped a trickle of moisture from her cheek. Would the sense of loss never fade? Would she ever have a normal life again?

Or maybe she'd never had a normal life in the first place. How would she know anything about normal?

Brittany stirred next to her, yawned deeply. "Mama?"

Willow tightened her arm around the girl's shoulders. "She'll be home later. Do you feel okay? You girls seem awfully lethargic tonight." She pressed the backs of her fingers against the side of Brittany's face. Not overly warm.

"You and Mama made us get up late last night," Brittany said.

"No, they didn't," Lucy said. "We just woke up."

"Last night?" Willow asked. She had been here until two o'clock in the morning. "How did your mother and I wake you up? We're always careful not to wake you." Not that they needed to take much care; these children were both deep sleepers.

"Mama was yelling at you," Brittany said.

"Your mother never yelled at me."

"Yes, she did, she yelled your name. I heard it," Lucy said.

"Why are you crying?" Brittany asked.

"I'm fine, sweetie," Willow said, mystified about last night. Had Sandi been arguing with someone else?

"Sissy, you're not supposed to talk about people crying," Lucy said.

"Why not? Mama cries sometimes," Brittany said softly to Willow. "She cried last night. I think she misses our old house. And I think she has a boyfriend who makes her cry."

"Brittany!" Lucy said. "That gross man isn't her boyfriend."

Intrigued, Willow asked, "Your mother's been spending time with a man?"

"He's not her boyfriend," Lucy said. "They just talk

sometimes. We hear them from the bedroom when we're supposed to be sleeping."

"And shout," Brittany said. "A lot."

"Maybe that was who shouted last night," Willow said. "Maybe my name just came up in the conversation."

"He's her boyfriend," Brittany insisted. "Mama says that's what boyfriends do—they're mean and they fight."

"It isn't like they kiss or anything." Lucy's voice betrayed the deep disgust she felt at the idea.

"Maybe they do. We don't see them."

"We don't even know his name," Lucy explained to Willow. "Mama doesn't bring him inside when we're up."

"I know it's different when the man isn't your own father," Willow said.

"We don't have a father," Brittany said. "He died. Mama says we don't need no man to tell us how to live our lives."

Willow suppressed a smile. The comment was so typically Sandi—at least, what she knew of Sandi. "What about your grandparents?"

Lucy shook her head. "Don't have any of those, either. Mama says we're the only family we've got, and that's all we need."

Brittany yawned loudly, rubbing her eyes with her knuckles. "Can I go to bed? I'm really sleepy."

"Me, too," Lucy said.

Unaccustomed to their eagerness for bedtime, when

they ordinarily found multiple, creative excuses to stay up later, Willow saw them to their bedroom, tucked them in and left them snoozing.

Only moments after she left them in their room, the telephone rang. She answered.

"Willow? This is Carl Mackey down in Two B." A panicked male voice came over the line. "I heard you were a nurse."

She hesitated, frowning. "Yes, but how did you know—"

"Sandi said you were keeping an eye on the kids for her, and I saw your car. You need to get down to Four B. Mary Ruth Blevins has something bad wrong with her, and she's down there moaning in pain."

"Then you need to call for an ambulance."

"She doesn't want an ambulance, and I'm not calling for one or they'll make me pay if she refuses. She needs medical care."

Willow hesitated. "But I can't leave the girls—"

"I'll come straight upstairs and keep an eye on them while you're out, so leave the door unlocked."

"No, I won't do that."

"Well, then, I can just stand guard at the front door. Just get down here fast! Mary Ruth could croak on us."

Willow closed her eyes and sighed. "I'll be down."

She checked on the children quickly, then rushed through the apartment and out the front door, locking it securely behind her.

She reached Mary Ruth Blevins's apartment without encountering Carl Mackey, but took for

147

granted they had merely taken different routes to their destinations.

When she reached Mary Ruth's door, she was surprised to see no lights coming through the window. She knocked and rang the doorbell. "Mary Ruth? It's Willow. Are you okay in there?"

She peered through the window in the door, and finally saw a light come on inside. When a blurry-eyed Mary Ruth Blevins answered the door, she didn't seem relieved to see Willow, and she wasn't grim-faced with pain. She looked sleepy.

"Carl Mackey called me," Willow said, noting that Mary Ruth's color looked good. "Are you okay?"

Mary Ruth scowled at her. "Why wouldn't I be?"

"He said you were sick and moaning in pain. He said you didn't want an ambulance, but you needed medical attention."

Mary Ruth's scowl remained. "Carl said all that?"

"He called me just now."

"I haven't even seen that man since yesterday. Why would he call you?"

Willow deflated. Then she frowned. "You're not having any kind of pain right now?"

"Not me. I had gas a couple of days ago, but that happens when I eat too many onions with my beans for dinner. Thanks for checking, Willow, but tell Carl he's hallucinating."

Willow excused herself and returned to the apartment. She did not find Carl Mackey diligently watching the girls. No one was there.

When Willow checked the bedroom, she cried out in horror. The girls weren't there, either.

Graham raced through the darkness toward the complex with the echo of Willow's panicked voice still ringing in his ears—"I can't find the girls! Someone took the girls! Graham, help!"

Once again he saw the emergency lights flashing through the darkness, reflecting from the treetops. Multiple lights. Two little children were missing, and the police and other emergency workers would be out in force.

Because this had been the site of another emergency less than a week ago, and because that emergency was thought to be connected to two other arsons in the city of Branson, the Branson police would be here, even though this wouldn't ordinarily be their jurisdiction.

He turned onto the property drive, going slowly to avoid the inevitable pedestrians out to see the excitement, and as he drove he endured flashbacks of Monday's fire. Emergency vehicles lined the drive, and flashlight beams dotted the woods like giant fireflies.

Could Monday morning's fire be connected in any way to tonight's emergency?

Since the arsonist hadn't used particularly complicated methods to start the fire, the captain felt he probably wasn't an expert, but just wanted to get at Preston for some reason.

But why? Preston was in the hospital now. Those

little girls had nothing to do with him. The only connection was . . . Willow.

This time the crowd was congregated on the lawn in front of Sandi's apartment. Graham parked quickly and got out.

"Dr. Vaughn!" Carl Mackey shouted from the porch. "The police call you?"

"No, Willow did. Where is she?"

Carl pointed toward Sandi's apartment. "Inside with Sandi and the detective and some policemen. We've been scouring the place. The police need your keys to the other apartments so they can search."

Graham pulled a set of eight keys from his pocket.

"They're bringing in a search-and-rescue dog," Carl said. "Police are questioning everybody, even me! Said I was supposedly the one who got Willow out of the apartment. As if I'd do something like that."

"Where is Sandi?"

"The police just brought her in from her job a couple of minutes ago. Did you know Willow was babysitting?" The man shook his head sadly. "This doesn't look good. All this time leaving those little kids alone at night, and now, with a babysitter, they disappear."

A loud snap of female outrage filled the air, shooting through the open front door of the apartment. "What did you do to my kids?" It was Sandi's voice, sharp and angry.

Graham excused himself and crossed the threshold into the living room to find Willow seated on the sofa between a uniformed officer and Detective Trina Rush.

Sandi stood in the middle of the room, the center of attention, wearing a white Stetson hat, tight white shorts, white cowgirl boots and a Western-cut red-and-white-plaid shirt with several buttons undone. It was her uniform at the Stetson Bar and Grill, a popular nightspot downtown where she worked.

Her face was flushed, long tawny hair splayed across her shoulders. "Now I know why you wanted to babysit so badly this week," Sandi accused Willow. "You practically begged to stay with them!"

"Sandi, you know why I stayed with them." Willow's voice was clear and calm.

"You threatened me!" Sandi looked at Detective Rush. "She threatened that if I didn't let her stay with my girls she'd cause me trouble."

"How?" the detective asked quietly.

"Does it matter how?" Sandi demanded. "The point is that she threatened me."

"That was not a threat," Willow said. "I merely stated the facts, and then offered to help."

"She forced me to let her stay here alone with the girls," Sandi told the detective. "Now my kids are gone. Don't you think that's just a little too coincidental?"

"Would you please have a seat?" The detective gestured toward the chair next to the sofa.

Instead, Sandi took a step closer to Willow. "You're not going to get away with this. Where did you hide them? How long have you been planning this? You don't care about those little girls or—"

"Ms. Jameson," the detective warned, "please sit down."

Sandi hesitated for a tense moment, then did as she was told.

"Is there anyone else to whom you've given a key to this apartment?" the detective asked.

"Just her." Sandi pointed to Willow.

"If I had taken Lucy and Brittany, do you think I'd still be here?" Willow asked Sandi. "Would I have called the police? You were leaving them alone at home at night, and that's a reportable offense."

"But you didn't report it, did you?" Sandi snapped.

"I wanted to give you the benefit of the doubt," Willow said. "I only offered to stay with the girls to help you during a bad time."

"Oh, and you sure helped, didn't you? Now my babies are missing!" She glared at the uniformed policeman. "Did you look in her car? You've got to look in her car! It's where you found the other things."

"Detective Rush?" Graham said. "I brought the keys to the other apartments."

Willow looked up at him, and he heard her sigh of relief. There was no mistaking the tension in the set of her jaw, the rigidity of her shoulders.

"Thank you, Dr. Vaughn." Trina Rush stood up. "We have officers making the rounds, but there are a couple of units where no one seems to be home."

"I'll check them out," Graham said.

"Thanks. I'll have Officer Tidwell go with you."

Willow watched Graham walk out of the apartment with the officer, then she reached into the pocket of her jeans, turning back to Trina Rush. "I didn't take Sandi's children, and I didn't start the fire, but in case someone is playing another cruel prank, an officer should look in my car." She pulled out her keys and held them out.

Trina looked at the keys, hesitated, then took them. "We have your permission to search your car?"

"Of course."

Trina handed the keys to another uniformed officer. "Go ahead. It's the dark red Subaru."

Obviously the officer knew which car was Willow's. Sandi started to leave the apartment with him.

"There's no need for you to go, Sandi," the detective said. "I need to ask you a few more questions."

Sandi turned back reluctantly and sank into her chair.

"Why don't you tell me what kind of trouble Willow was going to cause you?" Detective Rush asked.

Sandi glared at Willow. "Let her tell you herself."

The detective looked at Willow. "Well?"

"When I found the girls Monday night, Sandi wasn't there. I confronted her about leaving her children at home alone at night while she's working."

The officer came back inside with Willow's car keys and handed them to her. "Nothing there."

Sandi leaned back in her chair and covered her face with her hands. "Just tell me where you took them," she whispered. "Please."

"I'm sorry, Sandi," Willow said. "I shouldn't have left them alone, but it was only for a few minutes. I locked the door behind me." She had repeated this story several times already. "Carl Mackey was supposed to be right up, and he was going to guard the door until I got back. I wish I'd waited until—"

"You're lying," Sandi said. "You have to be lying. He said he didn't know anything about it."

"What about that man the girls were telling me about tonight?" Willow asked. "The one you fight with?"

Sandi's eyes widened for a fraction of a second. Then she shook her head. "You're the only one with a key."

"Sandi," Detective Rush said, "how often do you leave your children at home alone when you work?"

The interview continued, and as Willow sat back in silence, listening, she couldn't displace the memory of Lucy and Brittany talking about the man who made their mother cry.

Ten minutes later Graham and Officer Tidwell entered the apartment carrying Lucy and Brittany.

Graham watched Sandi's reaction as he and Tidwell set the sleepy little girls on their feet. She burst into tears, rushing across the living room to grab her daughters.

"Where have you been?"

"Where did you find them?" Detective Rush asked the officer.

"In apartment Four A," Tidwell replied.

"That's Mrs. Engle's apartment," Sandi said. "Kids, you need to tell me what happened. Lucy? Did you and

Brittany play a joke on Willow?"

"No, Mama," Lucy said.

"No, Mama, we like Willow," Brittany said. "She's nicer than that man—"

"Then tell me what you were doing in Mrs. Engle's apartment."

"They were asleep," Graham told her. "All snuggled together in Mrs. Engle's bed."

"Lucy," Sandi said, "do you remember how you two got there?"

The older child shook her head, dark brown eyes wide but still groggy. "We didn't know we were in her apartment until they woke us up." She pointed at Graham and Tidwell.

"Well, then you must have woken up when you went to Mrs. Engle's apartment," Sandi said.

Brittany shook her head. "Uh-uh. I'm sleepy. Can I go to bed?"

"We went to bed in our own room." Lucy looked over at Willow. "Didn't we, Willow? Even before our bedtime."

"That's right, sweetheart," Willow said. "But are you sure you didn't wake up later, when I wasn't here?"

Both girls shook their heads.

"Why did they go to bed before their bedtimes?" Sandi demanded. "They never do that."

"We were sleepy tonight, Mama," Brittany said. "Remember? You kept us up late last night when you were shouting at Willow."

Sandi shot a quick glance toward Trina Rush, who

held the gaze, eyes narrowing slightly.

"Go on to bed, you two," Sandi told her girls. "We'll talk about it in the morning."

"They'll need to sleep elsewhere until our officers have gathered all the evidence they can find in their room," Detective Rush said.

"My bedroom, then, girls," Sandi said, then muttered, "I'm not going to be sleeping much tonight, anyway."

"Do they ever sleepwalk?" Graham asked as the girls disappeared down the hallway.

"Never," Sandi said.

"But according to Willow," Detective Rush said, "you aren't always home with your children at night. So you can't know that for sure." She motioned for the uniformed officers. "Check out the apartment where you found them. Do a fingerprint check of every room." She turned to Willow, and her gaze searched Willow's face, as if already gathering evidence. "I'll need you to come to the station with me."

"Again?"

"That's right. And Sandi, I want to ask you later about this mysterious man. I would also advise you to take the girls to the hospital emergency department to be checked out."

"They're fine. You saw them—they're just sleepy." Sandi folded her arms over her chest. "Willow wouldn't hurt them, and you can't make me take them in."

The detective sighed, obviously tired herself. "That's

156

right, I can't. But I will need to question you before I leave tonight, so have a seat."

It promised to be a long night.

Chapter Twelve

The closest parking spot Graham could find to the Stetson Bar and Grill was two blocks away. Obviously this was a popular place.

He pulled in behind a pickup truck beside the curb and got out, studying the low-slung building constructed of cedar and brick. He'd heard interesting stories about this place, how the police had to come here often to check out complaints about the noise. Sometimes the music got too loud. Word around town was that this was the place to come for a good time.

He couldn't help wondering what they meant by "good time." He doubted they meant a good country music show, though they did advertise live music on Friday and Saturday nights. Since Branson was known for its live music shows, he doubted a band would draw crowds.

He had called Ginger to update her on tonight's events, and she was on her way to the police station to intercept Willow when the police released her.

Judging by the last time Willow had been questioned, she would be there awhile, and he wanted to follow up on a hunch.

Sandi Jameson could be covering for someone. Preston had remarked that something didn't seem quite right about her, that she'd seemed "whacked" at times.

Graham wanted to know more about the man Sandi's little girls had mentioned. Could this whole thing be drug related? Could that man be Sandi's supplier?

And Sandi had seemed so convinced that Willow had been the one to take the girls—even desperate to convince the police of it. Why? Was she trying to deflect suspicion from herself? Or from the mysterious man?

He didn't want to be judgmental. He knew Sandi was in a tight spot, trying to take care of her children, struggling to support them. But he still couldn't overlook the fact that she'd left those little girls alone at home often, had made a habit of it. And then she'd had the gall to shriek like a shrew at Willow for leaving them alone for five minutes.

He'd hoped the police would question Sandi more thoroughly, but it seemed that, once again tonight, they had decided to focus their efforts on Willow.

No one could blame them, of course, but he did hope they would follow up on that man.

The music blasted Graham as soon as he stepped into the foyer of the restaurant-bar. A woman wearing the same type of outfit Sandi had had on this evening— white Stetson, tight white shorts, white boots, red-and-white-checked shirt—greeted him at the door, looking harried, with a smile that wasn't quite in place.

"You want smoking or non?"

"Actually, I'd like to ask you a few questions, if you don't mind."

The not-quite-there smile slipped further. "Honey, it's Friday night, we've got a full house and we're short a server. You want a table or not?"

He glanced toward the bar and hesitated. She wasn't in the mood to talk, obviously, but maybe someone else would be. "I'll take that stool at the bar if it's open."

She looked relieved. "Suit yourself." She grabbed a menu and walked him to the stool. "The server will be with you shortly."

He thanked her, making no effort to peruse the menu. He had no appetite after tonight's excitement. Still, he would have to order something. This place didn't make money without selling their food and drinks. He felt foolish about the reason he was here. The police would most likely have already been here, asked their questions and reached their conclusions.

Why did he feel as if he had to check up on the police? They had proven time and again that they were perfectly capable of doing their jobs.

But this concerned Willow.

He ordered coffee and asked the middle-aged man next to him about his experience here, how often he came, who waited on him. The guy was a newcomer. But the man on Graham's other side overheard his questions.

"Oh, yeah," the younger blond man said with a smile. "Sandi works a lot when I'm here. She's a sexy lady, and she knows it."

"Really?"

The guy spread his hands. "Sure. She's quite a head turner. Real friendly."

Graham took a sip of his coffee. "I'm curious. The apartment complex where Sandi lives caught fire on Monday night, and she and her children had to move out for a few days."

"Children?" the man asked, obviously surprised. "Sandi has kids?"

"Two little girls."

"Married?"

"Not that I know of."

The man shook his head sadly. "It's a shame a woman has to stay out late at night when she should be home tucking her little girls into bed. Everything okay with them?"

Graham nodded. "They're already back in the apartment. You come here often?"

The guy grinned. "Too often."

"The fire struck early Monday morning. I don't suppose you were here then."

The man hesitated and frowned at Graham. "Matter of fact, I was. They close at one o'clock on Monday morning. Weekend business is the best."

"Even on Sunday night?"

"Sure is. Folks hang out along the street after closing. It's a real friendly group."

Judging by the loud talk and laughter that seemed to rock this place, Graham guessed the man knew what he was talking about.

"I don't suppose you'd have noticed a good-looking

woman like Sandi hanging around after closing?" he asked the man.

"You bet. She was talking to some customers outside the grill when the police cruised by and stopped. Wasn't long after that Sandi left. I just figured the cops were breaking up the party, since they were getting a little loud."

Graham glanced around the room. "Like now?"

"That's right."

"So you're saying she was here at the grill at the time?"

"Well, now that you mention it, I heard one of the other girls complain because she had to cover Sandi's customers, but she was here after closing."

"Did you notice who she was talking to?"

The guy shrugged. "Couldn't see a face."

"She has a boyfriend?"

"I'm not sure if you'd call him a boyfriend, but I know some man came around a few times when she was working. She'd step outside for a few minutes, then come back in alone. One time she didn't come back. The other server was mad."

"I don't suppose anyone here could give me the name of the guy she was talking to," Graham asked.

"Doubt it. The girl who complained doesn't even work here any more."

"Were you here earlier tonight?" Graham asked. "Say, about eight?"

"Sure was. I had dinner, then stayed around for the band. Good stuff. They'll have their own theater someday. If you wait, they'll be back out after break."

"Was Sandi here?"

"She sure was, but she went hightailing it out about the time the band started. Don't know why. Maybe she had a short shift."

Graham didn't fill in the blanks for the man. He would most likely read about it in tomorrow's paper. Especially if the notorious reporter Jolene Tucker had any inkling of what was happening.

Graham couldn't say why he found the information about Sandi's caller intriguing. So she might have a boyfriend. That was not a crime. There was nothing suspicious about it.

Still, he would have a talk with some of the other renters and see if Sandi ever had visitors in her apartment.

Graham's cell phone chirped, and he recognized Ginger's number on the tiny screen.

He excused himself and took the phone outside to answer. It was too noisy inside. "You can't be telling me they've dismissed her already," he said as he stepped out onto the sidewalk.

"Have some faith, Graham," Ginger said. "I've been praying my heart out here on the steps in front of the station. They're releasing her. Where are you?"

"Out checking some alibis."

"Willow's?" Ginger asked.

"Sandi's."

"And?" Ginger prompted.

"Clear. She was here when the whole thing took place."

"You need to get to the station, and fast," Ginger said.

"What's so urgent? You've got your car in town."

"I need a sweet talker to convince Willow to go home with us tonight. I know she won't listen to me, but she might listen to both of us."

In spite of everything, Graham felt himself smiling. Willow was strong-willed, indeed, if she was able to withstand Ginger's powerful mothering instinct after everything she'd been through this week.

"I'll be there in five minutes." He disconnected and hurried toward his Dodge.

Graham made a mental note to call a man he'd met a couple of months ago at a Branson town meeting. The man had been passing out business cards. He was a private investigator. As he'd told Graham, a person never knew when he would need that extra bit of protection.

For now, Graham would keep this quiet. No one needed to know about it except himself and Larry Bager, P.I.

Willow paced to the edge of the pavement, her whole body trembling with fury.

"You're going to have to calm down, honey," Ginger said, following in her wake. "All that excess energy's going to make you sick."

"I'm not the one in trouble here, and no one seems to realize that," she snapped.

"What do you mean?"

"I told the detective those kids could be in real danger." She swung around and faced Ginger. "Think about it. Someone has the audacity to set me up, fake a phone call and steal those girls from the apartment. Then he carries them three doors down to an empty apartment—and how did he know it was empty? How did he have a key to both places?—and then he just sits back and waits for the fireworks to begin."

"You think it was the arsonist again?"

"I don't know. Maybe. He's just mocking everyone, Ginger."

"What do you think he'll do next?"

"Exactly my question. How much further will he take it?"

The dismay was evident on Ginger's freckled face. "Of course you're right, Willow," she said softly. "I'm sure the police will patrol the area very closely tonight."

"That isn't enough."

"Well, I don't suppose you convinced Detective Rush to place the children in protective custody, did you?"

"All she said was that I was to stay away from them, per Sandi's orders, and that they would make sure the girls were safe."

What really frightened Willow was that the game this person was playing seemed to be directed toward her. First the arson paraphernalia in her trunk, now the girls. And Detective Rush had received no helpful information from Kansas City, so no clues there. Willow wasn't surprised.

A pickup truck with a poor excuse for a muffler blasted past them on the road below, and Willow cringed. How could she know there wasn't someone lurking in the shadows right here outside the police station, watching her?

"I need to get back to my room," she said at last.

"No way you're doing that, Willow Traynor," Ginger said. "Preston would never forgive me if I let you go back to that motel room, in the dark, by yourself, after all that's happened."

"Ginger, it's after midnight, I'm tired and I just want some sleep."

"I can't believe you're still staying there when you've got so many other options. You could stay with Graham and me. You could stay in one of the condos on the lake. Why do you insist on—"

"Would you please let up?" Willow snapped, then was immediately contrite. Ginger might be just a tad overbearing, but she had the heart of a true saint.

"Look, I'm sorry," she told Ginger more gently, "but I'm not putting my tail between my legs and running to your house for cover."

"You know that motel door is about as sturdy as paper. You won't be safe there."

"Trust me. I have a cell phone, and I know how to use it. I'll put a chair against the door. No, wait, for you I'll put the dresser against the door."

"Don't pull that with me. I do not trust you to call me

if you get into trouble. You know what you're doing? You're rolling yourself into a tight little ball, like one of those roly-poly bugs, and you won't allow any friends into your life to help you through the bad stuff."

Willow sighed. "You're calling me a bug?"

"I'm talking armor. Protective armor. You've got it so thick I'm surprised you can hold up the weight."

"I'm sorry, Ginger. You're right. If that unit Sandi and her girls left is still empty, I'd be interested in moving there, in exchange for some work on the rental accounts."

"How about something even better?" Ginger said. "Graham's house is more like a large log cabin. It has five bedrooms with bathrooms, it's on the lake, close to a wonderful little town, and it's worth the price of admission."

"And that price would be what?"

"Putting up with Graham and me, of course. And you'll have to trust that we have your best interests at heart."

A red Dodge 4X4 came cruising down the street and parked along the curb in front of them. Graham got out, took one look at Willow's expression and grimaced. "Have I interrupted a catfight?"

"Your sister's just been waiting for you to arrive so she can hog-tie me and dump me into your truck and haul me to Hideaway," Willow said dryly.

He glanced at his sister. "Is this true?"

"You have a problem with that?" Ginger asked.

"I have a rope in the back. Grab her."

It spoke of Willow's affection for them that their silliness could make her smile at a time like this. "I don't do well in captivity."

"Graham, she's convinced those children are still in danger," Ginger said. "The police promised to keep watch on them, and she's been threatened with a restraining order if she doesn't stay away from them."

"Sounds as if she should stay away from them," he said.

"I'm *staying* away," Willow said.

"But you insist on going back to that dreary motel room," Ginger said.

"Which means her stubborn streak has become a detriment to her health," Graham said. "We'll need to excise it."

"Fat chance," Ginger said. "I think it's inherent."

"Of course it is, but those things can be—"

"Would you two stop talking about me as if I weren't even here?" Willow grumbled.

Graham folded his arms over his chest and studied Willow with an expression of sympathy. "Stubborn bullheadedness isn't going to sway us this time, Willow. Imagine what Preston would do to Ginger and me if we allowed anything to happen to you."

"So you're saying you do believe something could happen?" Willow asked.

"I think it's likely, especially after what happened to Lucy and Brittany tonight. You seem to be a target for someone."

Willow's rush of relief surprised her. She should be upset about having her fears confirmed, but instead she felt less alone. She wasn't being overly imaginative. Someone else believed her. Two other people.

And those people were becoming important to her.

"Willow, did your husband ever talk to you about his job?" Graham asked.

"Nothing specific. He couldn't. He talked in generalities sometimes, but I never knew what kind of case he was working on."

"Did he ever bring home reports from work? Anything like that?"

"Nothing. Why?"

"I'm just trying to find out if anyone from your husband's work could be worried that you know something."

She shook her head. "Travis never wanted to worry me with details of his job, so even if it hadn't been against the rules, he wouldn't have."

"Okay, but try to remember anything you can about Travis and his job, anything he might have mentioned in passing, or something he might have let slip. Meanwhile, you can do that in the comfort of a nice lakeside house. Ginger and I both want you to come and stay with us."

"She wants to stay in the condo where Sandi and her girls stayed this week," Ginger grumbled.

"Not secure enough," Graham said.

Willow smiled. "I think I remember Preston telling me you had an apartment complex in a gated community on Lakeshore Drive."

"That's right."

"And he also told me there was a vacancy in a furnished unit, which he was hoping to fill, but hadn't found a renter yet. I'd like to rent that unit, please."

Graham and Ginger looked at one another, and if it hadn't been such a tense evening, Willow would have laughed aloud at their expressions.

"I know how much you need for deposit and the first month's rent." Willow reached into her purse. "I can write you a check now, unless you need me to fill out an application—"

"That won't be necessary," Graham said. "I don't want your check. You can stay there, but you won't pay."

"I thought you only gave free lodging to your property manager."

"Good, it's settled," Graham said. "It just so happens I need a good property manager while Preston recuperates. Let's get your things from that room and load them in my SUV. You can follow us to your new apartment. We'll have ourselves a convoy." He easily mimicked the stereotypical drawl of a trucker, and Willow smiled.

For some reason, she felt safe. But she had felt safe before and she'd been wrong.

Chapter Thirteen

On April 14 Graham had wandered through the house three times, had walked to the dock and back twice, had tried to sit on the deck and enjoy the view of the lake. He couldn't sit still.

Not only did he feel at loose ends because it was late Sunday afternoon and he had no place to be—an unusual occurrence in the past few months—but he couldn't stop thinking about Ginger's advice last week. Forgive.

She was right, of course, which irritated him. He wasn't the kind of person to hold a grudge—or at least he hadn't been until the divorce. Now he found that the bitterness he carried with him against Dena sometimes threatened to spill over into other relationships. He should never have given her the power to do that.

Ginger was also right about something else, a fact that had become more apparent to him in the past two weeks as he got to know Willow Traynor better. She was a very appealing woman. He'd noticed it the first day he met her, of course. But now he saw more than just her outward appearance—he felt as if he'd had a few glimpses into her heart. He loved what he saw.

She had worked tirelessly in the past week to catch up on lodge repairs and book work that had piled up since Preston's hospitalization. When she wasn't doing that, she was either visiting Preston or Mrs. Engle, or volunteering her time at the clinic.

She continued to keep herself just a little apart from the rest of the world—not indulging in the casual banter at the clinic, not hanging around with the other volunteers at the end of the day. Graham had been granted the opportunity to get to know her better when she worked through the lunch hour filing charts and calling patients for follow-up care.

For the first time in over four years, since he and Dena had first separated, he found himself thinking about a woman. He watched for her to arrive at her scheduled time, and felt his heart leap when she dropped in unexpectedly to help out for an hour or two with the ever-present paperwork.

Though he told himself that he was silly to respond this way to someone he had known for only two weeks, the logic didn't seem to matter to his heart.

It was time for him to deal with the past. He couldn't continue to harbor resentment toward Dena and move on with his life. For the first time since the divorce, he glimpsed a possibility he didn't want to pass up.

He glanced at the clock. At this time of day, Dena would be home from her Sunday-afternoon golf game, if her habits hadn't drastically changed over the years.

She answered on the third ring, and she sounded wary—he knew she had caller ID. "Yes . . . may I help you?"

"Hi, Dena, it's Graham."

No further greeting, no comment, only silence.

"I hope I'm not interrupting anything."

"What do you want?"

"Do you have a few minutes to talk?"

"That depends on what we're talking about. Why should I give you a single minute of my time, Graham Vaughn?"

He swallowed a hasty retort and willed himself to remain calm—another aspect of his personality that he seemed to lose wherever Dena was concerned. Had it always been that way?

No, it had not. Once upon a time they had both been happy. Though theirs wasn't a match made in heaven, they had been compatible, civil.

"Hello?" It was a one-word command for him to speak, or she would hang up.

"Yes, I'm sorry, I'm trying to figure out the best way to go about this." He cleared his throat.

"Go about what?" There was suspicion in her voice.

"I need to apologize."

There was an unamused snicker. "For what? Don't tell me after all this time you're getting ready to come clean about the affairs."

This was a study in humiliation. Dena had tried to base her request for divorce on the lie that he'd had numerous affairs during their marriage. Of course, there'd been no proof, but the accusation had still struck bone.

Humility. Be like Christ and be humble. Again he took a deep breath and called on God's strength to help him keep his voice gentle. "I never cheated on you, Dena, but I know I let you down. I'm not calling to ask your forgiveness. I'm simply telling you that

I'm sorry things worked out the way they did."

There was a long, suspicious pause. "Why now, after all this time?" she asked at last. Her voice no longer carried quite the same sharpness.

"My sister came home from Belarus a few weeks ago, and we've had some discussions about the divorce."

"Oh, really? Sounds as if you don't have anything better to talk about. What's it been, three years? Why don't you just get on with your life, Graham? I did. I'm happily married with two stepchildren who call me Mom."

"I'm glad to hear that," he said. But something in the tenor of her voice, so familiar to him, told him she was forcing the assurance a little too much. She had never wanted children, which had been another point of contention between them. "I just wanted to wish you all the best," he said at last. "I'm sorry I didn't do so sooner."

Another silence, as if she were trying to read some sarcasm beneath the words. "Are you sick? With some incurable disease?"

"No incurable disease."

"You're acting strangely."

He laughed in spite of himself. "Don't worry. I'm fine."

"I don't worry about you anymore, Graham."

Still the nasty little barbs. "Well. Good. Look, I just don't like to fight, and I'm trying to make amends. I truly do wish you the best. I will pray for your happiness and leave you in peace. Goodbye, Dena."

He hung up before she could say more. It was one thing to apologize, but he didn't feel like wallowing in her verbal barbs today. He felt good about the fact that he'd called her, and relieved that for the first time in three years the conversation hadn't exploded into a shouting match. He supposed that was the best he could hope for.

Now for the strength to continue with this act of forgiveness.

Sunday evening Willow stifled a yawn as she navigated the winding Lakeshore Drive back to Pine Lodge Estates. The moment she'd stepped into the apartment in the gated community last week she had fallen in love with the expansive great room, fireplace, vaulted ceiling, well-equipped kitchen. The master bedroom had a walk-in closet that could have served as another bedroom, and the deck overlooked the woods in back. She'd seen deer twice already. She was in love.

Ever since moving in, she'd done her best to show Graham her appreciation for his generosity, and in doing so had rediscovered her love for nursing. It wasn't the ICU, of course, but volunteering at the clinic for a few hours every day had been fun. She enjoyed the interaction with the patients, and since she kept the hours limited to four a day, at most, the shifts were manageable in spite of her continued insomnia.

Graham was good to work with. He treated the staff as equals, while deftly directing the clinic operations.

He generally kept a positive attitude, no matter the situation.

Willow had imagined, on more than one occasion last week, that she sensed Graham watching her while she worked. Maybe she was being overly sensitive, since he knew more about her background than most people. Or maybe she was being hopeful.

She smiled, but the smile dissipated. She was attracted to him. The emotions, the attraction stirring in her ranged from pleasant surprise to guilt to a renewal of grief.

But still, maybe there was hope for the future.

She yawned again and readjusted her seat. She knew she shouldn't drive when she was this tired, but she desperately needed a good night's sleep. Therefore, she had driven to The Landing to buy melatonin, valerian root, chamomile tea and a CD of soothing music.

Her recent nightmares had become relentless, robbing her of rest, haunting her during her waking hours. Simple Benadryl no longer helped.

To further complicate matters, Preston had encountered a setback when his lung collapsed. She was now more worried about him than she had been since the night of the fire, and she had stopped by to make sure he was settled and comfortable for the evening.

Unfortunately, tonight she hadn't included the Branson traffic into her plans. She'd missed one of the shortcuts Ginger had shown her, and had been caught in the Highway 76 creep-a-thon as the shows ended. Tonight one of those shortcuts would have saved her thirty minutes of snarl time.

She forced herself to sit fully upright and take a deep breath. "Hang in there, Willow, not much farther." She had to break this spell of centerline hypnosis.

Strange how a person could lie in bed for hours, unable to coax sleep, but once behind the wheel of a car, the brain relaxed and gave up the fight.

The lake to her left reflected the lights from the Branson Landing, the major hot spot in this part of the state, promising to get hotter still as shops continued to open along the shoreline.

Headlights approached from behind, and she squinted as the inconsiderate driver flashed bright beams into her eyes.

"Don't even think about it, buddy," she muttered. No way should anyone try to pass on this winding road, which lacked any kind of shoulder or guardrail. She cautiously applied her brakes, hoping the flash of red lights would translate the message.

Unfortunately, the boor seemed intent on munching her rear bumper. To her dismay, she caught the glow of approaching headlights over the next rise, as well.

She adjusted her rearview mirror, unable to read the license plate with the glare in her eyes.

The oncoming car crested a rise, and bright lights once more flashed in her eyes. The lights quickly dimmed, the car behind her backed away and she relaxed, easing her foot slightly from the accelerator.

Nothing like a little excitement to chase away the grogginess. She'd be glad to get home, start a fire in the fireplace, kick back with some chamomile tea. A few more curves and she was there.

But the car behind her got impatient again. Its headlights torched via the side mirrors straight into her face.

She reached over to make another adjustment. A fraction of a second too late she saw the curve coming. With a squeal of tires she corrected, but something bumped her from behind. She slammed the brakes as her front tires left the pavement.

Another bump, and her headlights shot across open space to the gleam of water far below. She pumped her brakes, but her tires had nothing to grip. She cried out as her car plunged through an old sign and a bramble patch of brush, then soared out into empty air.

She slammed into an embankment and tumbled through the blackness with the sound of shattering glass and crumpling metal—and her own desperate screams.

Graham was startled from his reading by the ring of the telephone. He picked up, expecting it to be Ginger calling to tell him she'd be home late from church. They had committee meetings tonight, and she had just been voted onto the missions committee.

The caller wasn't Ginger.

"Dr. Vaughn? This is Rick Fenrow. I'm calling from the E.R. at Clark Memorial Hospital. You're friends with Willow Traynor, aren't you?"

A sudden chill gripped him. "Yes. What's happened?"

"She was just brought in by ambulance from a single-vehicle accident on Lakeshore Drive."

"What's her status?"

"We don't know yet. Right now she's unconscious, and they have her on a backboard and C-spine. Dr. Teeter is with her in the trauma room. Do you want me to ask him—"

"No. I'm on my way in." He gave Rick his cell phone number, then scribbled a note for Ginger and raced out the door.

Willow awakened to the sudden sting of pain in her arm and reached to rub it. Someone caught her hand and pulled it away. She opened her eyes, then closed them again against the bright lights that blinded her.

"She's awake." A deep female voice spoke from above and to her left. "Mrs. Traynor? You're in the emergency department of Clark. You've been in an accident."

Willow felt as though someone had their hands wrapped around her throat. Again she raised her hand, and again someone caught her arm and pressed it back to her side.

She was lying on something hard and uncomfortable.

"What happened?" she asked, forcing her eyes open once more, despite the glare of the lights. She couldn't focus on the faces around her, but she was definitely the center of attention.

"You apparently ran off the side of the road into a ravine," the woman said gently. "You're on a long board with C-spine immobilization."

That explained the discomfort.

"Vitals are stable, Dr. Teeter," someone said from somewhere above Willow's head.

"Willow, we're going to have you taken into radiology to take some films and make sure you can be removed from that nasty old long board," added a slightly familiar voice. Dr. Teeter. He'd been the E.R. doctor who treated Preston the night of the fire.

She closed her eyes and felt her bed moving. The next time she opened her eyes, she was being pushed down a hallway.

She looked up at the man wheeling her to X-Ray. A long, familiar face, smiling. Rick Fenrow. "Are you my guardian angel?" she asked, noting that her words slurred a little. "You seem to always be here when I'm here."

His smile widened. "I told you they call me down whenever they're busy. You have a talent for picking the busiest nights to have your accidents."

"Has it been a bad night?"

"I haven't seen a good night in this E.R. Don't worry, they give good care here. I was here when an older man was brought in the other night with end-stage Parkinson's. The entire staff treated him like royalty. That means a lot to me, since my own father has Parkinson's."

She closed her eyes. The pain in her head seemed to be spreading throughout her body. She felt a hand on her arm.

"Are you doing okay?"

"I'm fine."

"Good. I've never lost a patient on my shift yet."

She opened her eyes again. "I'm sorry about your father. It's hard knowing a loved one is suffering when you're surrounded by healthy people."

"Exactly."

"Not that I'm healthy right now, but it seems as if I'll be fine. I can wiggle my fingers and toes, and I can feel everything—every single ache in my body. Obviously no nerves have been severed."

"You have a great attitude. I hear you're friends with Dr. Vaughn."

"That's right. If things keep going the way they have been lately, he's going to rue the day he met me."

"I hope you don't mind that I broke the rules and called him. He's pretty worried about you, and he's on his way in."

By the time Graham reached the hospital parking lot he had been apprised twice of Willow's condition, had spoken to Dr. Teeter and promised to watch her closely. Dr. Teeter agreed she would be in good enough condition to be released when Graham arrived, or at least soon after. Willow had no apparent serious injuries. Her X-rays had been read as normal, and even her CT scans had been read as negative. She'd been one of the fortunate ones tonight. Seat belts and air bags were lifesavers.

When Graham walked into the E.R., he saw Dr.

Teeter engaged in resuscitation efforts on another accident victim. Graham found Willow in room four, slightly bruised, but not as badly injured as he'd imagined on his drive in.

"So here's my patient," he said as he entered and sat on the chair in front of her. Seeing her once more helpless, with bruises on her face and arms and a cracked lip, he felt an overpowering rush of tenderness.

"Graham, you have a full schedule tomorrow," she said. "I told them I'd be fine if I could just get a ride home."

"You're a nurse—you know better. You need to be with someone where you can be awakened every two hours so you can be checked. I told Dr. Teeter that Ginger and I would take care of you at my house, rather than leave you in the hospital overnight."

She scowled at him. "Since when did you start making decisions for me? He didn't ask me what I wanted to do."

He took her right hand and examined it, then slowly, deliberately, raised it to his lips and kissed it.

Her eyes widened, and she looked startled.

When she made no attempt to remove her hand from his grasp, he continued holding it. "I started making decisions for you as soon as I received a call about the wreck."

"Rick told me he called you."

"You can't know what I went through on my way here, and I'm not taking any more chances with your safety tonight. You should just be glad Ginger doesn't

181

know about this yet, or you'd have both of us to contend with."

She blinked up at him, lips parted slightly, but for once she didn't seem to have an argument for him.

"Dr. Teeter got you through in record time," he said. "I saw your X-rays and spoke to one of the paramedics who brought you in. God definitely was protecting you tonight. Your car is demolished. Do you remember what happened?"

Slowly, with apparent reluctance, she withdrew her hand from his grasp at last. "I've been told a resident in the area heard a crash and investigated. He called 9-1-1. All I remember is traffic, bright lights, sleeping aids and seeing Preston." Her eyes widened. "Oh, poor Preston. Does he know about this?"

"He knows. I've reassured him that I'll take good care of you tonight. You are not getting out of my sight for twenty-four hours. After that, I'd like you to consider staying in Hideaway with us for the next week."

She started to shake her head. Once again he took her hand—partly because he wanted to make a point, but mostly because he'd suddenly discovered that he very much enjoyed the feel of her hand in his.

"Willow, I discovered today that the police found traces of ether on Brittany Jameson's pillowcase. Someone meant business. You have retrograde amnesia and can't remember what caused your accident—"

"I might have fallen asleep at the wheel."

"But you might not have. I'm not willing to risk it,

even if you do live in a gated community. Fences aren't enough to protect you from someone this determined." Again he raised her hand to his lips and kissed it. "Come home with me? I promise not to let Ginger take over your life."

A suggestion of a smile touched her lips. "Promise?"

"Absolutely."

"Then let's get out of here."

Chapter Fourteen

A week after the accident, Willow sat up in bed with a cry. She stared into the darkness, her breathing echoing from the corners of the room.

The room. Her bedroom in Graham's house at Hideaway. Not in that place of white shadows and strange shapes and sounds that percolated in her dreams until it became almost tangible.

Still, she watched for that figure from the casket to come rushing at her, as if it could follow her from her dreams into the waking world. In memory, she could still see those ugly, angry eyes, gaping mouth and fingers that groped toward her, looking more like animal claws than human hands.

This time, however, the face had stripes, as if shadows fell across it . . . or as if bars kept it from her. The arms reached between the bars, fingers stretched as if to gouge out her eyes. That was what had awakened her. They had come too close.

A drop of perspiration trickled down the side of her face, and she blinked, her vision adjusting from her dream world to this one. The silhouette of the huge leather chair that faced the dark fireplace was barely visible in the dim gray light that filtered through the large picture window.

No one was here. She was safe. She caught her breath on a sharp sigh of relief and heard the quiver in that sigh. The lighted numbers of the clock at her bedside stand told her dawn was near. It was Monday morning, April 22. Travis had been killed two years ago today.

The grief made her want to curl back into a ball and cover her head with the comforter. She'd had, what, five hours of sleep last night? She needed more.

But she couldn't face another nightmare, and the significance of today's date guaranteed more of the same if she closed her eyes. Besides, five hours was more than she'd had on some nights since the accident.

The final vestiges of the lingering nightmare mocked her from the dark corners of the large bedroom suite—a face of ghostly white seemed to hover just past her field of vision. The bars between them had never been there before. Was it her subconscious trying to tell her she was being imprisoned?

She blinked again. *Stop it!*

In spite of the peaceful week she'd spent here in this house in the countryside that surrounded Hideaway, Missouri, she was still on alert.

And she couldn't get Travis out of her mind. Last

night she'd gone to sleep trying hard to recall his face, not from photographs, but from memory—just an image of his face. She couldn't do it. His image often eluded her nowadays, and she found herself forced to rely on photographs.

Worse, the face that had come to her in her dreams was not Travis. But she felt that, somehow, she should recognize that image. Should she know that man who resided in the white casket and lunged up at her when she least expected it?

Someone from her past? Someone she knew, but didn't recognize in her dream state?

She thrust the comforter aside, trying to throw off the clinging remnants of her dream with it. Time for a shower.

Standing under the sharp needles of warm water, she tried to dismiss the suspicion that the persistent nightmares might be evidence that she'd inherited the disease that ruined her mother's life.

She didn't even want to think about that today. Life was overwhelming enough right now. Preston had not healed as quickly or as well as the doctors had hoped. The physical stressors of his smoke-damaged lungs, one of them still collapsed; his internal injuries and his burned body, not to mention the metabolic demands of recovering from major surgery, were making progress painfully slow. He was still a guest at Clark Memorial Hospital, a very reluctant guest.

Closing her eyes, she tried to let the steam from the hot water soothe away her tension, the uneasiness that had escalated every time she considered leaving the house. This was the only place she had felt safe this past week.

She had no reason to believe that anyone had discovered where she was staying now, though she had thought a dark-colored sedan may have been following her in Branson traffic a few times—or perhaps she imagined she'd seen the same car.

Lately Willow had even felt apprehensive when she went to the hospital. Consequently, she'd chosen alternating routes to and from Branson. Silly, maybe, but she preferred to take any precautions she could.

Today her rental car was parked across the lake at the boys' ranch because yesterday she had taken the southern route out of Branson to Highway 86, along the far shore of Table Rock Lake—that was how cautious she'd become.

One of the boys at the ranch had brought her across in Dane Gideon's bass boat. If she needed transportation into Hideaway—a quarter of a mile from here via the shoreline—she also had access to Graham's jet bike or his canoe. It was much closer to town via the lake than by road, anyway.

Showered and dressed in a pair of comfy jeans and a bright red cotton sweater, she went downstairs with the intention of catching up on some paperwork for Graham's rentals. She had slipped into her brother's job easily under Graham's patient direction. She spent several hours a week in the roomy, tastefully decorated office, with a view of Graham's private cove.

The large, well-appointed kitchen was dark and quiet when she passed through it, but as she reached for the office door to push it open, she heard the sound of squeaking boards coming from the direction of the deck.

A large human shadow moved across the panes of the French doors, slightly taller than Graham, and broader.

Willow froze, unable to breathe, as her heart once more kicked into nightmare gear. Had someone followed her here after all?

Graham sat up in bed, frowning into the gray gloom of his suite on the top floor of the house. He heard no sound now, but a few moments ago he had awakened to the faint swish of water flowing through the house pipes. Either Ginger or Willow had been taking a shower, and he guessed it was Willow.

Several times in the past week he had awakened in the middle of the night to the sound of faint cries. At first he had dismissed them as coyotes, but then he realized they sounded more like a woman weeping. Each time he heard them, he noticed that Willow was groggy the next day, with dark circles under her eyes.

Obviously she was continuing to struggle with nightmares. She never mentioned a problem, of course. He hadn't asked her about it, because he didn't want her to think he was complaining because she awakened him. She was so sensitive to others, so afraid to disturb anyone or be an inconvenience.

He hadn't yet discovered how to reassure her.

Knowing he would get no more sleep now, he rose and pulled on a fresh pair of jeans. He would shower later. Right now he wanted to make sure she was okay.

The shadowed figure turned. Willow slumped with relief when she recognized Blaze Farmer, the college kid who called the boys' ranch home.

As she watched, he pulled a deck chair to the far railing so that it faced east, where the sun had barely begun to peer over the tree-lined horizon. He sat down, placed his feet atop the wooden rail, hitched his chair onto its two back legs and crossed his arms over his broad chest, looking content.

Willow had spoken to Blaze several times in the past week—or rather, he had gone out of his way to speak to her when he came across the lake to take care of the cattle, horses, goats and chickens on Graham's property.

She knew he had a heavy schedule with his college studies and the work program at nearby College of the Ozarks, in addition to his part-time job as a tech at Hideaway Clinic. He also took care of Graham's animals in order to earn extra money to save for veterinarian school.

Even so, he never gave the impression that he was in a hurry. He had a way of making a person feel significant.

Willow strolled through the great room to the French doors, then hesitated. Ordinarily, she would have left him alone so he could enjoy his brief time of peaceful solitude, but this morning, the remnants of her nightmare continued to disturb her. She didn't want to be alone. Nor did she want to awaken Graham or Ginger.

She had a feeling she had done so a few times. Graham didn't always look perfectly refreshed on those mornings after her worst dreams left her sleepless. The problem was, his suite was directly above her bedroom. He was likely to have heard her; several times she had awakened to the sound of her own voice, crying out in fear.

She unlatched the door and opened it. Blaze turned his head in greeting, his ebony skin a sharp contrast against the growing light.

"Willow, how're you doin'? Hope I didn't wake you up. Those hens didn't want to cooperate this morning, made all kinds of racket."

"You didn't wake me." She pulled up a chair and sank down beside him, glimpsing the basket of newly laid eggs and the container of fresh milk that he had placed beside the door. "I can't believe you already have the farm chores done. Don't you ever sleep?"

"Sure do. Now that I'm staying at the ranch again, I get to bed by nine." He sighed with contentment and returned his attention to the sunrise, its golden glow highlighted by streaks of pink and mauve. "Gotta love that sunrise, don't you?"

She nodded, then took a deep breath of crisp morning air. "It's so beautiful here." She heard the wistfulness in her own voice, and saw Blaze cast her a curious glance.

"It is that," he said. "Whoever named this area must've been a prophet or something. It's been a hide-away for a lot of people, and I'm not talking about just vacationers. You know Dr. Cheyenne Gideon?"

"Of course." Dr. Gideon was married to Dane Gideon, who ran the boys' ranch. She was also the founder and director of Hideaway Clinic. Willow had met her last week and liked her immediately.

"Would you believe she came right here to this farm for the first time two years ago?" Blaze said. "And I just happened to be here when she got here. Like to've scared her out of her skin."

As Blaze launched into a story about the night single, beautiful Cheyenne Allison had come to Hideaway, Willow leaned back, appreciating the tranquillity of the morning. By the time he reached the part where Cheyenne attacked Dane with pepper spray, Willow was relaxed enough to laugh.

"Folks who hide away here don't stay hidden, though," Blaze said. "Seems trouble does come after them, one way or another."

Willow looked at him, feeling a chill slide down her spine.

"I kinda figure it's God's way of tellin' them not to put their whole trust in places or people, but to trust in Him alone."

She held her tongue. Hadn't she done that? And look where she was now.

• • •

As soon as Graham reached the bottom of the stairs and entered the great room, he caught sight of two people sitting on the deck overlooking the lake, heads close together.

Blaze and Willow, engaged in lively conversation. As he stood watching, Blaze raised his hands in a broad gesture, emphasizing a point he was making. Willow burst into laughter, her voice drifting through the glass doors.

Graham hadn't seen her laugh like that since she'd arrived here last week. Leave it to Blaze. What was his secret?

Graham didn't need his sister to point out that Willow had been deeply hurt by the incident with the children. He had quickly learned that she possessed an overdeveloped sense of responsibility, a good trait for an ICU nurse, but not good for someone who had been unfairly accused—or at least suspected—of a crime.

He also knew the accident had left her with a deeper sense of danger. He had noticed her watching the clinic door more closely, studying the patients, even starting nervously at times when the phone rang. He wished he could reassure her, but she was right to be so watchful.

In spite of her concerns, however, she'd insisted on renting another car, until she could replace the one that had been demolished in the wreck.

"Coffee?" Ginger's sleep-thickened voice came from behind him.

He turned to find her dressed in scrubs, hair freshly

washed, makeup understated but definitely there. "Are you coming to the clinic with me today?"

"Sure am. Hope you don't mind if I ride in with you. Ted's picking up my car and taking it to his shop this morning. It isn't running right."

"I thought Noelle Trask was due to work with me this morning," Graham said.

"Noelle's having morning sickness, so she called me last night. Tomorrow I'll help out at Hideaway Clinic. No rest for the weary or the wicked."

Graham glanced at her, surprised. "Morning sickness?"

Ginger nodded, grinning. "She and Nathan found out a few days ago that she's pregnant. When did you stop listening to the office scuttlebutt?"

He glanced toward the window overlooking the deck.

"Ah. I see. Never mind. Stupid question." Ginger crossed through the great room toward the kitchen. "Anyway, if Noelle's having this much trouble now, I have a feeling I'll be on call quite a bit in the coming weeks."

"Willow's been filling in quite a bit. Why don't you take some of my cases and let Willow cover for Noelle?"

Ginger raised a brow, then nodded approvingly. "You might ask Willow if she wants to do that. You want that nasty decaf this morning or my specialty, which will curl your hair and make you happy for the rest of the day?"

"And keep me up half the night?" Graham grumbled. "I don't need my hair curled this morning. Do we have any of that herbal stuff left?"

Ginger gave him a look of disgust over her plump shoulder. "Oh, Graham, please tell me you haven't crossed over to the other side."

"Where's your loyalty to friends? I bought that stuff from Noelle's Naturals. Don't you want to support your pregnant colleague?"

"I'll support her, but I don't want to destroy my taste buds while I'm doing it." Her steps slowed as she watched Willow and Blaze outside, apparently now deep in conversation. "Willow must've had another bad night. She doesn't usually get up this early."

"I was thinking the same thing." Graham followed his sister into the kitchen and sat on the stool at the bar that separated the kitchen from the great room. Once again, his attention was drawn to the two people on the deck, particularly to one person.

"I'm worried about her," Ginger said softly, looking up from the coffee grinder.

"Why? Has she said something? I know she's still having nightmares."

Ginger filled the coffeemaker with water and turned it on, then stepped over to the bar to lean against it. "I'd be having nightmares, too, if I were her. Want to take those two some coffee once it's brewed? Or I could poison them with your weird stuff."

Five minutes later Graham stepped out onto the deck with a crocheted throw from the sofa draped over his arm, carrying two cups of bona fide coffee—one with cream, no sugar, the way Willow liked it. The other cup had the works, the way Blaze always drank his.

Two pairs of eyes looked up at him, and he was struck by the glint of laughter that lingered in Willow's expression. He'd missed that this past week. She'd been so quiet.

"I was just tellin' Willow about Hideaway's fall festival," Blaze said. "And the pig races, and how Fawn Morrison fell in the manure last year."

Willow accepted the coffee from Graham. "Thanks. Are you going to have your usual nasty brew?" She looked at Blaze and gave an exaggerated shudder. "That stuff tastes as if it might come from the pigpen after those races."

Graham rolled his eyes. "First Ginger, now you. Some people just don't know what's good." He held out the remaining cup of coffee to Blaze. "Ginger fixed your favorite. Mocha with honey."

Blaze took the cup and stood. "Mmm, mmm, mmm, she does know what I like." He took an appreciative sip. "She in the kitchen?"

Graham nodded, placing the throw over Willow's shoulders. She smiled her thanks. She had a beautiful smile, and he saw it far too seldom.

"Mmm, mmm, mmm," Blaze said again. Graham glanced around to find the eighteen-year-old watching him with a knowing glint in his eye. "Well, I'll go thank Ginger for my drink before I get back over to the ranch. I promised Cook I'd make breakfast this morning."

"Don't you ever have down time?" Graham asked.

"There'll be time for that after I graduate, if I can save enough money."

"Still planning to attend vet school?" Graham asked.

"If I'm accepted." He gave Graham a sassy grin. "If not, I'll have to settle for med school. Maybe I'll become a surgeon." Chuckling, Blaze stepped through the French doors and closed them behind him. Just before he turned away, he gave Graham a thumbs-up and a quick nod of approval toward Willow, who sat gazing across the lake.

Graham felt a brief twinge of envy toward Blaze. The kid had the ability to form a bond with a complete stranger within a few minutes of conversation. Graham had been that way once, but lately his social life had screeched to a dead halt.

He'd become increasingly aware of that fact this past week, even as he'd become more and more aware of how much he enjoyed Willow's presence in the house. For some reason, that awareness made him revert to sharp memories of insecure adolescence—or something even worse: the overwhelming conviction that he was not worth knowing. That had become obvious to him when Dena filed for divorce. The one woman who knew him best in the whole world, who shared his heart, and his deepest secrets about himself, had decided that she wanted him only if she could also have the money he earned as a surgeon.

But that kind of thinking was exactly what he'd decided not to indulge in. He said a quick, silent prayer for forgiveness, and for help to continue forgiving Dena.

Chapter Fifteen

"What's Blaze's real name?" Willow asked, once more turning her attention to the shimmering surface of the early morning lake.

Graham sat down in the chair Blaze had vacated. "Gavin. He nicknamed himself when he arrived at the ranch two years ago, insisted he be called Blaze."

"Why was that?"

"He was once unfairly accused of arson."

Willow looked up sharply. "By whom?"

"By his mother."

Willow suddenly grew very still, hands wrapped around her coffee cup, seeking warmth. As Graham provided Willow with details, she suddenly felt like such a whiner. "These past couple of weeks I've felt sorry for myself because I was suspected of arson and kidnapping. Blaze lost his home and both of his parents, and was sent away to a ranch for delinquent boys. He has such a good attitude."

"I was just thinking the same about you, considering all you've been through in two years," Graham said. "You're not exactly hiding away in your room. You help me, you handle patients and rental property, you visit the hospital every day."

"Okay, so I'm a saint," she said dryly, but she couldn't prevent a smile. She took another sip of the delicious coffee and leaned back in her deck chair, appreciating the warm throw Graham had brought out for her.

"Speaking of those rentals," she said, "I did some more background checks on Sandi. I tried calling the previous landlord with no results, so I sent them a letter. I received a reply yesterday. They didn't know much more about her than we do. She only lived in Columbia two months. Before that, she lived in Blue Springs, which is a suburb of Kansas City."

Graham frowned. "Interesting that she once lived in the same city you did."

"A lot of people live in K.C. For instance, Carl lived in K.C. briefly before moving farther south in search of warmer weather. I did some research online."

"Where did he live before that?"

"Carl had a pharmacy in Minneapolis until he retired five years ago."

"Have you found any interesting information about the other renters?"

"Nothing that strikes me as significant. The Jasumbacks are from the Pierce City area, retired. Rick worked at a hospital in Columbia before moving here. A lot of the renters are retired. I can't see any of them skulking around Preston's cabin, soaking it with fuel and lighting a fire around it."

"Never underestimate the senior citizens. Have you

been able to glean any more information from the neighbors about any visitors Sandi might have had?" Graham asked.

"None," Willow said. "But I did find out that Social Services paid a call on her last week. They're apparently keeping a close watch on Brittany and Lucy. I'm glad."

"So am I."

Willow knew he wasn't just saying that. He obviously loved children, judging by the way he coddled the youngest of his patients.

She studied his face. He had kind eyes, the color of dark amber, and generous laugh lines. She often heard him and Ginger bantering, laughing, teasing one another comfortably. And for some reason they had welcomed her into their family circle this past week as if she'd always belonged.

There were times she couldn't help wishing . . .

"You're up earlier than usual this morning," Graham said. "Is your room warm enough at night?"

"Perfectly. I still don't sleep the best, and I decided long ago that it's easier to just get up than to lie there and try to get back to sleep."

"Would that possibly be due to more of the nightmares you mentioned before?"

She closed her eyes and nodded. "Please tell me I haven't done anything outrageous like sleepwalk or scream or—"

"No sleepwalking. You can relax. Is it still the same dream?"

She nodded. "Sometimes it's more graphic than others."

"Do you have a clear memory of it when you wake up?"

"Not always. This morning I did. A man, lying in a casket lined with white. He's angry with me, and he sometimes sits up, or even stands up from the casket, reaching for me as if he wants to strangle me."

Graham frowned. "You know that would be a very difficult thing to do. I know, because our church youth group conned me into playing a dead man who sat up in a casket in a play."

"This is a dream, Graham, not reality."

"You never recognize the person?"

"Never, except to tell that he's a man."

"And the setting? Always a casket?"

"Always."

"You're sure it's a casket? It isn't as if he's stepping through a door or a window of light, or something else rectangular?"

She hesitated, trying to bring to mind an image from one of the dreams. But as with most dreams, the edges of it had always grown fuzzy as soon as she awakened, and with time the images dissipated completely. "No, I don't think so, because he sits up from it. Or he stands up and lunges toward me. I think the reason I feel it's a casket is because he's so deathly pale."

"In this dream, does he ever catch you?"

"No. Believe me, I've tried to figure it out."

"Remember what Ginger said about it? That it might be a message from your subconscious?"

"Of course, but what kind of message? I just don't know."

He shrugged. "My immediate impression is that you might have seen someone or noticed something that could be the cause of what's been happening. The detail could be so seemingly insignificant that you've dismissed it consciously. I'm certainly no expert in dream study, however."

"I just assumed it was grief. This man could even be a representation of my husband, Travis, and possibly a reflection of my residual anger at him for leaving me as he did."

"Or it could be anger at yourself," Graham suggested. "Perhaps you're feeling guilty because you're still alive when your husband isn't."

She took another sip of the coffee, then set the cup down and folded her hands in her lap. "Today is the second anniversary of his death."

Graham was silent for a moment. "I'm sorry. That could account for an active dream life. But what if it isn't? How do you feel about talking to a friend of mine at church who is a psychologist?"

"No."

Graham blinked at her, surprised, and she realized she'd snapped the word a little forcefully. "Preston urged me to do that once when we were talking about the possibility of inheriting Mom's illness."

"I'm not talking about psychoanalyzing you. I'm

talking about trying to get to the bottom of this dream. What if it really does have something to do with everything that's happened to you?"

"No. Call me paranoid, but that would make me nervous."

"You're not psychotic, Willow. Trust me."

"And you're an expert on the subject?"

"Not even close, but I find psychology fascinating, and spent some time on rotations with a psychiatrist. I found it so interesting I gave up some free time to study with her further."

"Why would a surgeon want to do that?" she asked, relieved the former subject had been so easily deflected.

"It never hurts to have a little extra understanding about the human psyche. It comes in handy now, especially, since I'm no longer strictly a surgeon."

"I noticed you were taking quite a few general medical cases."

"I feel that's what God has called me to do."

She shook her head. "I don't understand His methods. Look at all you've given up to follow that calling. He sure has an interesting way of dealing with His children."

Graham didn't reply, and she stared out across the lake.

"Would you like a refill?" he asked.

She glanced at him. He wasn't going to argue with her about her take on God? "No, thanks."

"I think my nasty concoction is finished brewing."

He reached for her cup and stood up. "Would you wait here for a minute? I'll be right back."

Graham took a large mug down from the cabinet, glancing at Willow through the window. He knew enough about the grief process to recognize it when it stared him in the face. He'd gone through that himself, and he was still praying daily to continue forgiving Dena. His bitterness wasn't aimed toward God the way Willow's was, but it was there.

Lord, give me wisdom. Show me what to say. If You would, touch her through me with Your healing grace.

He took his time preparing his drink, and he fixed Willow another cup in spite of her polite refusal.

When he carried their cups back out to the deck, she had nudged the throw from her shoulders and formed a pillow with it. She had her head back and was soaking up the early morning sunshine.

He handed the cup to her. "I thought you might change your mind. It's still a little cool out here."

She thanked him and accepted it, watching him with an expression of wariness as he settled. "No sermon?"

He shook his head. "That would be hypocritical. There have been times I've felt the same way you do about God."

She clasped the cup in both hands and raised it to her lips, inhaling quietly. "I don't seem to be able to over-come this . . . this resentment." She took a sip of her drink and closed her eyes. "Believe me, I know all the trite platitudes anyone could offer, because I've offered them myself in the past. Not anymore."

"Have you ever considered that platitudes become what they are because of the truth in them?"

"You mean like the one such as 'Nothing happens to God's children without a reason'? Or maybe the one about good coming from our trials? Sorry, I'm not to the point where I can deal with that yet."

"Most people aren't when they're in the middle of the crisis, which you are."

"I wish someone would tell me how long this crisis is supposed to continue, because to me it seems as if God's allowing me to be hit over and over again, driving me to my knees."

"Believe me, I understand. Some might say on our knees is exactly where we should be."

"Another platitude," Willow said. She stretched her long legs out in front of her and sighed. "Did you know I catch myself in the middle of automatic prayers even now, when I'm trying so hard not to speak to God? I never realized how difficult the habit would be to break."

"Maybe it isn't just a habit," Graham said. "Maybe it's God pursuing you. One of my favorite passages of scripture is in Psalm 139. " 'Where can I flee from your presence? If I ascend into heaven, you are there; if I make my bed in hell, behold, you are there.' "

Willow finished the passage. " 'If I take the wings of the morning and dwell in the uttermost parts of the sea, even there your hand shall lead me.' " She sighed. "I know all that. Honestly, I do."

"Sorry, I guess I was preaching."

"Do you want to know what worries me the most about all this? Preston isn't a believer, and I'm torn between putting on a good front for him or letting him see how much I'm struggling with God right now."

"You're afraid you'd be lying if you try to tell him God is the answer to every struggle?"

"Exactly. I'm blaming Him for everything right now."

"He's big enough to shoulder the blame," Graham said. "Remember He did that when He walked this earth."

"Okay, now you're preaching," she said. But she didn't seem annoyed.

He only wished he could do or say more to help her.

But one preaching service was enough. "I noticed you haven't gone into town in the past couple of days," he said, changing the subject.

She hesitated. "No. Preston has several friends who visit him on the weekends. He doesn't need me every day."

Graham waited. Something in her tone was different. "Willow, you're understandably tense about the events that have taken place lately, but is something else wrong? Has something happened at the hospital that made you nervous?"

"Well, there was something that bothered me," she said softly. "Probably nothing at all, but I'm hypersensitive lately."

"You're allowed," Graham said. "You've been

through enough to warrant it. What did you see?"

"I think someone was following me."

His hands tightened around the mug. "Where? When did it happen?"

"The first time I noticed it I was on Shepherd of the Hills Expressway, last Wednesday, when I glanced into my rearview mirror and saw a black late-model car. Possibly a Ford, though I'm not good at identifying makes of cars."

"How often did this happen?"

"Once on Wednesday and twice on Friday, but as I said, I'm not sure it was the same car."

"This happened three times?" He'd have to talk with his P.I. again. "Do you think it was the same car, or do you think you've just become particularly alert to that type?"

"I don't know for sure. After what happened to Preston, and to Lucy and Brittany, I can't risk allowing someone to follow me back here and endanger you and Ginger, as well. I always managed to lose the car in traffic before I came here—if it truly was following me in the first place."

"Were you ever able to see the driver?"

"I could never get close enough to get a clear view of who was inside, but it looked like a man alone."

"Willow," he said with a sigh, "I wish you'd told me about this sooner."

"As I said, it could have been my imagination."

"After everything you've been through, you're ready to dismiss something like that as imagination?" He heard the sharpening of his tone, and saw Willow's eyes widen a fraction.

She didn't say anything.

"I'm sorry," he said. "I probably should have told you about this, but two weeks ago, after the girls were kidnapped, I hired a private investigator."

For a moment Willow didn't react. She continued to stare across at the horizon. But he saw her hands clench into fists, and he realized he'd given her quite a shock.

She pressed her lips together, her chin jutting forward a fraction. She swallowed, then turned to meet Graham's gaze. "You've been having me watched?" Her quiet voice betrayed deep disappointment.

"I've been having your background investigated, your husband's previous cases checked out and, yes, I've instructed my investigator to do some surveillance."

She closed her eyes. There was a long silence.

"Willow, I was worried about your safety."

She looked back at him, and the hurt disappointment had metamorphosed into anger—vivid anger. "If you were worried about my safety, shouldn't you have told me what you were doing? The problem is, you don't trust me."

"I didn't want to place more worry on your shoulders right now. I just wanted to make sure this monster didn't have another chance to get at you."

She studied his face for a moment, as if she were trying to read fine print in a contract. "Are you sure that's what you wanted?"

He met and held her gaze. "I'm sure."

"It had nothing to do with protecting others from me?" Her tone held reproach.

"Of course not. Willow, I'm sorry. I didn't intend to upset you with this. I merely wanted to put your mind at ease, and it seems I've handled things poorly."

She sighed and reached down for her half-empty coffee cup and the blanket throw he had brought out for her. She stood up.

"Willow, we need to talk about this."

"What is there to talk about? You seem to have taken matters into your own hands without consulting me. That implies that you don't have a high enough regard for my emotional stability to trust me with *your* plans to secure *my* safety."

He winced. "I'm sorry. I didn't see it that way."

"I do," she said, not looking at him. She sounded suddenly tired. "When you talked me into coming to stay here, you promised not to allow Ginger to take over my life. She hasn't. It seems *you* have."

"Please sit back down and talk to me about this. All I did was arrange for extra protection for you. I haven't taken over your life."

"I think I'll pay Preston a visit. May I use your canoe to cross the lake? My car's at the ranch."

"Please use the jet bike. It'll be much easier."

"I need the exercise," she said. "And I need the peace and quiet of the canoe right now."

He'd stepped over the mark again. He'd learned

before she arrived here that she did not like to be over-protected or coddled. Which was one reason he had hesitated to tell her about Larry Bager, because he'd been concerned that if he did tell her about the P.I., she would protest.

"Take the canoe with my blessing." He knew he sounded irritable. Her determined independence irritated him.

"Thank you."

A few moments later, as he watched her paddle the canoe across the lake, he was very aware of his own disappointment. Why hadn't he handled that differently? And why wouldn't she at least stay and talk to him about it?

And then he realized why her response meant so much to him. It was because *she* had come to mean increasingly more to him.

What he was dealing with here was an old-fashioned crush. This transparent, hurting, loving woman had touched a place in his heart no one had touched in a long time—a place no one had been allowed to reach.

He felt a deep need to help Willow, to protect her, but would she believe that? Apparently not. He was surprised, himself, by his instinctive response.

"Oh, Lord, please keep her safe," he murmured as he continued to watch her progress across the water. *"And please, Lord, draw her back to You."*

Chapter Sixteen

Monday morning, April 22

Willow drove over the rough country road that led to Highway 86 south of the lake, unable to enjoy the burgeoning colors of vibrant Ozark springtime. A heart-healthy canoe ride across the lake had served only to give her time to brood.

Did Graham really think she was so helpless he couldn't even trust her with information about safety measures he had taken for her? He certainly never treated others like that. Oh, sure, he was considerate of his sister, and seemed to dote on his patients, but he was straightforward with them. If a patient needed particular treatment for a physical condition, he didn't just prescribe it for them without explaining what he was doing and why.

She slowed for a pothole in the road. Okay, she wasn't being completely fair—she knew that. He'd been honest about his fear that she might be in danger, but to hire someone to watch her without her knowing?

It hurt. She couldn't help it.

What mystified her was that he'd been a little miffed by her reaction, as if he'd expected her to gratefully welcome his attempts to control her life without her input.

What if he really did suspect her, down deep, as the police had?

Stop it, Willow. You're overreacting.

Instinctively she glanced in the rearview mirror and caught movement in the distance on the road behind her. Someone was speeding toward her.

Her hands tightened on the steering wheel as her heart rate soared with a rush of adrenaline. Then she saw the flashing yellow light on the car's roof. It was a rural mail carrier.

True to its mission, the vehicle pulled over at the next mailbox, and the driver, sitting on what was typically the passenger side of the automobile, shoved mail into the box.

Willow had definitely overreacted. Again.

"Relax," she muttered as she slowed at the stop sign, then turned left onto Highway 86. "It's nothing. You're just scaring yourself."

Surely Graham couldn't have been that surprised at her reaction to his news. Why couldn't he just have told her immediately that he'd hired a detective to tail her? The logic remained the same. If he trusted her, why not tell her what he was doing? Therefore, he didn't completely trust her.

Of course, there was also the possibility that he was afraid she would never agree to a P.I., and therefore he'd decided to hire one quietly to avoid conflict. That was still wrong. She still resented it.

But would she have refused if he'd asked her first?

Okay, yes, she probably would have, even if a P.I. was a good idea. She was well aware that she over-emphasized her independence, even when it could be to her detriment.

As she passed the turnoff to Blue Eye, she finally, grudgingly, reached the conclusion that although Graham had gone about it all wrong, he had probably done the right thing by hiring the P.I. Maybe that was why nothing else had happened the past two weeks. Maybe he'd scared off her stalker.

But had he, really? Her enemy was still holding her hostage, if only in her mind. She couldn't relax, she was always on her guard, and when she slept, the nightmares plagued her.

Somehow she had to break free from the constant heart-pounding tension she'd lived with for so long.

Graham dialed Larry Bager's cell phone number, wondering if the P.I. would be in range to intercept Willow this morning. *Why didn't I tell her about hiring Larry? This could all have been avoided.*

If he'd told her two weeks ago that she had a licensed private investigator on her case, it was possible she might have been willing to cooperate with the investigation. And maybe she wouldn't have been so alarmed by the car following her. He felt remorseful about that.

The call connected. "Bager," the investigator said curtly.

"It's Graham. Can you get to the hospital? Willow's on her way there to see her brother."

"Finally," Larry muttered. "When we set this up you told me she would probably be at the hospital every day. Not only isn't she there when I expect her to be, she shows up at odd hours, when I'm not expecting her. It's hard to keep up with that lady."

"She spotted someone following her in traffic and she's a little spooked," Graham said. "Can't say I blame her. Do you drive a dark sedan?"

"Nope. I trade off between a tan pickup and a silver sedan."

Graham felt fear tighten his gut. "So you never tailed Willow in a dark car?"

"Never. The only time I've tailed her was when I happened to catch her at the hospital, and then she only drove to the clinic. I saw no one following her. When did she see this car? Is she positive that's what she saw?"

"It happened more than once," Graham said. "She admitted she might have been imagining things, but I don't want to take any chances. How long will it take you to get to the hospital?"

"It'll be at least an hour. I'm in Bolivar, but I'm in my car now. I'll get there as quickly as I can."

Graham glanced at his watch. His first patient was due at the clinic in an hour. "I think I'll call Detective Rush. Maybe the police can make a pass by the hospital just to check on things."

"If you were that worried you could've gone with her," Larry said.

"At the time she left, I thought you were the one she'd seen following her. Besides, you obviously don't know Willow very well if you think she'd docilely allow me to bodyguard her."

"Whose fault is that?" Larry grumbled. "I could have been best friends with her by now if you'd introduced us. Look, just relax, okay? If she's as watchful and as smart as you're saying, it's unlikely a nonprofessional has followed her out of Branson without her noticing."

"Which means, if he's watching for her, he'll likely be at the hospital, where he will know he can find her if he waits long enough," Graham said.

"And if he makes a move on her, it probably won't be in a crowded hospital corridor."

"True." Graham willed himself to relax. Larry knew what he was talking about.

"I managed to cadge a copy of video footage from hospital security. I've marked every place where Willow is either entering or leaving. I don't see anyone following her from the building or the parking lot. If someone's waiting for her, they could be parked off hospital property."

"If we can meet with her this morning at the hospital, maybe we'll have time to run through some of that footage with her, see if there's anyone she recognizes," Graham suggested.

"I'll make some still shots to show her. The video is time-consuming. Maybe I can meet with her later today."

"Have you found out anything more about Sandi Jameson?"

"A few things," Larry said. "I was going to call you when I got home today. I've still got some buddies on the force in K.C. Jameson is her maiden name. There's no record she's ever been married, and there's no record of the father of the children, so far. There *is* a police record on Sandi, though it's old."

"A record of what?" Graham asked.

"Drug trafficking in Kansas City."

"How long ago?"

"Four years."

"Jail time?"

"None."

"Any connections there?"

"I'm still looking."

"Let me know."

"Will do. Later." Larry disconnected.

Graham knew that if Larry said he would be at the hospital in an hour, he would be there in forty-five minutes. He had proven to be prompt with information delivery, and he had good contacts with the police in Kansas City, having worked there for ten years before his transfer to Branson.

After burning out on police work a couple of years ago, he'd taken a year off to work as a car salesman, hated it, and started his own investigation company. Graham had checked his credentials and found he had a clean record with the force.

Graham dialed Willow's cell, and as he'd expected, got no answer. She didn't use her cell phone when driving because it wasn't hands free. Besides, if she saw who was calling, she might still be angry enough to ignore him.

He wasn't surprised when her voice mail kicked in. "Willow, this is Graham. The car you saw was not my investigator. We need to talk. Call me."

Willow was pulling into the covered hospital parking lot when her cell phone beeped for the second time that morning. She checked her call screen and saw that this time it wasn't Graham. This time the call was coming from Sandi Jameson's telephone.

This was the pits. Her cell phone hardly ever rang, and now that it did, it was announcing calls from two people she did not want to talk to right now.

She allowed it to ring four times while she found a parking space and stopped, then she relented and answered.

"Willow? It's Sandi. Is everything okay?" Her voice was high-pitched, her words clipped. It didn't even sound like Sandi. "I haven't heard anything about the investigation for at least a couple of weeks—you know those police won't talk to me. I'm always scared when the girls take off for school in the morning."

Willow frowned. "Why are you calling me? I don't even think we should be talking."

"Please don't . . . don't be that way," Sandi said. "I called to apologize for the things I said to you. You've got to understand that I was more than a little freaked about the situation. I mean, my babies were missing. But I shouldn't have blamed you, I know that now, because you were the one person who cared enough to try to get involved and help me with them. And what did I do? I spat all over you. I knew better than that, because I knew who—"

"My impression was that you felt I had ulterior motives for wanting to keep Lucy and Brittany," Willow said, intentionally interrupting the blast of Sandi's monologue.

"I was wrong, okay? I'm just so worried about them. Now I'm afraid to leave them alone for a minute, or that DFS woman will come tromping into our home and try to take them away, and I can't—"

"I'm sure that won't happen without good reason," Willow said.

There was a short silence. "What's that supposed to mean?" Sandi demanded, her voice suddenly even more shrill.

What was wrong with her? "Those people are already so overworked, it isn't as if they're searching for children to snatch from their parents," Willow explained.

More silence, then, Sandi said, "The girls ask about you a lot, you know." Once more, Willow found herself scrambling to keep up with the racing emotional roller coaster Sandi seemed to be on. "They keep wondering when you're coming back to sit with them again. They miss you."

Willow missed them, too. "Last I heard, you felt that I was dangerous to them," she said.

"Okay, but I wasn't thinking straight. You're obviously not a mother, or you'd know how hard it is to raise two little girls alone."

Willow felt the sharp edge of Sandi's words. "You're right, I can't possibly understand. So why did you even bother to call me?"

"Because they like you a lot, Willow. A whole lot. They keep talking about you, and they ask about you, and wonder where you are and why you don't ever come to see them, and I don't know what to tell them because you never call us anymore."

A chill slid down Willow's spine. Why was Sandi chattering and repeating herself? *And why would she expect me to call her?*

Willow closed her eyes, her hand gripping the hard plastic of the cell phone. What kind of person were those children living with? "Sandi, where are the girls now?"

"What do you mean? They're at school. Where else would they be? Brittany's in kindergarten this year, and I'm trying to work when they're in school, but I can't make a living just working days, and those people—"

"Did you drive them to school this morning?"

"No, the bus picks them up, and I try to be here when they get home, but sometimes I can't because you know how the traffic is, and—"

"Are you on some kind of medication?" Willow asked.

There was silence.

"Sandi, what's really going on with you? Are you okay?"

More silence.

"Look, if you called me to—"

The line went dead.

Willow shoved her phone into her purse, mystified and clueless. Why had she even bothered to talk to the woman?

She knew the answer, of course.

Those two little girls. If it was within her power, she couldn't allow anything to happen to Lucy or Brittany.

Graham gripped the steering wheel tightly as he drove the sharp curves of Highway 76 toward Branson. He had called and left a message at the hospital for Preston to have Willow contact him as soon as she arrived.

If she ignored that message, she wouldn't have to worry about her stalker catching up with her, because Graham was going to personally strangle her. How inconsiderate to needlessly worry people who cared about her.

"Graham, you're going to break that steering wheel in half," Ginger said beside him. "What's going on with you?"

"Nothing. I'm just a little tense."

"You mean you're still stewing over that fight with Willow this morning?"

He glanced sideways at his sister. "You were eavesdropping?"

"Nope, but it sure didn't take a genius to read your body language."

"Willow's ignoring my calls. That woman is the

most stubborn, self-sufficient person I've ever met."

"Last I heard, self-sufficiency wasn't a sin."

"No, but it's extremely rude to ignore a helping hand from someone who wants only the best for you. I had to tell her this morning about hiring Larry."

"Well, maybe if you'd been up-front with her to begin with—"

"Thank you, Miss Manners. I've been through that routine three times already this morning. Don't start it again."

"Three times?"

"Once with Willow, once with Larry, once with myself. Now she won't answer my calls."

"Well, relax and slow down or you'll get us killed on this next curve."

Graham eased his foot slightly from the accelerator. "I realize now I should have told her, but I didn't expect her to freeze me out completely."

"You'd be upset if you were in her situation," Ginger said. "You know she values her independence, and yet you didn't respect that."

"I did apologize."

"Fine, then give her a chance for the apology to sink in. And stop being so controlling. What's she supposed to make of your behavior? She's never seen you falling in love before."

The words hung in the air unchallenged for a long moment as Graham navigated an S curve. "Don't start with me this morning."

"I'm not starting a thing. I'm just commenting on

what I see, and what I see is quite interesting."

"I give Willow the same respect I hope someone would give you in the same situation. You call that interesting?"

"Very. I see the way your gaze seems drawn to her every few moments during dinner at night when we're all home, and the way you try hard not to act as if you're interested."

Graham couldn't prevent a grin. "You're a hopeless romantic."

"I can cut the attraction with a steak knife around the house lately, and the fact that you avoid being in the same room alone with her on some occasions is, to me, very revealing."

"Attraction is a dangerous thing. It can make you do dangerous things, make dangerous decisions."

"Attraction is a vital part of a promising relationship," Ginger said.

"Need I remind you that we've both made some bad decisions based on attraction?"

"I learned from those stupid blunders. You have, too. You just don't trust yourself. Deal with Dena so you can get on with your life."

"I've dealt with her, thank you."

"What do you mean?"

"I called Dena and apologized. Last week, in fact. I did it just to get you off my back. So get off my back."

"So you do realize Willow is special."

"I'm not blind. She's struggling with a lot right now. She doesn't need further complications in her life."

"You wouldn't complicate it," Ginger said. "You'd make it better."

"You know that for a fact?"

"I sure do," Ginger assured him. "Being around you has made my life better. Give yourself some credit."

Graham turned left on Highway 76 in Branson West. Fifteen more minutes, and he would see for himself if Willow was safe at the hospital.

Chapter Seventeen

The volunteer information clerk looked up from his place at the reception counter when Willow entered the hospital lobby. "Mornin', Miss Willow. How's that brother of yours?"

"Hi, Harry." She stepped over to the desk, where the partially bald, fiftysomething man greeted newcomers and regulars alike as if they were long-lost friends. "He's almost healed and ready to get out of this place."

"I heard he's hoping to get sprung today, tomorrow at the latest," Harry said. They had discussed Preston's condition at length in the past weeks, as well as the latest news about the best music theaters in town, the best places to eat, the state of the economy. Harry knew a little about everything and everyone.

He motioned for her to come closer. "Word's out that you and Dr. Vaughn are sweet on each other. Is that just a rumor, or should I be looking for a wedding gift?"

Her smile grew wooden even as she felt the blood rush to her face. "Now, Harry, where did you hear something like that?"

"Carl from the lodge is the one who said something to me about it."

"Well, that just goes to show never trust rumors."

Harry looked disappointed. "Too bad. That Dr. Vaughn's a fine man."

She forced her smile back into place and winked at him. "Does he pay you to say that?"

Harry chuckled as she walked away.

She nodded to three more familiar faces as she stepped down the hallway toward the bank of elevators. Though Clark was a large state-of-the-art hospital, it had a small-hospital atmosphere, and she had become acquainted with several of the staff who attended to Preston.

She had discovered, visiting with Mrs. Engle, that the older lady was quite popular. This meant Willow often encountered neighbors from the apartment complex both when she was visiting Preston and when she was with Mrs. Engle. She had encountered the Jasumbacks twice, Mary Ruth Blevins once, and Carl Mackey made it a point to visit with Esther Engle and Preston every time he pulled a shift in the pharmacy, which was three times a week.

Willow stepped into an elevator to find a man already there—another familiar face. Rick Fenrow.

She'd become more acquainted with him in the past week, encountering him in the hallways or in Preston's room. She had come to look forward to his quick smile and encouraging words.

Today he carried a set of patient charts under his arm. The smile was in place, as always. In fact, today, as had been the case for the past week, the smile was a little friendlier.

"What a great way to start the week," he said. "Riding in the elevator alone with the prettiest woman in Branson."

She laughed. "Rick, you know how to turn on the charm."

"With a face like this, a guy's got to have an alternate plan to woo the ladies. Preston might be sleeping. He was up half the night last night, probably too excited to go to bed. He wants out of this place as badly as I do this morning."

"Maybe tomorrow."

They reached the fifth floor just as Willow's cell phone beeped from her purse. She grimaced. There were signs telling visitors to turn off their cell phones in the hospital, and she usually complied, but this morning she'd been preoccupied. She'd forgotten. But since she knew she wasn't in an area of the hospital where cell phone activity could interfere with medical equipment, she checked the tiny screen, saw it was Sandi and answered as she stepped out of the elevator.

"Sandi, why did you hang up on me?"

"I'm sorry." Now the woman's voice was wobbly, as if she were crying. "I've ruined everything. This is all my fault."

Willow's steps slowed automatically. "What do you mean?"

"Can we talk in person?" Sandi asked. "Will you meet me somewhere?"

Willow glanced back toward the closing elevator doors and gave Rick a wave. "I don't think that's a good idea."

Sandi gave a watery sniff. "Please," she whispered. "I'm so sorry. I can't stand this anymore. I n-need help. I've got to talk to somebody. I was going to talk to you before, but . . . but he warned me not to."

"He? Who are you talking about?"

"He's the one who took the girls. I know that now. It wasn't you."

Willow's hand tightened on the phone. "Sandi, if you know who took them, why didn't you tell the police?"

"I couldn't face it. Don't you see? I wanted you to be the one who took them. I knew you wouldn't hurt them."

The woman was living in a fantasyland. Either she was high on drugs at this moment or she was psychologically unstable.

"Sandi," Willow said more gently, "tell me who took them. Why couldn't you face calling the police?"

"Because . . . I couldn't. I don't have proof, and if the police checked him out or took him in for questioning, he'd know I was the one who called. It's all falling apart."

"What is, Sandi? What's going on with you?"

"Not on the phone. I'm so . . . scared, Willow, and I

can't do this alone anymore. He doesn't want me talking to you. He hated it when you were staying with them at night, and if he finds out I'm talking to you right now he might take the girls again. This time we won't find them."

"If you'd just tell me what's happening to you, maybe I can find a counselor or someone to help—"

"No! No, please, can I meet you somewhere? Where are you now? I could drive to wherever you are."

"I'm at the hospital visiting Preston," Willow said. "Do you want to meet downstairs in the lobby?" That way they could talk in full view of others.

"Not the hospital," Sandi said. "Too many people. I can't take the chance we'll be seen."

Willow hesitated. *Tell her no, Willow. She's up to something. She's tricking you.* But she sounded genuinely frightened.

"Please?" Sandi said softly. "There's something you need to know about . . . about the fire. And about some other things. I can't talk any more over the phone. I can't risk it. I think he might have some kind of bug in my apartment."

"Where are you calling from?"

"I'm in my car on my cell. Willow, this is bad stuff, and it's getting too scary."

Sandi couldn't possibly be confessing to arson, could she? "Like what?"

"Meet me at the marina at Big Cedar."

"There will be people there, too."

"Tourists. Not locals. Just meet me, okay? And

225

please, don't bring anyone with you. I don't trust anyone, and you're the only one I'll talk to."

"No," Willow said. "You're not the only person in danger here, Sandi."

"I know. You are, too. But the marina is out in the open, and it's busy. I can't risk . . . anything else. I'll be there at ten this morning." She disconnected, and Willow found herself standing outside Preston's room, wondering how on earth she'd allowed Sandi to believe they would meet.

What did Sandi know about the fire?

Graham dropped Ginger off at his clinic on Fall Creek Road and drove on to the hospital. As a licensed physician's assistant, Ginger could open up and see the first scheduled patient for him, though the first patient wasn't due for another twenty minutes.

At his request, Ginger had tried once more to reach Willow on her cell phone as they'd traveled into town, and it was busy.

At the hospital Graham spotted Willow's dark red Subaru Outback in the covered parking lot. Relief washed over him. He'd been more worried than he had allowed himself, or Ginger, to realize.

When he stepped to the open door of Preston's room moments later, Willow was sitting at her brother's side, her voice soft and urgent.

"I never said our hardships just suddenly disappear when we believe in Christ. Look at my life, Preston. Would I believe something like that?"

"Mom and Dad said it enough," Preston grumbled. "I grew up being told God hears our prayers and cares for us, and yet I watched Mom fight to retain her sanity for as long as I can remember."

"I know. I had a hard time with that, too."

"So tell me how you can keep hanging on to faith in a God who allows you to go through what you have."

Graham knew he shouldn't eavesdrop, but he certainly couldn't interrupt them right now, and if he retreated they might be distracted from a very important conversation.

"Because there have been too many times when He was all I had," she said softly. "I believe what I read in the Bible, and though it does say God loves us and blesses us, I haven't found a single verse taken in context that convinces me God will prevent me from experiencing life's trials. He's there with me through them, though. And He continues to be with me."

"How do you know?" Preston's gruff voice was gentle.

"You're alive, aren't you? And God placed Ginger and Graham in our lives at just the right time." Her voice wobbled, and for a moment there was silence.

"Why does God have to come into that? They're just good people who are supportive friends."

"Of course they are," she said. "But their presence in our lives is no coincidence. Nothing is coincidence."

"You mean like the fire? Or Travis's death? God decided to let those things happen?"

"Yes," Willow said. "These past two years, there've

been so many times that I've awakened in the middle of the night wondering how I could go on, but I would recall certain times when God sent something or someone special into my life at just the moment I needed to be reminded I wasn't alone. Though I was often angry with God, I knew He was there, and His Spirit was with me in the darkness. I knew there was more than just this miserable life. I have an eternal future."

Silence, and Graham was just about to knock on the threshold and announce his presence when Preston said, "You never told me before that you were angry with God."

Willow took her brother's hand. "I didn't want to shake what faith you had with my own doubts. But I've discovered in the past couple of weeks that, in spite of my anger, He pursues me with this supernatural, relentless love that I can't escape. Now I'm not so afraid to be angry, or to talk about it. And I've found that when I do that, my anger isn't nearly as harsh."

Graham cleared his throat then and stepped into the room. "So you're saying that what you're going through has increased your faith?"

Both brother and sister looked around at him in surprise, Preston with a smile of welcome, Willow simply startled.

"Graham?" she said. "I thought you had clinic today."

"I do. I'm sorry, I truly didn't intend to eavesdrop."

"No problem," Preston assured him. "It was getting

a little too serious for this early in the morning."

"Willow, I tried calling you on your cell phone," Graham said. "I understand you don't like to talk when you're driving, but this is important, very important."

He glanced at Preston and hesitated, but he would not insult the man by taking his sister out into the hallway to talk to her in private. Besides, Preston needed to hear this, as well. "My investigator does not drive a dark sedan."

Willow's blue-gray eyes widened, and her face paled. She gave her brother a brief glance, then looked away.

The silence in the room quivered with tension.

"Does someone want to enlighten me?" Preston asked.

"I'm sorry," Graham said. "I knew you were worried about Willow, so after the police took her in for questioning the second time, I called a private investigator."

"But that was two weeks ago," Preston said. "You never said anything to me about it."

"He never told me, either." Willow's dark, well-defined eyebrows lowered.

"I wanted to do this quietly," Graham said. "I didn't want to upset anyone or get your hopes up. I also felt that the fewer people who knew, the less opportunity there would be for your stalker to get wind of the investigation."

"So you do believe there's a stalker?" Preston asked.

"I'm becoming more and more convinced of it. Larry, my investigator, said Willow's car showed evidence she might have been rammed from behind. It isn't conclusive, but it's enough for me to be cautious."

"What else is Larry doing?" Willow asked.

"He's been doing background checks on our most recent renters."

"I checked their references when I rented the apartments to them," Preston said.

"Sure, you checked with their employers and their previous landlords, but you couldn't have done a criminal background check," Graham said.

"Has he found anything?" Willow asked.

"He has a few leads. I also asked Larry to keep watch over you when you were at the hospital, to see if anyone followed you from here."

"And?" Preston asked.

"Your sister doesn't make a habit of telling people when she's going to be here."

"So what's this you said about Larry not driving a dark sedan?" Preston asked.

Willow's eyes narrowed at Graham.

Preston turned to his sister. "Willow, what are you up to? Keeping secrets again?"

"Obviously I didn't keep this one from the right person."

Graham would never have believed his emotions could go from tender to provoked in the span of a few seconds.

"Has it occurred to you that I'm about to get out of this place tomorrow at the latest?" Preston snapped at her. "And that I'm not an invalid, and I don't need to be protected from reality? It would help to know what we're up against."

Willow apparently realized Graham was irritated, because she had the wisdom to drop her gaze. "I'm sorry, Preston, maybe I should have told you, but—"

"Told me what?"

"I thought I saw a car following me in traffic a few times. I managed to lose it, and it never followed me out of town."

"How do you know?" Preston asked.

"Because I'm not blind, okay? It isn't hard to lose someone in Branson traffic." She glanced at her watch and casually rose to her feet. "And now, if you'll excuse me, I have other visits to make this morning."

"Do you have somewhere you need to be?" Graham asked. "Because if you don't, Larry's on his way here, and I want you to meet him."

She hesitated and once again looked at her watch. "I have an appointment a little later this morning. Right now, I'd like to visit Mrs. Engle. If you'll ring her room when Larry gets here, I'll come back, or meet you wherever you want."

Graham couldn't hide his surprise. She was actually being cooperative? "Speaking of which, how's Mrs. Engle doing?" he asked. "I haven't seen her in a few days."

"She hopes to be able to go home soon," Willow said, walking from the room with a wave. "I'll see you all later."

Preston groaned and rolled his head back on his

pillow. "Graham, if I don't get out of this place tomorrow I'll go crazy. Willow's going to be the death of me."

Graham sat down in the chair she had vacated, glancing at his watch. Ginger was perfectly capable of spelling him this morning, at least for a while. He had a surgery consult later, but there was time.

"Remember those times you went out of your way to tell me what a wonderful person your sister was?" he teased Preston. "You're saying this is the woman who's going to be the death of you?"

"She's been so bullheaded since she lost Travis and the baby."

"Did it ever occur to you that her independence is an integral part of her grief process?" Graham suggested. "Maybe she feels she depended too much on Travis, and when he was killed, she lost that support. She wouldn't want that to happen again."

"No." Preston sat up in bed and swung his legs over the side. "It hadn't occurred to me." He watched Graham for a long moment. Burn marks lingered on his arms, face and neck, but he was on his way to complete recovery. Even his eyebrows and mustache had grown back. "I have a feeling that might be changing in the future."

"How?"

"I think she's met someone else she can depend on."

"She can depend on a lot of people. She just won't do it."

"Give her time," Preston said. "I think she'll come

around. You're a patient man."

Graham nodded. He hadn't been very patient with her this morning, but Preston was right—patience was exactly what she needed right now. The realization hit home that Graham cared enough about her to give her that patience.

His only question was how far she would stretch it.

Chapter Eighteen

Willow was visiting Esther Engle when she received the call from Graham. The private investigator had arrived.

As she reached Preston's door once more, she checked her watch. She still had plenty of time to decide if she was going to meet with Sandi. She remained reluctant to do it.

She entered the room to find Graham and Preston talking to a man in a short brown leather jacket and jeans. He had dark brown hair, dark brown eyes and about a three-day growth of beard.

Where had Graham found this guy?

After cursory introductions, Graham invited her to sit next to Preston, who was dressed in pajamas and seated on the side of his bed. Except for the IV port still in his arm, which would be removed prior to his discharge, and the fatigue obvious in his face from lack of sleep, Preston appeared almost back to normal.

At least he was shaved, which was more than Willow

could say for their so-called expert, Mr. Tough Guy.

"Willow told me something this morning that could have a bearing on this case," Graham said. "This is the second anniversary of her husband's death."

Preston closed his eyes and groaned. "Willow, I'm sorry. I forgot."

"That's another reason I wanted all of us to have a brainstorm session today," Graham said. "I may be totally off track, but we don't have any other leads right now. These incidents have taken place awfully close to Travis's death."

"You think our perp might have some kind of hang-up about dates?" Larry said.

"You've been investigating under the assumption that someone was angry with either Preston or me for some reason to do with the rentals, or seeking revenge against Willow because of her husband's actions on the job. We haven't seriously considered the possibility that Willow is the direct object of someone's hatred. She is the fulcrum for everything that's happened."

Larry's heavy eyebrows lowered. "She's an ICU nurse. Who could she have offended?"

Graham turned to Willow. "Do you remember any incidents on the job or off in which you might have upset someone who might become vindictive?"

She stared back at him blankly. "As Larry said, I was an ICU nurse."

"Exactly. Not all ICU patients live. Do you remember any patient deaths that might have taken place at this time of year? Possibly from the first of April and throughout the month?"

"I've had patients die, of course, but I've never been blamed for a death. I've never been named in a lawsuit."

"No accidents took place on your shift? Nothing like that?"

"I was a nurse for thirteen years, Graham. There's no way I could remember every case."

"If we're talking about someone wanting revenge," Larry said, "that would probably be from something more recent, but not necessarily."

"What about the dream, Willow?" Graham asked. "I can't help feeling that's significant."

"Dream?" Larry asked.

Willow scowled at Graham. Did he have to share the most intimate details of her life with this stranger?

"She has a recurring nightmare about a corpse sitting up from his casket and chasing her. Willow, what if that isn't a casket, but a bed in ICU? What if, as Ginger suggested, your subconscious is trying to tell you something important about who might be doing this to you?"

"Don't you think I've already racked my brain over and over again with possible scenarios?" Willow asked.

"Try again. What might have happened on April first, April fifth, April fourteenth, April twenty-second, sometime before Travis died?" Graham asked. "Something might have happened on one or more of those dates that would cause someone to get revenge on you by killing your husband."

"That makes sense," Larry said. "If this perp's into symbolism he might choose those dates to start a fire, kidnap children and ram Willow's car off the road."

She closed her eyes and tried to recall the details of the dream. She saw the white face, the casket, which Graham had suggested could be an ICU bed, the angry eyes, the pointing finger.

She had never seriously considered the casket in her dream could be anything but a casket. As always, the vividness of this morning's dream had dissipated. However, she did recall the change in this one. There were bars between her and the monster. He was reaching out through the bars, his hands almost grasping her.

This morning she had believed those bars to be her own prison, but what if they weren't hers, but the monster's?

A memory teased the edge of her mind, impressions from a previous dream. *Other people . . . innocent people . . . helpless people depended on her for protection . . . the rhythm of a heartbeat sang through the room in mechanical tones, a familiar sound she worked with every day . . .*

"Helpless people depended on me for protection." She opened her eyes. "Bars between us. April fool!"

Graham felt the sudden focus of Willow's gaze on him. "What happened on April Fool's Day?" he asked.

"It wasn't a dead patient at all, Graham. You were right."

"What was it?"

"Several years ago I had an incoherent patient in a drugged state, which isn't unusual. But while I was sitting with this patient the day after he was brought in, he started muttering details of a high-profile crime, and I knew Travis was working the case. We were dating at the time. I couldn't just ignore his muttering and take the chance that innocent people could be hurt or killed, so I reported it."

"How long ago was this?" Larry asked.

"About seven years ago, because I hadn't turned thirty yet, and I hadn't been dating Travis long. Though my testimony wasn't admissible in court, the information I gave the police helped them secure enough evidence for a conviction. The police nicknamed him the April Fool, because that was the day he started talking to me."

"Sperryville!" Larry exclaimed.

Willow blinked at him. "That was his name. How did you know?"

"I remember that case," Larry said. "Everyone knew about it. I was working in K.C. then." His dark eyes suddenly glowed with respect. "You were the one who helped crack that case? That was a crooked attorney we'd been trying to catch for years."

"You were in Kansas City?" Willow asked.

"Sure was. The sleaze made his millions keeping organized crime members out of jail, and he didn't

237

mind getting dirty himself, often and with great enthusiasm."

"In the end, he couldn't keep himself out of jail," Willow said. She frowned at Graham, then looked back at Larry.

Graham couldn't miss the sudden apprehension in her eyes.

"Amazing he's still in prison," Larry said. "I've got some shots I'd like you to look at as soon as I can get them printed. Will you be available later?"

She glanced at her watch. "Uh, yeah. Later. Look, I have an appointment in a few minutes, but I should be around this afternoon. Call me on my cell." She stood from the bed, lightly punched Preston on the arm, then looked at Graham and jerked her head toward the door.

He followed her out and closed the door behind them, leaving Larry and Preston sharing details of the April Fool, like big kids sharing details of their favorite comic book scenes.

"Where did you find this guy?" Willow asked, strolling in the direction of the window at the end of the hallway.

Graham fell into step beside her. "I met him a couple of months ago at a town meeting. He's an ex-cop."

"Did he approach you or did you approach him?"

"He gave me his business card after the meeting, then followed up a few weeks after that with a visit to the clinic. Willow, I checked him out—he's got a clean record. Everything was in order."

"Call me paranoid, but a clean record doesn't necessarily mean the guy's an honest, upstanding citizen. Don't you think it was a little coincidental for him to suddenly be available when you just happened to need a private eye?"

"I don't believe in coincidence. I believe he was a nudge from God."

"Excuse me? We're talking about the same God who let my husband and baby be killed? That God?" She reached the window first and stood staring out at the cars racing past on the highway below them.

He didn't know what to say to her. He had prayed about this decision to use Larry—though perhaps Willow would say he hadn't been quite as diligent in prayer as he should have, considering the fact that he'd neglected to tell her about Larry from the beginning.

"Willow, after what you've been through, I know it's hard to trust again. I'm not going to lie and say I'd be able to do it. You *can* trust me, and I believe you can trust Larry. It's a sure thing that you can't do this on your own. Please, promise me you won't try."

She turned to him and as if on impulse reached up and gently traced her fingers across his jaw. "I'm sorry," she said softly. "I can't make any promises right now."

Willow watched the rearview mirror as much as she watched the traffic ahead when she drove the short distance to Highway 65. She took the on-ramp and headed south toward Big Cedar, an exclusive resort ten miles south of Branson. Due to the traffic and her lack of familiarity with her destination, she'd known she would have to leave herself thirty minutes to find her way.

A car raced past her and cut into the lane in front of her. She pressed the brake, studying the car and trying to catch a glimpse of the driver inside. She couldn't tell if it was a man or a woman, but it wasn't a dark sedan—it was a red sports car.

Slowing even further, she allowed the car to pull ahead. If a car followed her out of town, she would have to lose it before she reached Big Cedar. Unfortunately, she could easily get lost if she tried, and end up on some dead-end back road.

She'd been to Big Cedar once since coming to stay with Preston, and that was only for Sunday brunch at the Worman House on the resort grounds.

The resort was tucked deep in the woods on the shore of a protected cove of Table Rock Lake. She knew the marina was nearby, but she wasn't sure how to get there by car. Preston had been driving when they came, and she had quickly lost her sense of direction on the roads that twisted and turned through the hills and forests. She couldn't afford to do that now. She needed to find out what Sandi knew about the fire . . . and other things.

She glanced again in the rearview mirror as the four-lane highway became two lanes. Difficult to tell, but she didn't recognize any of the cars.

Poor Graham. It must be difficult for a man like him to put up with someone like her. Was he doubting his sanity for taking her into his home?

Worse, would he doubt *her* sanity when he discovered whom she had come to meet?

Graham entered his private office at the rear of the clinic, already tired of the day, and it wasn't even noon. If not for Ginger, he'd be busy, but for the time being she was in the treatment room with the only remaining patient.

He leaned back to stare out the window. The woods that surrounded this clinic on three sides—kissed now by spring green—had always been his favorite aspect of this location. He didn't often have the chance to enjoy it, busy as the clinic had become since its inception.

This building and his own house were the only pieces of property on which he did not have a mortgage. Those mortgages had initially made him nervous—he owed the banks well over a million dollars for the rental properties from which he supported himself and the daily operations of the clinic. If necessary, he could borrow more money against them to make payments, but he didn't want to do that.

He'd learned long ago, however, that he often had to do things he didn't want to do in order to make the wisest choices for others. He was determined to do anything he could to keep this clinic up and running.

The phone rang and he picked it up, knowing Ginger was the only other staff in the clinic, and she was busy.

It was his ex-wife. He didn't feel like another fight today of all days.

"Well, surprise, surprise," she said by way of greeting. "I guess you didn't expect to be hearing from me."

Forgive. "Hi, Dena. Is everything okay?"

There was a pause, then a sigh. "Did you mean all those things you said the other day?"

"Of course I meant them. I wish you all the best, and I don't like being at odds. I realize our marriage is permanently ended, but I don't believe bitterness is the best way for it to end."

"You aren't going to believe this, but I don't either. That doesn't mean I'm going to give you back the house or the car or the money."

"That wasn't why I called." *Bite your tongue, Graham.*

"Just so you know that."

Forgive. "I understand."

There was another long silence. Graham heard Ginger walking out with Mrs. Henderson, an elderly lady on a fixed income who had osteoporosis.

"I haven't been able to stop thinking about what you said," Dena said at last.

"Which part? I know I'm not that memorable an orator."

"True, but when you said you hoped I'd be happy, you sounded like you meant it."

"I did."

"Did you mean it when you said you'd pray for me?"

"Yes, and I have." He didn't think it wise to add that most of his prayers had been for help to forgive her.

"Thank you," she said quietly. "I could probably use a little more of that."

"Anything I can help with?"

"I don't think so. This is something I have to do myself." She was quiet for a moment, then said, "It wasn't all my fault. I know you think it was. I know practically everybody thinks so, but you abandoned me long before I filed for divorce."

"I'm sorry, Dena. I know I should have discussed my decision with you before giving notice at the clinic."

"Yes, you should have. It was as if my opinion didn't matter at all—just yours and your God's."

He thought about Willow's anger with him this morning for not telling her about Larry. Some habits died hard. But this habit, he was determined, would die. "My behavior was unbecoming to a man who calls himself a Christian," he said quietly. "I hope what I did won't give you a faulty impression of God. You are as important to Him as I am."

"All those patients you wanted to rescue?" she said, this time more softly, almost sadly. "They were more important to you than I was." Her voice was threaded through with old bitterness that had an underlayer of hurt disillusionment.

"That isn't true," he said. "I can understand, now, how you could have felt that way. For that, too, I'm sorry." He knew she had expected so much more from him. And why shouldn't she have? Maybe once upon a time she had expected a Christian to behave differently, perhaps to show her more grace, more gentleness, as well as more strength.

"I should have taken your needs into consideration," he said. He realized, at last, that her angry response to his decision to leave his practice, as well as her frantic demands for an overly generous settlement, were a result of fear. There was greed involved, too, of course, but there was also fear.

If he had responded with gentleness in the first place, instead of hurt anger when she filed for divorce, it was possible their marriage could have been saved.

"I just want you to know that I made sure my new husband wasn't planning to be a missionary in Africa or something," she said at last.

Graham chuckled.

When they said goodbye this time, he felt as if a major weight had been lifted from his shoulders.

Chapter Nineteen

Willow walked along the deck of the Bent Hook Marina, listening to her footsteps echo over the surface of the lake. The picture-book surroundings, the gentle ripple of water against the shore, the caress of the breeze against her face did nothing to soothe her nerves. Sandi was fifteen minutes late.

Pulling her cell phone from her jacket pocket, Willow sank into a deck chair and studied the cabins on the opposite shore of the cove. The forest seemed to engulf them as smoke drifted from chimneys and mingled with the morning air. Someone could be watching her from any of those cabins, or from anywhere along the shore.

This could be a setup.

She punched in Sandi's number and waited. The answering machine picked up on the fourth ring. Willow didn't leave a message.

She had just folded the phone and was sticking it back into her pocket when it chirped in her hand, startling her. Irritated by her own jumpy reaction, she checked the screen and saw that it was Graham's cell phone number.

Still studying the forest across the cove, she hit the silence button. Graham could leave a message. The line needed to stay open in case Sandi called.

As she placed the telephone back into her pocket, she saw a speedboat leave a dock several hundred feet along the shore from where she sat. The driver gunned the motor and the boat leaped through the water toward the marina where she sat.

She watched as the boat kept coming toward her. Growing nervous, she got up from the deck chair and started inside, but as the boat reached the no-wake zone it slowed, then glided into a slip. It was one of the employees.

She closed her eyes, allowing time for her breathing to return to normal. What was she doing here? Was it irrational to think she might finally be able to find some clue to the fire from Sandi?

Judging by Sandi's behavior over the phone earlier, she was obviously unbalanced, and Willow suspected drugs. The Ozark forests were rife with methamphetamine production; a few years ago Missouri had won the title for having the highest number of meth lab busts.

Was it possible Willow had been jumping to conclusions all this time? Maybe they all had. Granted, being hauled to the police station tended to make one a tad sensitive to such things, but what if Preston had stumbled unknowingly onto a meth lab, even in one of the apartments? Obviously if he had, he didn't realize it, but what if the perpetrator thought he had? And then, to redirect suspicion, the same person might have set Willow up.

She glanced over her shoulder toward the marina parking lot, searching for Sandi's gray Toyota Camry. It wasn't there.

There was a flaw to Willow's theory. After the fire, the fire department had gone through every unit to investigate damage. They knew what to look for. They would have found any drug-manufacturing paraphernalia at that time, unless someone had packed up all supplies and left.

Fifteen minutes later Willow punched Sandi's number again. When the answering machine picked up, she allowed Sandi's voice to complete its spiel. "Sandi, I've waited long enough. I'm on my way to your place. I want to know what kind of joke you're trying to pull on me. I'll see you shortly."

She refolded the cell phone and slipped it back into her pocket.

She was walking the ramp from the floating marina to the parking lot when her phone chirped again. This time it came from the main number at Graham's clinic. She answered as she walked toward her car. To her relief, it was Ginger.

"Lady, are you playing hide-and-seek? Graham's pacing the floor like an expectant father, especially since you didn't answer his call."

"I'm fine," Willow said. "I would have called sooner, but I needed to keep this line clear."

"Is everything okay?"

Pausing at the car door, Willow sighed and took a final glance at the peaceful setting that surrounded her. The serenity of this place had been wasted on her for the past thirty minutes while she'd stewed over Sandi.

"Everything's fine, except my meeting seems to have been delayed. I don't suppose anyone's heard from Sandi in the past hour or so, have they?"

"Sandi Jameson?" Ginger's voice rose with alarm. "Why? What's up between you two this time?"

"She called me and wanted me to meet her."

"You didn't!"

"I tried. It was to be in a public place, perfectly safe. Unfortunately, she isn't here."

"Where is *here?*"

"Big Cedar."

"Well, would you please get your hindermost parts back here before everybody has a meltdown?" Ginger exclaimed. "We're worried about you, especially after your discussion with Larry this morning. We can go together to meet with Sandi, and take Larry along with us for good measure, but this gallivanting all over the county alone when you know someone has been following you, that's just asking for trouble."

"Sandi wanted to see me alone. She hinted that she knew something about the fire."

"Oh, sure she did. That's one of the oldest tricks in the book—you should know that."

"Yes, I know. I thought that, too, and now I know why it works so well," Willow said. "She's messed up, possibly on drugs, but she doesn't have any reason to try to hurt me."

"Honey, to go off like that alone to meet her—"

"As I said, we were to meet in a very public place, with plenty of witnesses. Ginger, I need to know what she was talking about when she mentioned the fire. We could get to the bottom of this whole thing with one conversation."

"Hold it. Graham just stepped into the front office. He wants to talk to you."

"Not right—"

"Willow?" Graham's voice came over the line. "Would it be possible for you to return to the hospital now? Larry just called and he has those prints. Also, Preston just called and is wondering where you are."

"I'm not in town right now."

"Oh?" That one word held a polite request for more information.

"That's right. Ginger can tell you about it. Do you mind if I call you later? I need to get off the phone right now. I promise to return to the hospital and placate Preston as soon as I can."

There was a pause, then a sigh of frustration. "Can you give me a time?"

She glanced at her watch. "Twelve-thirty." That would give her plenty of time to see about Sandi. This meeting had been a bust, and she only hoped she would find the woman at home. "Do you need help at the clinic?" she asked.

"How did you guess?"

"Don't you always? I'll come straight there after I leave the hospital, okay? Then if Larry has those shots for me to look at, he can bring them to the clinic."

"Is that your way of trying to placate me, as well?" he asked.

In spite of herself, she smiled. "Believe it or not, I like helping at the clinic. I'll see you before long."

Graham replaced the receiver and sank onto the chair in front of the computer. "She said she'd be here by twelve-thirty," he told Ginger. "Any other patients in the waiting room?"

"Nope." Ginger seemed distracted. "The next one's due in fifteen minutes."

"Good, then you have time to explain to me where Willow is and what she's doing. You look worried."

"I'm just praying right now."

"What's going on?"

"She's trying to meet with Sandi down at Big Cedar, and she's been stood up."

He closed his eyes. He probably should have seen this coming. "*Why* on earth is she trying to meet with Sandi?"

"You'd better relax," Ginger warned. "Willow's a grown woman with a mind of her own."

"But Sandi of all people!"

"I know. I've already chewed her out about it, and she realizes the risks, but Sandi apparently implied she knew something about the fire, and you know Willow's determined to find out what happened. You also know how she hates to drag anyone else into her problems."

"And she certainly wouldn't have told us this morning about her plans, because she knew no one would have approved."

"So there you go. You can chew her out when she gets here. Meanwhile, relax." Ginger leaned back in her chair and raised her arms over her head, arching her back as if to get the kinks out. Her red-gold hair glowed in the light of the overhead fluorescents. Even in the harsh brightness, her skin did not betray her age. Graham envied her. He felt as if he were aging at an accelerated rate lately.

The phone rang, and Graham snatched it up without checking the caller ID. "Vaughn Clinic."

"Hey, boss." It was Larry. "I've done some more

checking with my buddies in K.C. Get this—Sandi Jameson was a courier for Sperryville before he went to jail."

A sudden burst of adrenaline raced through Graham's system. "What kind of courier?"

"She did anything he wanted done—carried drugs, documents, did some spying, you name it. Word is she got a little too cozy with Sperryville's son, though, and she was out the door."

"Where are you now?" Graham asked.

"My condo here in town."

"How fast can you get to Big Cedar? You're a lot closer than I am, and I'm afraid to leave Preston vulnerable right now."

"Why Big Cedar?"

"Willow's supposed to meet Sandi there."

"You've gotta be kidding me. That Willow's got a death wish."

"Hurry."

"I'm on it, boss."

As soon as Graham disconnected he called Willow's cell. She didn't answer.

Willow ignored Graham's call as she turned onto the hilly, tree-lined lane that led to the lodge. Although she hadn't seen anyone following her to Big Cedar from Branson, she found herself glancing in the rearview mirror every few seconds. It was easier to evade someone in the crush of Branson traffic than it was out here in the countryside.

After turning off Highway 65, however, there had been no cars in her wake.

Rounding the final curve through the trees, she saw the lodge and the carport. Sandi's car was still in its spot. As Willow parked in her usual spot, she shook off her annoyance. Sandi had certainly sounded high when they spoke. She might have totally forgotten calling. Or she might be sick.

Sandi didn't answer the doorbell. Willow couldn't see any lights through the window, but the shades were closed, so that didn't mean much.

She knocked hard on the door. After receiving no response, she returned to her car, grabbed her purse, and slung the strap over her shoulder. In the past two weeks, she'd begun carrying an extra set of keys to the doors of all the apartments in the lodge, in case Mrs. Engle needed something or in case Graham requested that Willow run an errand to the complex while she was in town.

Ginger was right—this could be a setup. If that were so, then perhaps Sandi was sitting inside right now, prepared to call the police if Willow entered.

But Sandi had sounded genuinely frightened on the phone. Acting as an agent for the owner of this property, Willow had the authority to enter any of the apartments if she felt there could be a problem. She definitely felt there was a problem.

She rang the doorbell and knocked one more time. When there was no answer, she used the key to enter.

A lamp glowed in the far corner of the great room

and, as usual, the kitchen sink and counter were piled high with dirty dishes. The trash can overflowed with empty hamburger wrappers and frozen-food cartons.

"Sandi?" Willow called. It occurred to her that even though Sandi's car was here, she might have left with someone else. But who? The man the girls had told Willow about? Or maybe Sandi's car wouldn't start and she'd begged a ride from one of the other renters.

But if her car wouldn't start, it would have made sense to call Willow and let her know. Not that Sandi had been making sense this morning.

Reluctantly, feeling like an invader, Willow called out again, then walked down the hallway toward the bathrooms and bedrooms.

She peered into the hallway bathroom. Aside from a mess of dirty clothes and towels on the floor, she saw nothing. The girls' room was even messier. The door to the master bedroom stood half shut. She pushed it open.

Here, total chaos reigned, and Willow frowned as she stepped inside. Beside a pile of clothing on the floor was a figurine, broken in half, with spatters of red staining the pastel porcelain. A pillow lay on the floor. The bedspread was half on, half off the bed. A picture hung askew on the wall.

"Sandi?" Willow called again, this time more timidly.

She stepped toward the master bathroom. She was halfway through the room when she saw the foot—

dainty, nails painted with bright pink polish, contrasting with hideous clarity against the white skin. Deathly white.

The scent of copper permeated the room. Blood.

Sandi!

Willow rushed to the bathroom and found Sandi lying prone, right arm flung out to her side, legs twisted unnaturally, hair splayed around her like a shroud.

Then Willow saw the blood on the bathroom floor beneath Sandi's face. Far too much blood.

Willow pulled the hair back, then nearly retched. Sandi's face was barely recognizable. It was bleeding profusely.

Or rather, it had been bleeding. The blood no longer flowed. Willow checked for signs of life but didn't find any. Sandi was dead.

Chapter Twenty

Graham was pulling on his jacket and walking out the front door when the phone rang beside him. He saw the caller ID listing. It was the hospital. He rushed to the phone, nearly jerking off the right sleeve of the jacket in his haste to answer. Patients turned to look at him curiously from the waiting room.

Amazing how quickly the influx could hit. Two patients were early for their appointments, and two walk-ins had arrived soon after, one with a cut that needed sutures, another with a sprained or broken ankle.

"Vaughn Clinic," he said, glancing down the hallway, wishing Ginger would take over at the desk.

"Am I speaking with Dr. Vaughn?" A slightly familiar female voice came over the line.

"Yes."

"This is Sheila Jackson, one of Preston Black's nurses at Clark Memorial Hospital. We tried to reach your house, since we know Preston's sister is staying there. I didn't want to leave a message, so this is the next number on our list for emergency contact."

She suddenly had his complete attention. "What kind of emergency?"

"There's been an incident here at the hospital. Preston has gone into anaphylactic shock."

Graham closed his eyes. This could not be happening. "When?"

"They're working on him right now."

"What caused it?"

"We're not sure yet. Dr. Teeter is in the room trying to intubate him. It's been kind of touch-and-go. The doctor said he might have to do a cricothyroidotomy. Do you know if Preston could be allergic to anything besides penicillin?"

"That's all I know about," Graham said. "He didn't list anything else on his papers with check-in, did he?"

"No."

"Has he been placed on any new medications recently?"

"No. In fact, his medications have been titrated down, since he's getting so much better."

"Have you or any of the other staff noted any signs of reaction prior to today?"

"None, Dr. Vaughn. I've always felt that people who react to one drug might develop the same reaction to other drugs, so I pay more attention to physical signs."

"Sheila, I know better than to ask, but I have to. Could there have been a medical error?" Sheila was a good nurse, and Clark had excellent staff.

"We've already checked that," she assured him. "Preston was getting ready to go home, and I gave him his medications myself. I triple-checked everything, as I always do."

"I'll try to contact his sister by cell phone," Graham said. "Meanwhile, I'm on my way there." He hesitated, reluctant to share his darkest suspicions with Sheila, but the sooner a search was made, the more likely they were to find a culprit, if there was one.

"Sheila, one last question. Have you had any new personnel working in your unit in the past couple of days?"

"No. Our nurses have all been here for at least a year, and you know they're the only ones who are authorized to dispense medications."

"Thank you. I know this might sound strange to you, but I must request that Pharmacy take an inventory of the penicillin."

"Now?"

"Yes, and I'm sorry. This may be a matter for the

police." The moment he disconnected, he dialed Willow's cell phone. No answer. He was torn. He needed to get to the hospital to check on Preston. But he couldn't help worrying about what Sandi was up to. He could only pray that Willow and Sandi truly were in a public place at Big Cedar.

He also needed to find out from Willow if Preston had any other allergies. Where was she?

A scream ricocheted through the apartment as Willow stumbled to her feet. She didn't realize, until she caught her image in the mirror, that she was the one screaming.

She staggered backward as the edges of the room blackened around her and stars flashed in that blackness. Her stomach protested violently. She thought she would vomit.

She leaned over, breathing in through her nose, out through her mouth, pressing the side of her cheek against the tiled wall. Even with her eyes closed, she couldn't get the imprint of Sandi's bloodied face out of her sight.

As an ICU nurse, Willow had often seen the worst of human suffering and death, but this was different. Here, she had no buffer of doctor orders and machines and backup staff.

And Sandi was dead.

Willow dug her cell phone from her pocket and, with fingers numb with shock, she dialed a number she had memorized two weeks ago. Detective Trina Rush.

When the detective herself answered, Willow sagged with relief. "This is Willow Traynor. I just found Sandi Jameson dead in her apartment." Her words spilled from her in a spiral of panic. "Somebody needs to get here quickly. She's been bashed in the face!" She heard the trembling in her voice.

"Where are you now, Willow?" The voice sounded efficient and calm.

"I'm here with her in the bathroom. Please send help. Please!"

"It's on its way, and I'll be there shortly. Meanwhile, is anyone else there with you?"

"N-no." But even as Willow replied, the question took on a more sinister meaning. She caught her breath and glanced around the shadowed room. Had the killer left?

"Willow," Trina Rush said calmly over the line, "I need you to leave the building while you're on the telephone with me. Don't hang up."

Resisting the urge to cower in a corner, Willow turned away from the grisly sight of Sandi and glanced once more through the shadows as she retreated from the room.

Taking care not to touch anything, she was halfway down the hallway when she saw a figure standing between the kitchen and the great room. It was the form of a man. He didn't move.

Willow stopped in her tracks, suddenly paralyzed with terror. She gripped the cell phone in her hands as if it would protect her. But she was on her own. The person at the other end of the line was just too far away.

Oh, Lord, help me! Is this the killer? Am I going to die just like Sandi did?

"Willow?" It was the detective's voice. "What's happening right now?"

Willow remained frozen, unable to speak.

Graham called Larry and gave him a brief overview of the situation.

"You don't lose a lot of time, do you, boss?" Larry said. "You'll have the whole staff mad at you, accusing them of medical error."

"Preston was nearly killed in a fire in which his place was singled out and torched," Graham said. "In my opinion this is a murder attempt until proven otherwise. And quit calling me boss. How long before you reach Big Cedar?"

"They're doing roadwork up ahead, but I know a back road. Shouldn't be more than another fifteen minutes. Relax, boss. I'll find her if she's there."

Graham hung up, muttered a quick apology to Ginger, who was just stepping out of an exam room, and left her juggling four difficult cases by herself.

Ginger was a lifesaver.

The man took a couple of steps toward Willow, then stopped. Willow briefly considered running into the children's bedroom and climbing out the window to escape, but then the man spoke.

259

"Hello? Sandi, that you?"

Willow released her breath in a whoosh of air—breath she hadn't realized she was holding. "Carl? No, I'm not Sandi. It's me, Willow Traynor."

Detective Rush's voice came like bullets from the phone. "Willow, get out of there now! Get out of that apartment. I don't care who you think that is, he could be dangerous. He could be the killer!"

But escape was impossible. The man was blocking her way.

"Willow?" Carl said, stepping toward her. "What was all that ruckus? Either somebody was screaming like a banshee a minute ago, or my hearing aid's messing up again. Where's Sandi?"

"Stop right there, Carl. Don't come any farther. We've . . . we've both got to get out of this apartment now. We could be in danger."

The man stopped. "Danger? What are you talking about? What's going on here?"

"Willow?" Trina Rush said over the phone. "I told you to get away."

"I can't right now," Willow told the detective, keeping her attention on the man in front of her. "Please, Carl, somebody attacked and killed Sandi. I just found her in the bathroom, and whoever it was might still be here."

The man started, eyes bugging out behind his trifocals, lips parting like a landed fish. "What? She's dead?"

"I've already called the police, and I have Detective

260

Trina Rush on the phone right now." She held up her cell phone to show him.

Carl glanced dazedly at the phone, then back at Willow. "Somebody really killed her?"

"That much is obvious, and I don't know if the killer's still here or not. She's still warm. She hasn't been dead long." Willow glanced over her shoulder into the shadows, and those shadows posed much more threat to her than did Carl.

"But are you sure she's dead?" Carl moved as if to push past Willow.

She blocked the way. "I'm positive. She's beyond our help, and the detective has ordered us out of the apartment immediately." The hand that held the cell phone began to tremble violently, and her knees threatened to buckle beneath her.

"You okay?" the man asked.

"Please, let's get outside. I just need some fresh air."

Still dazed, Carl took her by the arm and gently led her outside. "You do seem a little wobbly. Let's go sit you down in the gazebo. You say the police are on their way?"

"They'll be here any time." She raised the phone to her face. "Detective Rush, can you tell me how long before help is here?"

"Five to eight minutes." The reply came swiftly. "I'll be there soon after. Willow, are you out of the apartment?"

"Yes."

"Good. Stay away from shadows, and since you

insist on talking to Carl, and it seems he isn't a threat, then stay with him until someone comes."

"I don't plan to let him out of my sight."

"Can you tell me what you were doing in Sandi's apartment this morning?" the detective asked. There was no inflection of disapproval or of accusation. She just sounded curious.

Willow explained about Sandi's telephone call earlier. "She wanted me to meet her at the Bent Hook Marina at Big Cedar. I waited there for thirty minutes and she never showed up. I didn't want to let it go, because she sounded frightened, and worse, she sounded like she might have taken drugs."

"What made you think that?" the detective asked.

"Wasn't acting like herself. She was highly agitated, talking nonstop, showing strong signs of paranoia."

"You're sure it was Sandi?"

"Of course. I've spent some time with her. I know her voice."

"But you thought you were talking to Carl the night the girls were taken."

"I had only spoken to him in passing once or twice. That was different."

"Okay, what about Sandi? What was she agitated about? Did she say?"

"She suggested that her apartment might be bugged, which was why she said she wanted to meet me somewhere else. She didn't want to meet at the hospital, because she was afraid someone might see her, though she never said who that someone might be. Except it was a male."

"No name, no description?" Trina asked. "No hint about where she knew him from, or what, specifically, he might do to her?"

"Not that I remember. She wasn't completely rational. She told me that she had only accused me of taking the girls because she wanted it to be me. Crazy stuff." Willow grew aware that Carl had fallen into step beside her and was obviously listening to every word she said. But then, who wouldn't?

"Did she say why she wanted it to be you?" Detective Rush asked.

"She seemed to feel it was a better alternative than who had really taken them. She said that he—whoever he was—had taken them as a warning to her that he could do it, and that he didn't want her talking to me."

"Did she say why he didn't want her talking to you?"

"No, but I get the impression it was because she knew who had started the fires. Do you remember the man the girls mentioned the other night—the one the girls said their mother was shouting at the night before they were abducted?"

"Yes, I remember."

"That could be the person Sandi was afraid of."

"She said that?"

"No, she didn't actually say it."

There was a brief silence, then the detective said softly, "Willow, I'm going to ask you some questions, and I want you to answer yes or no. Is Carl still there with you?"

"Yes."

"Do you still feel he could have been the one who called you at Sandi's the night the girls disappeared?"

Willow hesitated. "Not anymore."

"But you can't be sure, either way."

"No."

"Then be very watchful until the police get there."

Willow felt the skin tighten at the back of her neck. "I will."

"Are you still . . ."

At that moment the cell phone broke connection. Willow checked it. Her battery wasn't dead, but it was low, and she often had trouble with connections from this location when her battery wasn't fully charged.

She could call Trina Rush back and probably get through, but she decided to reserve as much power as she could in case of another emergency.

Chapter Twenty-One

Graham rushed down the wide corridor toward Preston's room. He had raced halfway across town to the hospital, thanking God for green signal lights and moderate traffic as he prayed for Preston to be okay. After all the poor guy had been through, to die from an allergic reaction . . .

What was he allergic to? Graham couldn't believe any of the nurses on that floor would have given

Preston the one thing that could kill him. His penicillin allergy was well-known, marked plainly on his chart. Even the greenest nurse would recognize the warning sign.

By the time Graham reached Preston's room, Preston had been intubated. His head looked like a gorged pumpkin and his lips looked as if they would split. He was not yet out of danger.

"Dr. Vaughn?"

Graham turned to find Sheila Jackson coming toward him. She looked agitated. "I can't believe this. Pharmacy did the inventory check you requested. They can't account for a 2.4 million-unit vial of penicillin G IV."

"So someone did give Preston an injection of penicillin?"

She shook her head, her dark hair feathering around her face with the movement. "I never gave him penicillin. I never would! I'm well aware of his allergy to it. I'm the one who cautions the others about checking for drug allergies."

Graham saw the IV port in Preston's arm, which would remain there until he was discharged. "I didn't ask if you did, Sheila. I asked if someone did. Have you seen anyone in this room who shouldn't be?"

She spread her hands in a gesture of helplessness. "I didn't see anything suspicious, but I wasn't looking. We don't monitor visitors. We can't possibly do that."

"I know. I'm not accusing you." Who would have the audacity—and the hatred—to slip into Preston's room when he was sleeping and inject a deadly poison into his IV port?

Or was Graham jumping to conclusions? Was he just being morbid today? Even in the best of hospitals, accidents did happen.

"I'm sorry, Sheila. I'm going to have to call the police about this, and Preston will need constant observation, even after he's out of danger. There was already one attempt on his life. This may be the second."

Willow remained awkward in Carl's presence as she sat beside him in the gazebo, waiting for the police to arrive.

"I'm surprised no one else came running when they heard my screams," she said, glancing back toward Sandi's apartment.

"Doubt anybody heard you. Only reason I did was because I was outside tending the roses. You know the Jasumbacks play their music so loud down there they can't even hear their phone ringing or someone pounding on the door half the time. Mary Ruth's deaf as a post without her hearing aid."

Willow shivered and hugged herself. "The lodge is well built. Besides, most of the neighbors are accustomed to hearing Brittany and Lucy scream and laugh when they play outside."

"Believe me, I didn't have any trouble telling the difference between those little girls and you. Besides, I don't hear them a lot, since I'm on the lower level."

"I know we never talked about the night the girls disappeared, but I was so sure I was talking to you."

"I may be getting a little forgetful now and then, but that's something I'd have remembered. I didn't even see Mary Ruth that day."

"That was what she said."

"Guess you know there'll be folks moving out over this," Carl said. "Place like Branson, there oughtn't be this much danger involved in just living."

"Will you leave?"

"Good question. Guess that depends on what else happens around here. Minneapolis seems tame in comparison."

"And Kansas City?"

For a moment he was silent. In the far distance Willow thought she could hear the first cry of a siren.

"How did you know I lived in Kansas City?" His voice was suddenly hushed, barely above a whisper.

"I did a background check on all the renters for Graham."

A flush crept slowly up his neck. "You checked my background?"

"I checked everyone's background. Relax, Carl, you're not under suspicion."

His eyes narrowed and grew hard. "What else did you turn up while you were digging for dirt on me?"

A second siren made a counterpoint melody to the first, echoing through the trees that bordered the lane. No other neighbors had ventured out yet to see what the noise was all about. Willow suddenly wished someone would. She didn't know what to say.

The first vehicle to round the last curve in the lane was a police cruiser, followed by another, and then an ambulance.

Willow and Carl rose from the gazebo bench, and Carl took her arm. She froze.

"Are you going to be okay?" he asked, his normal, gentlemanly demeanor back in place.

She nodded, then walked with him across the driveway to meet the first police officer who stepped from his car.

"I'm Willow Traynor, and I'm the one who called Detective Rush." She turned and gestured. "I found Sandi's body in apartment One A, the master bathroom."

"Okay, ma'am. Detective Rush is on her way. Would you please wait for her here?" He opened the back door of the cruiser. "If you wish you can sit in the car."

Willow looked at the seat, and at the protective barrier between the front and back that literally rendered this seat a jail cell on wheels.

"Are you detaining me for some reason?"

"No, Detective Rush only wants to ask you some questions." The officer glanced over his shoulder toward the apartment from which Willow had escaped. The other officers were entering, and he obviously didn't want to miss the excitement.

"I was with Willow in Sandi's apartment," Carl said. "I came running when I heard her scream. Guess the detective wants to ask me some questions, too?"

"No, sir. For now, I was only told to speak with Mrs. Traynor."

"She told me to wait outside for her, and that's what I'll do," Willow said.

He nodded and closed the door, then turned toward the apartment. "She'll be here in just a few moments."

She watched him walk down the sidewalk, and was relieved when Carl followed him. She had learned from Travis that often the person who reported a crime became a suspect. This was too close for comfort.

As another siren blasted through the trees and another police cruiser arrived, Willow felt as if her nightmares truly had followed her into her waking hours. Reality had a harsher edge to it than her dreams. Sandi's bloodied face would forever haunt her.

Within a few minutes, the drive was lined with vehicles. A small knot of neighbors had gathered on the lawn, drawn by the sirens, watching the excitement with obvious fascination. Doubtless, Carl had explained to them what was happening. Willow watched the man as he spoke with Mary Ruth and the Jasumbacks.

He wasn't as old as she had thought him to be when she first came here. His face wasn't as deeply lined as someone who would be nearing seventy. Perhaps he'd retired early.

"Good, you waited for me." A strong female voice spoke from behind her.

Willow turned to find Detective Rush walking toward her. The woman wore a fitted brown pantsuit today. As before, her only jewelry was a watch and a wedding band. Her face was devoid of makeup. "Of course I waited."

Willow gestured toward her car, which was blocked by two police cars. "I couldn't go anywhere anyway."

"I'm sorry, Willow, I still have to question you, but I also need to stake out the crime scene. I want you to stay here for a while longer." She turned to leave.

"Wait." Willow followed her up the sidewalk. "Can you tell me what's going to happen to Lucy and Brittany?"

"That isn't for you to worry about," Trina said without breaking stride.

"Excuse me, but I'm very worried. They don't have anyone else."

Trina Rush stopped and turned around, her expression guarded. "You have some way of knowing that?"

"They told me. They said their father was dead and they didn't have any aunts or uncles or grandparents. In fact, they talked more about Preston than they did about any other man, except for some stranger who made their mother cry."

Trina's expression softened momentarily. "You're in no position to do anything about the children, and neither am I. The DFS has already been notified of the situation, and the caseworker will take the children from school and find a relative who will take them, or place them in a foster home until someone can be found."

"Detective, please. They know me and they like me.

Can you imagine how horrifying this will be for them? First, to find out their mother—the one person in the world they trust and depend on—has been murdered? And then to be taken away by strangers?"

The detective studied Willow in silence for a moment, but the softness slowly drained from her face to be replaced, once more, by firm determination. "I'll be back when I'm finished."

She turned abruptly and strode toward the apartment, leaving Willow to wait.

Graham walked to the far end of the hallway and pulled out his cell phone. This time when he tried Willow's number, it went through. She answered almost immediately.

"Graham?" Her voice sounded tense, and the reception was bad.

"Yes. Willow, can you come back to the hospital soon? There's been an incident here with Preston."

There was a soft gasp. "What kind of incident?"

"He was given penicillin. He's out of danger for the moment, but it would help if someone knowledgeable about his medical history could answer some questions for the doctor."

There was static on the line. "What! Who did that? He's . . ." There was more static and her voice cut out.

"I'm sorry, Willow, I can't hear you. I'm trying to figure out what happened. As I said, he's out of the woods now, though they had to place him on a respirator. The police have been called."

"The police?"

"Yes. I don't want to take any chances. I was hoping you would be on your way here already."

"Are you at the hosp . . ." More static. Her voice cracked, disappeared.

"Willow? Are you still there? Yes, I'm at the hospital. Where are you?"

"I'm . . . something awful has . . . Graham, I need . . ." Her voice broke into white noise. The signal ended.

He punched her number again. This was a rotten time for interference.

No answer. What was happening with Willow?

He entered Larry's number, but the line was busy.

Graham seldom lost his temper, but right now he was frustrated enough to lob this little cell phone out the window onto the highway below. He resisted the temptation.

Willow tried to redial Graham, with no result. She would have to be in an area with better reception before she could reach him again. She shoved the phone back into her purse and studied the police cruisers blocking her from her car. She circled them, measuring distance to see if she could somehow squeeze between them, but there was no way.

She had to get to the hospital. She should never have come on this insane trip in the first place.

But as she thought about it she realized, with a sharp pang, who would have discovered Sandi if she hadn't—Lucy and Brittany.

She ran down the sidewalk to the apartment, where two husky uniformed officers stood guard, talking in low tones, jotting notes.

"Please, would you ask someone to move one of those cruisers?" She turned and pointed toward her car. "I have to get to the hospital, and I'm blocked into my parking space."

"Ma'am, you need to stay here until Detective Rush is finished with her work inside."

"No, you don't understand. My brother is in critical condition at the hospital, and I have to get to him." She moved as if to go past them.

"Hold it right there." The officer on the left took her by the arm, pointing to the crime-scene tape at the doorway. "No one is allowed inside right now. You're in danger of impeding an investigation."

"Then would you please help me get to the hospital?"

"Willow!" called Carl from the edge of the small cluster of neighbors and onlookers huddled beside the gazebo a distance from the door. "What's happened now?"

She gave up on the officers and crossed the lawn to the others.

"What's going on?" Carl stepped over to meet her.

"Preston's in trouble at the hospital, and I need a ride there. My car's blocked."

"Mine isn't. What's wrong with Preston?"

"He's having an allergic reaction to penicillin."

"What!" The man's eyebrows rose in alarm. "Who'd

do something like that? It says on his chart, plain as day, he's allergic."

"I don't know. My connection was interrupted. I need to get to the hospital."

"I'll take you to him."

"Willow?" It was Detective Rush.

Willow turned. The detective was stepping up to her across the grass. The lines of her face seemed to have deepened in the past few moments, and though her expression remained calm, her complexion was a shade paler than it had been. "You wanted to talk to me?"

"Detective Rush?" Willow hurried to meet her. "My brother—"

"Is in the hospital, out of danger." She sounded irritable.

"You knew about it? And you didn't let me know?"

"I just found out myself," she said. "Look, he's in good hands and there's an officer being sent to guard him, so there's nothing you can do for him at this point."

"I need to get to—"

"You're where you need to be right now. The hospital will give Preston excellent care."

"You're not going to have those cars moved?"

"No, I'm not."

Willow bristled at the harsh finality of the detective's tone. "Am I under arrest?"

"Not at this time, but don't push me right now." She fixed Willow with a level look. "What were you doing in Sandi's apartment? You were warned to stay away from her and her children."

"I told you, she's the one who contacted me—"

"And what about the call on her answering machine? Some would consider your message to be threatening."

"I wasn't threatening her. I was—"

"Save it for the interrogation. I'll be out when I'm finished here. Meanwhile, the longer you detain me now, the longer you will have to wait."

Willow glared at her, but the glare was wasted. The detective had turned away and marched stiffly back toward the apartment.

Graham stood in the doorway of Preston's room, waiting for a police officer to arrive. They were posting a guard. Meanwhile, he'd tried twice more to reach Larry on his cell phone, without success. He dialed the clinic and left a voice message for Ginger to contact him between patients.

Preston was improving. The swelling in his face had decreased considerably and his head no longer resembled a pumpkin. Now Graham wondered if he should have been quite so adamant with Willow about returning to the hospital. Still, she needed to stop trying to play detective on her own.

Preston would most likely be off the ventilator in a few more hours, once his doctor felt he was out of danger.

"Dr. Vaughn?" Sheila Jackson came striding down the corridor from the direction of the nurses' station, looking harried, eyes darting up and down the hallway as if a killer might jump from any of the patient rooms. "I need to talk to you." She entered Preston's room and waited for him to follow, then closed the door.

"What's up?" Graham asked.

"I just finished speaking with the pharmacist." She glanced toward Preston's bed, where he lay watching her intently. She smiled and stepped closer to him, including him in their conversation. "They're doing a comprehensive inventory to see if anything else is missing."

"Have they found anything yet?"

She bit her lip, then nodded, her friendly hazel eyes filled with concern. "Multiple quantities of dopamine and haloperidol. The police are coming in force."

"Those aren't even drugs of abuse. Why would anyone take them?"

"I don't know. We've never experienced anything like this before."

"Does anyone know how this happened?"

Sheila nodded. "Rosie Quick, our head nurse, always keeps a set of keys in the right pocket of her scrubs. She's the only one with a key to the pharmacy on her shift. She just told me that about a week ago she reached for her keys and they weren't in her pocket. Later she found them in the top middle drawer of her desk."

"Couldn't she have accidentally left them there?"

Sheila shook her head, frowning. "Everyone knows she never leaves them unguarded. She's convinced we have a pickpocket. The whole hospital's going to be in an uproar over this. As if it isn't already."

"Someone could have lifted those keys, made a wax impression of the key to the pharmacy and placed them in her drawer later," Graham said. But even as he said it, he considered another possibility. It might not have been necessary for the thief to lift Rosie's keys if he had a key of his own for the pharmacy door.

"When Mr. Black was sleeping this morning—he didn't get much sleep last night—someone slipped into his room and injected the penicillin into the IV port in his arm," Sheila said. She looked at Preston again, and her gaze seemed to linger on him a moment.

Graham noticed Preston holding her gaze. Right about now, if Ginger were here, she might be making some remark about attraction and steak knives. "Sounds like you're convinced this was no accident."

Sheila nodded. "It's hard to look at it any other way, now that we know the drugs were stolen. I'm just worried who else might become a victim."

Chapter Twenty-Two

Willow warned herself not to let her temper control her actions. The police were doing their jobs. As a cooperative citizen, she needed to obey Trina Rush's orders and wait.

"You still need a ride to the hospital?" Carl said, once again meeting her halfway across the lawn.

"I've been told to wait here," she grumbled. "Detective Rush says Preston's in stable condition."

"Are you under arrest?"

"No, but legally they can detain me without placing me under arrest."

"Even in an emergency situation like this?" he asked.

Another car came speeding down the drive past the police vehicles. It was a red Firebird.

"Rick's getting off late today," Carl said.

The car didn't park in its assigned spot, but pulled onto the grass as the driver window slid down. Rick Fenrow's face was, for once, devoid of a smile. He looked worried. His long face held a grimace.

"Willow Traynor, you're a hard person to find. Has anyone called you about Preston?"

"Graham did a few minutes ago." She stepped over to the car. "The police informed me he's in stable condition."

Rick's brows lowered. "That just shows the police don't know everything. He's had a setback."

Oh, no. Please, Lord. "What kind of a setback?"

"His breathing isn't as good, and he's swelling again. You might want to head to the hospital."

"I can't—my car's blocked." She glanced over her shoulder toward Carl.

"What's all the commotion here, anyway?" Rick asked. "Did those little girls disappear again?"

"Sandi Jameson's been killed." She saw the shock spread across the man's face. "Rick, do you have a cell phone I can use?"

"I can do better than that. Hop into my dream machine and see how well this baby handles."

She made an instant decision. "Carl, when Detective Rush comes out, will you tell her I've gone to my brother at the hospital? He's had a setback. I'll talk to her later."

She ran around the front of the car and got in. Trina Rush would just have to understand.

Graham walked out the front door of the hospital, relieved, at last, of his duties with Preston. An officer had been assigned to monitor anyone entering the room. The police had taken Graham's warning seriously.

He reached his SUV, and was reflecting on how quickly he had become dependent on a tiny electronic device he carried in his pocket, when it sang to him. He answered the call. It was Larry.

"You'd better sit down for this one, boss," Larry said by way of greeting.

"What's going on? Have you found Willow?"

"I haven't seen her yet, but I know where she is. I've been burning up my battery since I talked to you last. First of all, she's not at Big Cedar. Are you sitting down?"

"Just tell me." Graham unlocked and opened his door. Sometimes Larry reminded him of a ten-year-old kid playing cops and robbers.

"Sandi Jameson was murdered in her bathroom sometime this morning." Larry paused for dramatic effect. "I just heard it from the sheriff's deputy."

Graham did sit down then, stunned to silence, unable to wrap his mind around Larry's words.

"Want to take a guess who found her? And while you're at it, want to take a guess who's their top suspect?"

When he could find his voice, Graham asked, "Where is Willow now?"

"Last I heard she hasn't been taken into custody yet, and the police are all swarming the crime scene, so she's probably still at the lodge."

Graham slumped back in his seat. "Unless she's on her way here in response to my call. Where are you?"

"On Highway 65 headed toward your lodge, where else? I should be there in five minutes, maybe less if I take the curves on less than four wheels."

Automatically Graham made a mental note to call Ginger and have her check into applying for emergency guardianship of Sandi's children. If he understood correctly, Willow had told him last week that Sandi had no close family. Lucy and Brittany needed to be with someone they knew. They had at least met Ginger on one or two occasions.

"There's more, boss," Larry said.

"How can there be more?" How much worse could it get?

"Listen to this. Before I talked to the sheriff's deputy, I called my old partner in K.C.—I told you I've been wearing down my cell battery—"

"What else do you have?" Graham couldn't quite curb his impatience.

"My old partner talked to someone who worked the Sperryville case. Now that I know what questions to ask, the news is flying hot and heavy. Seems Sperryville developed Parkinson's after he went to prison. His health has deteriorated rapidly, and he hired an attorney a little over two years ago to try to get him released due to the illness."

"Did they get him released?"

"No, but the attorney he hired did a little more investigating, questioning some people at the hospital from which Sperryville was arrested seven years ago. Care to guess what he found?"

"I'm not up to guessing games right now, Larry," Graham snapped.

"He found that a certain ICU nurse helped with the investigation. He tried to use federal regulations to convince the judge that the evidence they uncovered due to her loose lips should have been inadmissible in court."

"Please tell me the judge dismissed it."

"That's right."

"So now we probably know the origin of the attacks, but we still don't know who's doing the footwork."

"Have you been able to get any information out of Preston?" Larry asked. "How's he doing, anyway?"

"His swelling is still going down, and he's fighting the tube down his throat like any self-respecting man should do. He doesn't remember seeing a thing. An officer has arrived to guard his room."

"Good. You need to leave something for the police to do."

"I could, but I have no guarantee they'll act on this until it's too late."

"I take exception to that. I was on the police force once, and they bust their behinds to catch the bad guys."

"Well, in this case, I'm helping, and they'll just have to put up with the insult."

"Hang on a little longer, boss," Larry said. "I'm going to make another call on my way there."

Graham disconnected and decided to try Ginger's cell phone this time, instead of the main clinic number. She was undoubtedly swamped with calls and patients and would not find much time to listen to messages.

Why would someone kill Sandi? She'd worked for Sperryville at one time, but she'd been fired for apparently fraternizing with his son. So who had sent her here? Sperryville? Why would someone suddenly kill her?

He wished he knew why she had come here. According to his research and Larry's, she'd been at work the night of the fire and the night her children had disappeared, so what had she been sent here to do?

Or maybe she hadn't been sent here at all. Maybe she had come on her own. There just wasn't enough information to go on.

Had someone overheard her call to Willow this morning?

But Willow had told no one about her call before she left to meet Sandi. He needed more information.

At long last, Ginger answered her cell phone, sounding stressed.

"Brace yourself, Ginger," Graham said. "I think you should sit down."

As quickly as possible he filled her in and dealt with the emotional fallout. With her promise to call DFS as soon as he hung up, he got off the phone and called Larry one more time.

"Hi, boss. I'm almost there," Larry said.

"Your friend told you Sandi was fired for fraternizing with the son? Did you happen to catch the son's name?"

"Nope, but I can probably find out."

"Do that and get back to me." He disconnected and drove out of the parking lot.

Willow sat tensely watching the road as Rick took the sharp curves of Highway 265 with smooth grace. "Did you see Preston before you left?" she asked.

"Sure did. He looked bad. You knew they had to intubate, didn't you? I've never seen anything like it. Even his eyelids were swelled. The doctor thought he might have to cut."

Willow cringed at the sound of excitement in his voice, as if he'd have loved to watch that procedure. "You should go to med school," she said. "Med students live for that kind of thing."

"I tried. I couldn't get in."

"How many years have you been an orderly?" she asked.

He hesitated. "Not that long."

"Thanks for driving me," she said. "I hope I don't get you into trouble. The police didn't want me to leave yet."

He chuckled. "That's the least of your worries. Besides, I know how it feels to need help. My father, you know."

"Of course. How's he doing?"

Rick stopped at the intersection of 265 and 165, and he remained stopped for a long moment. "Funny you should ask. He isn't doing well." He glanced at Willow. "Not at all."

"I'm sorry."

He glanced in his rearview mirror, looked both ways, then instead of turning right, as he should have done to take her to the hospital, he turned left.

"No, wait. Rick, we're going the wrong way. It's faster to—"

"You know, now that you mention it, I'm glad you're sorry about my father."

"Well, of course. Look, we were supposed to turn right back there. My brother's life is hanging in the balance, and—"

"My father's life is hanging in the balance, too, Willow, and thanks to you it's never going to get any better."

Her stomach tightened, and she felt a numb, tingly sensation along the back of her shoulders and scalp.

"What are you talking about? Where are we going?"

He negotiated another tight curve, then glanced at her, that characteristic bright smile back in place. "I'm going to conduct a little medical experiment."

From the time Willow was a little girl, when other children were making fun of her on the playground because of her mother, she had learned a useful tool— never let 'em see you sweat. "I'm not interested in an experiment right now. I need to get to the hospital, and if you're not going to take me, just drop me off right here and I'll—"

"I'm sorry," he said softly, almost sweetly. "I can't do that, because I need you in particular for my experiment. You see, they've been experimenting with medications on my father in prison for years now, trying to come up with the right combination to give him the fewest side effects for his Parkinson's."

The numb tingle of horror spread across her body, tautening each nerve fiber.

"He's had an especially bad time of it," he continued. "Other Parkinson's patients can do fine for years with the right drugs, but I think being tried and convicted and thrown into prison might have accelerated his disease."

She looked at him, then looked at the road ahead. It had been dawning on her since the turn that she was in the car with Sandi's killer. Now her background information took her a step further. "Sperryville is your—"

"Father," Rick supplied for her. "And you're the person I hold directly responsible for ruining his life.

My life. My whole family's life." His words grew clipped, his voice harsh, and his eyes narrowed and filled with anger.

"You don't hold him responsible for committing the crime in the first place? He personally killed two college students who were witnesses to another murder."

"He was injured and helpless in that ICU bed, and you betrayed his trust!"

"Whose trust would I have been betraying if I hadn't reported it?"

He didn't answer. She had always known that someday her bluntness would get her into big trouble. However, she didn't think this was that time. She'd been in trouble the moment she stepped into this car.

"So you're going to help me conduct this little experiment, in which I inject you with my father's dopamine dose . . . actually, several of them. After you go totally psychotic on me, I have another little surprise. It's called haloperidol, and a large injection of that might send you into neuroleptic malignant syndrome. Then your body will stiffen until you can't move, and your brain will cook. A fascinating experiment, don't you think?"

She wanted to spit in his face. It would be more proactive, however, to jump on him and scratch his eyes out before he could carry through on his threats.

She sighted the gray balustrade of Table Rock Dam ahead of them, and braced herself for escape. Sightseers. Help. If only he were forced to slow his speed as he drove over the crowded road across the dam. She would make sure someone noticed.

But even as she lowered her hand to the buckle of her seat belt, Rick reached for the lock mechanism on his door. "Don't try it, because it won't work."

He engaged passing gear and blasted across the dam in a fury of squealing tires, earning looks of disgust from the women and whistles of admiration from a couple of teenagers. Willow couldn't risk grabbing the steering wheel; if he lost control, he could hit someone.

She slapped the passenger-side window in an attempt to catch someone's attention. No one noticed.

She heard Rick's soft chuckle.

Willow closed her eyes and saw Sandi's battered face. Would she soon look like that?

Maybe not. While Rick negotiated the traffic signal below Chateau on the Lake, she slid her hand into her purse and withdrew her cell phone, praying her battery would hold out and her reception would be strong. She pressed what she knew to be the speed dial number for Graham's cell, then to mask the sound she momentarily pressed the face of the phone against the side of her leg as she returned her attention to Rick. After it had had time to connect, she laid the phone faceup on the seat beside her.

Chapter Twenty-Three

Graham was speeding down Highway 65 when he received a call. With heavy traffic, he didn't take the time to check his caller ID screen, so he pressed Answer, adjusted his earphones and had opened his mouth to speak when he heard the unmistakable contralto of Willow's voice.

"You killed my husband, didn't you? And my child. How you must hate me to be so willing to turn to crime yourself, in order to avenge your father."

"Willow? It's me. Graham. This is no time for jokes. What are you—"

"I gave you fair warning." Another voice spoke. A man's voice, slightly familiar, though in his state of growing horror Graham couldn't place it. "I said you would pay for what you did."

Fair warning. Those were the words the killer had used when he'd called her.

"You killed innocent people, Rick! I simply reported a guilty one."

Rick Fenrow. The orderly who smiled a lot and paid his rent on time.

A sudden, jarring vibration of the steering wheel startled Graham. In his distraction, he had veered from the highway onto the shoulder. He readjusted, still listening with amazement and growing terror to the conversation taking place . . . where? Were they still at the lodge?

Willow must have somehow managed to press speed dial without Rick's knowledge.

"Oh, come on, you think your husband was going to stay innocent for long? He was a narcotics agent," Rick growled. "How many times did you think he'd resist temptation before he gave in?"

Graham thought he heard the sound of an accelerating motor.

"And my baby?" Willow asked. "You ran me down like an unwanted dog on the road and killed my baby."

"How was I supposed to know you were carrying? I was just disappointed I didn't get you."

Graham's grip tightened on the wheel. *Where are you, Willow?*

"Is that the hypodermic needle you're going to shoot me with?" Her voice sounded angry, belligerent, but Graham had come to know her well enough to recognize the undercurrent of fear she was trying to conceal. "You can't possibly believe I'll hold still for that."

"You don't have to hold still. You get close to me and I'll plunge it into you up to the hilt. This little baby makes an effective weapon, don't you think? You try anything, you'll deprive me of some of my fun, but you'll be just as dead in the end." There was a wicked chuckle. "I can live with that."

Graham's whole body chilled at the possibilities, remembering the drugs that had been missing from the pharmacy. Dopamine and haloperidol would be a wicked combination. Dopamine was the drug used in the treatment of Parkinson's disease. It was a very symbolic choice, considering Willow's history, and the fact that dopamine could trigger schizophrenia.

"You can't possibly believe I had anything to do with your father's illness," Willow said.

"You're about to," Rick said. "In a few minutes you're going to discover the wild thoughts that rage through his mind. Come on, Willow," the man taunted. "You're a compassionate ICU nurse—don't you want to be able to identify with your patients?"

Graham flinched instinctively, imagining the horror Willow must be feeling.

"Where are you going?" she asked. "You can't possibly be in the mood for Silver Dollar City."

Good girl! Graham slammed on his brakes, checked traffic, made a U-turn. He had passed Highway 165 barely two hundred feet back. If they were headed toward Silver Dollar City from the lodge, they would be driving south of the lake on 265. He could reach that point more quickly on this road. And he'd better hurry.

Keep talking, Willow.

Willow prayed Graham was on the line. When her phone had good reception, it could last for several minutes on a low battery. Highway 265 followed a ridge around the southwest perimeter of Branson. It should provide good exposure for reception. From where she was, she could see the observation tower at the Shepherd of the Hills center.

"How did you get a job at the hospital?" she asked.

"They do a meticulous background check on their employees."

"What makes you think I have a criminal record?"

"Oh, I don't know," she said dryly. "Maybe the fact that you're a killer has something to do with it."

"Don't be so naive," he said. "I'm not a criminal— I'm an avenger."

"So why change your name?"

"I never changed my name. It's always been Fenrow. It's my mother's name."

"Your parents never married?"

"Why should they?" He placed the syringe on the dash, well out of her reach. "Keep an eye on that for me, will you?" He laughed again.

She stared at his weapon of choice, willing herself to do something, to grab the steering wheel and jerk them from the road, to attack him, but she couldn't. If she did, she had no doubt she would immediately feel the prick of that needle. Terror paralyzed her. That syringe was more effective with her than a gun or knife would have been.

She glanced out her window and saw the city of Branson far below the ridge, a blur of hotels, shops and restaurants on the roadside. How easily a crime could be committed in the midst of a crowd, and no one would be the wiser.

"You followed me with a black car," she said.

He patted his steering wheel. "This baby's far too noticeable, and there are lots of car rentals in town. They weren't too happy when I brought in a dented front fender, but insurance pays."

"So you did run me off the road."

"I shouldn't have, I know. Too risky. You might have remembered something, and then where would I be? Lucky for me you didn't. I needed to make sure you would be killed."

She cringed at his words. "Of course," she muttered. "Can't take any chances with my death."

"I got into the habit of volunteering a lot of free time to the hospital. That way I had a good excuse to be there to enjoy the results of my labors, and, of course, everyone realizes what a nice, compassionate guy I am. They wouldn't dream of suspecting me."

"Of course not. You must have charmed Mrs. Engle long enough to get a copy of her keys. Did you manipulate Sandi the same way?"

He ignored her, focusing on the curves and traffic as they neared Highway 76 west of Branson.

"Some thought you were Sandi's boyfriend."

He snorted. "That piece of trash was not my girlfriend. She couldn't even follow simple orders."

"To do what?"

"She was supposed to seduce Preston and kill him, but she couldn't even get him to look at her." He gave Willow a leer. "Imagine my surprise and delight when you suddenly moved in with him."

"You came here just to kill my brother?"

"You destroyed my family. You needed to see how it felt. I could have taken you out in Kansas City easily, but I decided to make you suffer a little longer."

She winced at the insanity in his voice. Why had she never picked up on that? Had he actually appeared so sane to everyone all these weeks?

"Sandi got scared. Sandi felt wrong." He said it in a singsong voice, mocking and filled with bitter anger. "Sandi suddenly decided you were a nice person. She was as stupid as—"

"So you killed her and left her little girls alone, orphans in the world."

"An ape at the zoo would be a better mother than that woman was, anyway."

"Try telling Lucy and Brittany that."

She thought of his killing methods. He'd used a gun, a figurine, fire and, several times, a car. He must have mistaken Jolene Tucker's car for a Subaru the night of the fire, when he ran her off the road. But then he had obviously discovered differently when he saw Willow's Subaru in its customary spot in the carport. So of course he had planted the arson materials in it. She had no doubt he would have tipped off the police about it, if they hadn't checked first.

He slowed at the intersection of 265 and 76, but instead of turning left, as she had expected him to do, he turned right on 76.

"We're going back to Branson?" she asked.

He slanted a glance at her. "Before long it won't matter to you where we go." He frowned, glancing down at the purse at her side. It was open. "Why have you been giving a running commentary on our route?" He reached over and grabbed the purse, knocking her

293

open cell phone from the seat. It bounced on the floor-
board, landing faceup.

The battery was dead. She had no idea how long it
had been that way.

Graham stomped on the accelerator, streaked past a
delivery truck, then swept back into the right lane with
a racing heart. Branson. The last words he'd heard
were "back to Branson."

But why would Rick return to the city when he could
more easily turn left and find himself in the wilderness
of the Mark Twain National Forest in just a few miles?
Then he could easily do what he was threatening with
no interference.

Of course, Rick *was* from the city. He had no knowledge of Branson or the surrounding area. He could be
headed for someplace close, especially if he felt he
wouldn't be able to control Willow much longer. She
wasn't exactly a controllable person.

There were still some places between the 265 intersection and town where Rick might be able to turn into
the forest and be almost immediately concealed by
trees.

Still speeding, Graham passed two more cars,
switching on his flashers as he dialed the police.
Quickly he gave them all the necessary specifics, then
disconnected and dialed Larry.

After explaining the situation, he asked, "Have you
ever been to the top of the observation tower at the
Shepherd of the Hills center?"

"Sure have, boss," Larry said. "Great view. Are you thinking what I'm thinking?"

"Call there. Describe Rick Fenrow's car to one of the security personnel—it shouldn't be too hard to spot on the road, twisting around those mountain curves."

"I'll do it now." He hung up before Graham could say any more.

Now Graham could do nothing more, but drive and pray.

The sound of crashing plastic compartments echoed through the car as Rick slammed Willow's cell phone against the window, smashing it to bits in a fit of rage. Willow cringed against her door.

She didn't know this section of road well, except there was a lot of forest on both sides. She could see the ridge that they had driven on a few minutes ago. Was Graham following? Had he even received her call? If not, she was totally at the mercy of this madman.

She leaned her head back, constantly aware of the position of Rick's hands and the syringe. At last, as she had feared for two years, her nightmare truly had followed her into her waking hours.

Rick was now forced to focus totally on the curves. Were she able to open the door, she could jump out when he slowed for one of the tightest curves.

But he had been keeping close guard on the lock. If she went for the door, he'd grab his lock mechanism again and keep her from switching it. Or he'd grab the syringe.

After all the brave, positive talking she'd done with Preston about God's relentless love, she'd neglected to tell him that there were times in a person's life when God seemed to step back and watch.

And yet, she had not lost her faith. As she stared at the forest racing past her window in flashes of green, she knew that even if her life ended today, in truth it would only be the beginning.

Life here on earth would always have pain and hardship, but as Travis had once loved to remind her, this life was a testing ground. She wanted to face her test today with grace. If she didn't live to see tomorrow, then she would see Jesus—and Travis and her baby—that much sooner.

That thought reminded her that she wasn't truly alone, even now, locked in this speeding car with a killer.

Again she looked at the syringe that he had placed in a slotted holder in the dashboard. She couldn't allow fear to paralyze her now.

She waited until he entered a sharp hairpin curve to the left, then grabbed the steering wheel and jerked it toward her.

He jerked it back easily, but with his concentration broken, he didn't see the eighteen-wheeler come speeding around the tight curve, breaking past the center line. The front bumper of the truck came within inches of the driver's-side window.

Rick swerved. The tires left the pavement. As he fought to regain control, the syringe rolled from the dash to the floor beneath his feet.

Seizing her chance, Willow flung off her seat belt, reached for the lock of her door with her left hand and grabbed the handle with her other. Centrifugal force flung the door open as she unlatched it.

"No!" Rick grabbed her by her jacket.

She tried to wrench free, but he jerked the steering wheel, sending the car lurching. In his panicked effort to hold her, he lost control. The vehicle left the road, took a nosedive off the steep hillside and rammed a tree. An air bag caught Willow in the face. Her vision went out of focus.

A sharp jab in her forearm shot a jolt through her body. She screamed and jerked away, striking out blindly at Rick. He grunted as the syringe flipped from his grasp.

She shoved the door open again. This time when he grabbed her jacket she slipped out of it and stumbled into the brush, dizzy with terror.

"Help me!" she screamed, praying someone had seen them from the road above.

She heard Rick's footsteps behind her and ran blindly back toward the road. The footsteps drew closer. She heard his heavy breathing.

He caught her just before she reached the road. She pivoted, striking out at him wildly again, scratching his face with her nails, still screaming for help, kicking up with her knee.

He threw her to the ground and fell on top of her, but just as his weight pressed her cruelly into the jagged rocks beneath her, he grunted and fell free.

She rolled over to see Graham wrestling Rick to the ground and three uniformed guards scrambling down the hillside toward them.

It was the last thing she saw before she lost consciousness.

Chapter Twenty-Four

Graham carried a bouquet of books in a basket down the corridor toward Willow's hospital room on Tuesday morning. He had planned to bring flowers, but he knew how much she loved to read. Books would last longer and give her more enjoyment.

He entered the room to find that someone else—actually, three someone elses—had thought of the flowers. He also saw that she wasn't in the room. Had they already released her? It was possible.

It hadn't taken long to discover she was as impatient a patient as her brother. Though she had taken a substantial hit of dopamine from Rick Fenrow's syringe—shooting her blood pressure skyward for a frightening ride to the hospital—she had recovered well enough to want to go home last night.

Graham knew that if the full amount of the syringe had been injected directly into a vein, Willow would be dead now. Fortunately, Rick had hit muscle, so even though the effects had lasted much longer than they ordinarily would have, they had not been as deadly.

Yesterday afternoon and evening had been torture for Graham. Of course, they hadn't exactly been a picnic for Willow, either.

The dopamine had, indeed, triggered periods of schizophrenia. They didn't last long, and though Preston worried about future episodes, Graham very much doubted that would happen. If it did, they would deal with it. He planned to be there for her.

He set the basket on her tray table between two bouquets.

As Preston had warned him last night, his sister could be the death of both of them. Graham doubted that would happen, either, though he couldn't be sure.

Graham had never believed in love at first sight, and he didn't believe in whirlwind romances. Physical attraction was heady and exhilarating, but it didn't necessarily lead to a lasting relationship.

All that aside, however, he knew that within three and a half weeks he had fallen head over heels in love with Willow Traynor. He still wouldn't rush into anything. For her sake as well as his own, he would take this slowly, giving them both time to get to know one another. He knew what he wanted, though. Someday he wanted to marry her.

Someone grabbed him from behind, wrapping long, strong arms around his midsection. He heard soft, feminine laughter, and turned to find Willow looking up at him with a broad grin. She was dressed in jeans and an electric-blue knit top that emphasized the color in her blue-gray eyes.

"So the knight in shining armor not only tracks down killers and rescues damsels in distress, but he knows exactly what the damsel wants on her tray table the next morning." She released him and pulled a book from the basket. "How did you reach us so quickly after we went off the road?"

"I wasn't that far behind you. Security guards had seen you from the tower and came running. Have they released you?"

"Not yet," she said, thumbing through the book as she sat on the bed. "But they will soon. I can't let Preston beat me out of here, and he's due to be released today."

"You're staying with us, of course," he said. "At least until both of you are stronger."

"No need. I feel strong as an ox, and Preston's swelling is gone, he's eating well and ready to get back to work. Besides, I love that condo with the deer in the woods and the fireplace."

Graham felt a sting of disappointment. As of this morning, he had learned that he and Ginger would be granted temporary custody of Lucy and Brittany. He had been looking forward to a houseful of people—or at least these particular people.

"Larry called me this morning," Willow said. "He explained the dates in April."

Graham pulled a chair up to the bed and sat down. "I know April first was the day Rick's father spilled the information about his crimes. What about the others?"

"April fifth, when the girls were taken, coincided with the day the police arrested Sperryville with enough evidence to convict him. On April fourteenth, the press found out and started harassing the family. That was one of the things Rick blamed me for—the loss of privacy. On April twenty-second his father had his first symptoms of Parkinson's, though they didn't know what it was for almost two more years. Rick blamed me for that, as well."

"Rick is a very unhappy man right now. He's facing some life-and-death decisions in the next few months, and they won't be his decisions to make."

"I feel sorry for him, Graham."

"Why? Because he's frustrated not to have killed you?"

"Because I doubt anyone ever told him God loved him. We fail people so often by neglecting to tell them there's another way to live, a more satisfying way."

"We can only tell them so many times. Some day they have to start listening, Willow. We can't take the responsibility for that decision."

"No, but we can make sure they are aware of the choices."

He studied her face. Gone were the lines of worry that had drawn her down for so long. She looked like a woman set free from prison. There were still shadows in her expression, from memories that would be with her for years. But Willow was strong enough to weather those memories and still find joy in living.

"Carl Mackey came in this morning," she said. "That poor man, he's really been through it, hasn't he?"

"How's that?"

"He was concerned that I had gotten the wrong impression yesterday. He'd been a little upset when he found out I'd researched his past, particularly in Kansas City. He had moved with his wife to Kansas City to come to a warmer climate and it turned out to be the worst decision of his life."

"Why?"

"His wife died soon after they settled in Overland Park and, in his grief, he made a mistake on a medication that cost a patient his life. Carl moved to Branson to put it all behind him and reminisce about better days, when he and Marty had come down to enjoy the shows. He never wants to think about that time again. When I mentioned it, he wasn't happy. I have to admit, there were a few moments I suspected him yesterday."

"So did I."

Graham watched her for a moment. She had the face of a young girl, but her eyes held the wisdom one gains from experience, by learning from failure and loss.

"Willow Traynor, I think you're the most beautiful, fascinating woman I have ever met and I would most definitely like to get to know you better."

Her eyes widened. "Wow. That's a great way to ask a girl on a date."

"You like that? Okay, how about this. When you get out of this hospital, would you consider going hiking with me? And then maybe we could visit Hideaway, take a float trip down Flat Creek to the lake, eat at Bertie's for lunch and then pack a picnic for dinner. If that doesn't work, we could attend a marathon of country music shows in Branson and go sightseeing. You haven't been exposed to the wild side of Branson until you've ridden the ducks."

"The ducks?"

"That's right. Are you willing to live on the wild side with me?"

She considered him in silence for a moment. "I can't think of anything I'd like better."

She slid from the bed and reached for him. Wrapping her arms around his neck, she smiled at him. "Believe it or not, I've been wanting to do this for weeks." And she kissed him, pressing her soft lips to his in a promise of more to come in their lives.

As Preston had warned, she could be the death of him. But she could also be the life of him. He didn't plan to pass up the opportunity.

He kissed her again, because he loved the feel of their lips together. He loved the feel of her face against his. He never wanted to let her go.

Center Point Publishing
600 Brooks Road ● PO Box 1
Thorndike ME 04986-0001 USA

(207) 568-3717

US & Canada:
1 800 929-9108